W9-BON-753

What the critics are saying…

Finalist for the *EPPIE Award.*

A Perfect 10! "…witty dialogue, compelling characters, and a great plot…" ~ *Kathy Samuels, Romance Reviews Today*

"…a laugh-out-loud book…sexy, hilarious, action-and-angst-filled romp…" ~*Sara Sawyer, The Romance Studio*

5 Angels! Recommended Read! "I laughed until tears rolled down my cheeks…" ~*Tanya, Fallen Angels Reviews*

"…hilariously funny and equally erotic…" ~ *Katherine Turcotte, Romantic Times*

5 Stars! "…a great read that had me laughing out loud…" ~*Julie Bryan, Just Erotic Romance Reviews*

5 Stars! "…ranks right up there with Laurell K Hamilton…" ~ *BJ Deese, eCataRomance*

SOMETHING WANTON

Jacqueline Meadows

SOMETHING WANTON
An Ellora's Cave Publication, March 2005

Ellora's Cave Publishing, Inc.
1337 Commerce Drive Suite #13
Stow, Ohio 44224

ISBN #1419951017

Edited by: *Raelene Gorlinsky*
Cover art by: *Syneca*

Warning:

The following material contains graphic sexual content meant for mature readers. *Something Wanton* has been rated *E-rotic* by a minimum of three independent reviewers.

Ellora's Cave Publishing offers three levels of Romantica™ reading entertainment: S (S-ensuous), E (E-rotic), and X (X-treme).

S-*ensuous* love scenes are explicit and leave nothing to the imagination.

E-*rotic* love scenes are explicit, leave nothing to the imagination, and are high in volume per the overall word count. In addition, some E-rated titles might contain fantasy material that some readers find objectionable, such as bondage, submission, same sex encounters, forced seductions, etc. E-rated titles are the most graphic titles we carry; it is common, for instance, for an author to use words such as "fucking", "cock", "pussy", etc., within their work of literature.

X-*treme* titles differ from E-rated titles only in plot premise and storyline execution. Unlike E-rated titles, stories designated with the letter X tend to contain controversial subject matter not for the faint of heart.

Also by Jacqueline Meadows:

SOMETHING WANTON

Chapter One

Magic. Sorcery. Witchcraft. Believe in any of those? Nah, neither did I. Not until three months ago, that is, when I smacked face first into a few hard, irrefutable truths. Truths that turned my entire world upside down — bombshell discoveries — not the least of which concerned the revelation about myself.

You see — cue the suspenseful background music — I am a witch.

Yep it's true, cross my heart. And not just an ordinary witch, either (if such a thing exists); I'm told I'm a Wiccan Queen, a High Priestess. Nice title, huh? I'd kinda thought that's all it was, too, a silly moniker, just words. Oh, I knew my powers were stronger than average but I hadn't quite realized how much stronger. And the title? Well, it comes with baggage, the heavy Samsonite kind. I found out all about it the hard way, this past doozie of a week.

What happened? Glad you asked.

I'm a P.I., and in addition to a normal workweek sleuthing cases of theft and adultery, I also fought two mystical battles, morphed a man into a toad, stopped a basement sexcapade gone awry, and rescued a tottering tree trimmer. I saved lives and took others. Did the week stop there? Give me a chance to catch my breath? No and no. It piled more atop me like a house of cards (and you know what happens eventually with those).

My week felt just as messy.

An example? Well, Thursday I came upon my 75-year-old aunt in a compromising position with the neighboring widower. *Very* compromising. Picture saggy birthday suits, tangled limbs, and septuagenarian sighs. My aunt raised me, she's essentially my mother, and everyone knows moms don't have sex. Ew. I'm still recovering from the sight.

But the real kicker? I discovered my best friend since childhood—one Nicholas Sage, and may I add the very married Nicholas Sage—has *feelings* for me, feelings that can't be filed under P for Platonic.

And oh yeah, I fell in love, madly, head-over-heels, crazy in love. Fell hard, too. I scraped my knees a bit but I'm fine now, better than fine, though I admit the fall was more "hard tumble" than "smooth descent". See, for three months I fought a full commitment to him, fought harder still the loss of my heart.

But he fought back stronger, and he fought dirty.

French, sharp, charismatic, and drop-dead-gorgeous. String those adjectives together and you've spelled Armand. Armand Bellamy. Add the fact he's a witch, a High Priest no less, and you've got Trouble with a capital T.

Last Sunday I finally began to admit my feelings for him ran rather deep.

For the better part of the previous week I'd been out of town on my latest case, a child custody battle. The frantic mother hired me to locate her ex-husband and their four-year-old daughter. It seems daddy neglected to return the little girl after their court-sanctioned outing. (Mighty forgetful.) Seems he also emptied his closets and bank accounts. It took me four days to track them over state lines to a shabby motel and only thirty minutes to alert my client, the authorities, and drive off into the sunset, case closed.

Melancholy accompanied me during the long drive home, slouching beside me glum and silent like a sulky youth. Pensive hours later I conceded why. Armand. I missed him, really missed him, ached and pined missed him. Oh we'd talked on the phone every night since my departure, long thoughtful conversations, but I needed to see him, touch him, even smell him. I discovered that sappy adage is really true—absence does make the heart grow fonder—and on that Sunday drive I knew one sure thing.

If it grew any fonder, I'd explode.

* * * * *

Buffered by lush gardens and mature trees, a circular brick drive led to a grand lakeside estate. The man dwelling within was cooking me dinner.

Maple, birch and oak leaves fluttered in the warm breeze like small waving hands, and in hula skirt fashion the trailing fringe of willows danced and swayed. Michigan was enjoying another beautiful summer's day. Since my state isn't exactly known for its consistent weather, residents held their collective breath during the clement streak.

I took a moment to appreciate the brilliant view before climbing the massive front stairs. The door opened at my second knock.

"Miss Desy! It's so nice to see you. Please, come in." Catalina, Armand's maid, beamed and stood aside. It took weeks to coax her to use my nickname. Desy is short for

Desdemona. I remain unsuccessful in persuading her to drop the "Miss" part.

I smiled. "Thanks. I haven't seen you in awhile. Has Armand worked you to the bone?"

She shut the door behind us and tsked. "That one! He hardly lets me lift a finger. It's not right. I clean, but that's it. I should do the cooking, too."

Armand loves to cook and, as his efforts always taste so divine, I suspect he sprinkles magic in each recipe. Catalina adores Armand. Control of the kitchen is just her pseudo-running argument with him. As a Latina spitfire with seven grandchildren and two more on the way, arguing is her passion, her hobby, one she practices in two languages with a fervent zeal.

My smile widened. "Ever taste his crepes? They're to die for."

"I've had the ones with shrimp." Catalina leaned and whispered, "Don't tell him, but they're the best I've ever had."

A deep voice said, "I heard that."

Armand entered the foyer and my parched gaze drank him down. Dark chocolate hair framed his sensuous face and fell to broad, ample shoulders. A black tee shirt and worn jeans covered muscles and smooth skin, emphasizing a strong natural build. He exuded a foreign blend of grace and carnality, somehow radiating both earthiness and elegance.

Barefoot, he crossed to me, cupped my cheeks, and the look in his eyes forced my heart to a fast pitter-pat. His dark gaze roamed my face, lingered hot on my mouth, and he whispered "*mon chou*" before kissing me. My hands fluttered about, then settled on his waist.

Catalina released a happy sigh and wished us a pleasant evening. Armand always gives everyone the night off when I visit.

He trailed his tongue along my lips. "Four days." His lips touched mine. "Six hours." His teeth caught my bottom lip and nibbled. "Twenty-three minutes," he whispered, and my fingers dug into his waist as he plundered my mouth. "Mmm, and thirty...long...seconds."

I moaned and surfaced for air. "I counted twenty-six."

He kissed me hard. "I rounded up." Armand swallowed my breathless laugh while I unsnapped his jeans. Taut stomach muscles jerked against my hands. "Not to interrupt you, but on the phone you said you were starving." He buried his hands in my hair with the next stunning kiss. "We're having salmon." He scraped his teeth on my chin in a soft nip. "Still hungry?"

"Famished." The downward rasp of his zipper flushed me with heat and my eager hand slipped beneath his underwear to curl in a tight fist around his cock. I squeezed, smiled when he groaned, "Jesus."

"Starved." I slinked my hand up and down and Armand hummed, backed me toward the staircase. Inside my pumping grasp his cock felt huge and totem pole hard. "Ravenous," I breathed against his parted lips as I shuffled backward, anticipation thrumming through me like an electrical current. My heel caught on the first riser and we fell in a tangled heap to the stairs. I pushed a small laugh around our entwined tongues.

Armand's hand stole under my dress, searing a slow path up my inner thigh. He cupped me, stilled, then shot his stunned gaze to mine. "Where are your—"

"Panties?" My hand continued to pull rhythmically on his cock. "In my Jeep." When his palm slid against drenched hairs, slick folds, I moaned and rocked my hips. Passion leapt higher in his eyes, and he reared up with a growl, shoved down his jeans and underwear, and plunged. "God!"

His cock plowed between my sprawled thighs, plunging balls-deep in creamy arousal. "Desy." He pulled nearly out. "You're so wet," he growled, driving his hips forward. "Tight." He drew back. "Perfect." His next lunge dug deep, urgent. "And mine."

I sank my teeth into his neck, my nails into his ass. Months with Armand taught he often liked it a little rough. I was always happy to oblige.

With a pleased grunt he began pounding a bracing rhythm. My pelvis rose to meet each circling thrust, his plunging cock stretched me taut, and long moments brimmed with smooth glides, breathy moans, circling hips, and rocketing tension.

I shuddered when his finger nudged my clit, whispered his name as everything within me tingled and pulled tight, then tighter still. My breath hitched before releasing on a sharp, cutting gasp.

I burst, spasming around his thickness.

"Jesus, you're beautiful." Armand hummed a rapturous groan, thrusting hard—five, six, seven times—before spraying endless streams of seed. I felt his contractions, his bucking cock—long, thick, rigid—and bursts of hot pumping cream. I moaned and he eased more of his weight on me, nuzzled my throat, eliciting a shudder with his soft nip.

I made a happy sound. "Is that the stair stabbing my back or did you maybe poke clean through?"

A puff of air feathered against my nape, followed by his ragged whisper, "I missed you."

My hands buried in the dark curtain of silk cascading about his shoulders. "Ditto."

* * * * *

Satiated on reheated salmon with papaya-mint salsa, we lounged poolside. The water shimmered deep blue, each ripple's crest sparkling beneath the sun's thick rays. My gaze took in the portico framed by large arches, the multitude of tall pillars, huge plants billowing from oversized pots, the manicured lawn, gardens and lake beyond. I shook my head.

"Troubling thoughts?"

I looked at him and sighed. "You have too much money."

"Is there such a thing?"

"Guess not. It's just I don't know if I'll ever get used to—" my hands gestured around "—all this. We've been together three months and I'm still uncomfortable with it."

"The size of my bank account aside, what matters most is our relationship." Armand paused a beat. "Will you feel comfortable with that anytime soon?"

"What do you mean?"

"I mean, in all our time together, *mon chou*, you've spent the night only five times."

He kept track? My mind whirred as I reached for my wineglass and sipped a fine French white that probably cost more than one month's car payment and electric bill combined. Staying overnight with Armand made me…uneasy, because sleeping all night beside him, waking curled—warm and cherished—within his arms, evoked yearnings for *more*. And *more* led to an engagement. And an engagement led to marriage. And marriage led to diapers and Fisher Price. And was I ready for all that?

Besides budding flowers and hay fever, spring had brought me Armand. We met under unusual circumstances. He showed me I'm a witch, taught me magic, and together we fought and won a mystical battle against a shared enemy. My attraction to him is volcanic. I fought against it then and to varying degrees still do. Spending the night with him thrust me to the next rung on the relationship ladder and I'm deathly afraid of heights.

Meeting him proved to be the watershed between ordinary and extraordinary in my life. It happened on an endless Monday as I entered unsuspecting my home's small sunroom in search of Aunt P. She sat beside a man, a stranger, a handsome, jaw-dropping-gorgeous, stunning package of foreign testosterone. He was visiting from Paris—his father, now deceased, had been a good friend of my aunt's. Armand's presence that night so rattled me it was a wonder I didn't speak in tongues, or Klingon.

He bought a house here in Michigan the very next day, just to be near me, he said. An entire life awaits him in France—homes, businesses, friends. His teenaged sister, Giselle, is there as well; she turns twenty next month. But he's here with me, says we belong together. And the scary thing? I'm starting to believe him.

Armand fixed me with an intent gaze. "I want you to stay the entire night. Will you?"

"I'm sorry, Armand. I drove straight here from Ohio. I haven't seen Aunt P in days. Tonight, I need to be home with her." I set aside my wineglass. "Do you understand?"

I live with my Aunt Penelope, who raised me from infancy after I lost both parents. I love her like a mother and although still spry, Aunt P has lived nearly three-quarters of a century. Not even the beguiling thought of playing footsie with Armand till sunrise could coax me to leave her alone another day.

He took my hand, swept his thumb across my knuckles. "I'm disappointed, but *oui*, I understand." Kissing my hand, nibbling there before lacing our fingers, he settled my arm along his thigh and looked toward the lake. "It's driving me slowly insane, you know."

I squeezed his hand. "I thought you understood."

Armand tilted his head toward me. "I do. I speak of the maddening fact you wear no panties beneath that dress."

I grinned.

"Show me," he coaxed low and sexy. "Draw up your hem. Let me see."

Draw up my hem? I drew up a shaky breath instead. The heat of his gaze alone could melt glaciers. Add in the seductive timbre of his voice and my eyebrows nearly singed off.

He released my hand. "Let me see."

Slowly I lifted my dress, watched his eyes darken with each new inch revealed. The sliding hem stopped when it edged past my vee of brown curls.

Armand breathed something in French, wispy words threaded with desire, and issued a soft command. "Spread your legs."

I watched him watch me. With nostrils flaring and eyes blazing lust, hungry desire suffused his face. His lips parted when my thighs spread wide.

"Do you have any idea how lovely you are?"

My heart leapt when he stood.

Bending one leg on my chaise lounge, he knelt between my thighs and used the blunt tip of his forefinger to trace a searing path round and round my opening. His voice burned thick and weighted under a heavier accent. "Shall I see if you're already wet?"

The Atlantic pulsed between my legs but why spoil his surprise? A giddy tremor scampered across my flesh at the mere thought of his touch, and I made a noise halfway between whimper and moan, then wiggled closer. He slid two fingers deep. I quivered and on a sharp inhale, curled my toes into the deck. His brown eyes sizzled with dark intentions, holding my gaze captive, as his fingers pumped from tip to web amid wet notes of squishy friction.

Armand held up his hand between us. "Look how ready you are for me." Fingers glistening with a shiny coat of arousal slid between his lips while I watched his tongue dart to lick them clean, saw pleasure sweep his face, listened to his low sensuous hum, and nearly choked on intoxicating arousal. Air burned thick and uneven from my lungs as our gazes held.

He viewed his clean fingers, then me. "I need more." Armand's long hair swung forward as he buried his face between my shaky thighs, and I grabbed onto the shiny strands, cradling his dark head against me. Before my breathy "God" had cleared, his tongue plunged. My heart stopped, then lurched with excitement, roaring reckless in my ears.

His smooth tongue slid and probed and wiggled, gentle teeth nipped, and my clitoris rejoiced in a tingling throb beneath skilful, wet nudges. Under the soft lace of my bra, fiery nerve endings pinched my breasts, swelling them, hardening my nipples to two aching points. Armand slurped and moaned while I rode his tongue with a slow, hazy rhythm, circling my hips, and the heat of a flush scorched my skin, settling in a wet prickle between my legs.

Hot and dizzy, I felt seconds away from my first swoon and wondered whether Armand would resuscitate me mouth to mouth. It sounded delightful.

He pinched my clit; I stilled and groaned, then imploded. Strong contractions pulled taut around his tongue, fluttering with a wild fierce beat, and Armand pushed a joyous moan deep inside me.

I saw stars…and constellations…and suns and moons and planets and…

He nipped my thigh. "Breathe, *mon chou.*"

Chapter Two

It was a heart-pounding, mouth-watering, mind-numbing, bone-melting, knock-your-socks-off, tonsil-sucking goodbye kiss. The kind that felt as if someone behind you hooked their arms under yours and spun you around in tight circles—your legs flying free in the air—so when it ended, your stomach performed dizzy somersaults while you stumbled around sideways. That kind of kiss. And after it Armand whispered goodnight, closed my Jeep door, and I drove home unaware of inconsequential things like stop signs and red lights.

I traveled from points A to B cognizant only of his taste still warm on my lips, the intoxicating scent of him encompassing me, and every inch of my flesh still thrumming with the memory of his hands.

We'd finally made it to his bed that evening, where he spent two enthusiastic hours demonstrating in minute detail just how much he missed me. Miles away, I still felt enveloped by him.

The man is lethal.

Quietly I entered my house and found Aunt P snuggled on the living room couch, her dear face awash in the television's flickering glow. She looked sleepy.

"Hi," I said. "Remember me?"

Her head swung up and she squinted. "No, sorry, I don't believe we've met."

I grinned and sat beside her. "I'm your long lost relative back from the trenches."

"Couldn't possibly be." She shook her head. "My only relative is a dear sweet girl who's enjoying hanky panky with her handsome Frenchman right now. I don't expect to see her until tomorrow." Her eyes twinkled. "Or the day after, if he's as good as I suspect."

I choked on a laugh. "Can I let you in on a secret?"

She nodded.

My voice lowered to a conspiratorial whisper. "He's even better than you suspect."

She hooted and slapped her leg. "There, proves my point. You couldn't possibly be my Desy. She has better sense than to leave a man like that alone."

I gave her a swift hug. "Yeah, but there's one important thing you're forgetting."

"That's doubtful." Her hand patted my knee, rested there. "I still remember when you wore your hair in a ponytail and danced around your room in frilly pink panties singing Motown into a hairbrush."

My tone scorched as dry as burnt toast. "That was last week, you ninny." Aunt P's cackle sounded like someone had goosed an ailing warthog. "What you've forgotten," I said, "is she's here because she loves her aunt oodles and gobs and heaps."

"I did say she was dear and sweet. But—" her voice turned serious "—she's also here because she's running scared."

"Ah." Back to that path of well-trampled conversation. Since they first met, my crafty aunt and the ever-craftier Frenchman joined in cahoots. Their objective?

To drag me kicking and screaming and bloody-kneed into his arms.

Stunning, smart, witty—why resist, you ask? He has it all. Trust, I suppose, is what it all boiled down to, and the fact he's way out of my league...out of my stratosphere...out of my solar system. I was *too* attracted to him. Armand reeks confidence and from day one his bold, suave demeanor raised my hackles and blood pressure. A wealthy playboy, I assumed.

But would a playboy give up gay Paree to bury himself in an obscure Michigan town? Would he take me out on our first official date and demand I see no one else? "You'll date no other man, *mon chou*," he said, his sexy brown eyes fixed on me. "We'll see only each other." Would a playboy be content, even seem to relish, spending long hours at home together, just talking?

Over time, somehow managing to slip under my radar, he earned my trust.

"By the look on your face, I'd say you have it pretty bad," my aunt remarked with a satisfied smile.

"All right, I admit it. He's given me a case of something. It...it's pretty bad."

"Case...case of what?"

"And there doesn't seem to be a cure."

Aunt P looked horrified. "Are you telling me he's given you a disease? An STD?"

"It's worse than that, I'm afraid."

Her hand tightened on my knee. "What? Just tell me." My aunt's face contorted into one large, concerned frown.

"Well," I said, "he's given me *Armand-itis*."

"Armand—" Her face cleared and she smacked my leg. Hard.

"Ow!"

"You're a horrid girl!"

"I thought I was dear and sweet."

"I'm 74 years old," she sniffed, "and obviously senile."

* * * * *

He snored like a defective chain saw low on oil.

My concerned gaze swept him from head to toe, taking in his mussed hair, one arm resting on his forehead, the other trailing to the floor, the dark circles under his eyes, his straight nose, parted lips, broad chest beneath a wrinkled blue shirt, and worn jeans. Legs dangling far past the couch's arm, his big toe poked through a hole in his left sock.

I'd known him forever. He is woven in my heart as surely as veins and arteries. Once next-door neighbors, we grew up in each other's pocket. I watched him mature into an all-American blond, blue-eyed, six-foot-one giant stud of a man. Watched females flock and cluck around him and determined early in life I'd never be one of them. No way. Nuh-uh. No siree.

We were just friends, the best of friends. Platonic. Though that morning I remained unaware our relationship would change as the week marched its merry way onward.

Nevertheless, he's always been there for me. Through first day kindergarten jitters and tears, algebra and braces, failed cheerleader tryouts and Goodyear-blimp-sized zits. Through college midterms and all-night cramming, boyfriends and failed relationships, I always turned to Nick.

When his parents retired to Florida he took over his father's private investigative firm. There was no question I'd be his partner. We've run the business together now for a couple years, and run it well. We make a great team and share everything, except the two darkest problems in our lives. Mine? I'm a witch, and not exactly ecstatic about the fact, either. He has nary a clue. His problem? Anita, and the fact he spends the night lately on the office's tweed couch instead of in his wife's bed.

Nicolas Sage, best friend and cohort, owns a troubled marriage. His wife and their rocky relationship stand like the proverbial elephant in the room. I pretend I don't see it, learned it was off-limits long ago by his monosyllabic answers, his slight frowns and body language. Nick doesn't want to discuss it, period. It makes him uncomfortable.

But on that Monday morning I knew my silence would soon end. For us both, the talk would be discomforting.

I ran my hand through his turbulent hair, smoothing it back in place. "Hey, handsome. Rise and shine."

He hummed, opened one tired eye. "Hi. What's the time?"

Wincing at his flesh-melting breath, I eased back. "Round eight-thirty."

"Shit."

I patted his chest. "You okay?"

"I'm fine."

He shifted to rise but my hand sat firm on his chest. "You smell like a six pack of tastes great, less filling. Want to talk about it?"

"Thanks, but no. There are tiny men excavating inside my skull." He rubbed his forehead, smacked his lips. "And something's crawled inside my mouth and died. I need coffee."

"Make you a deal?" I ventured. "I'll bring you fresh java, aspirin, and one of the bagels I brought in this morning if you update me on our caseload."

He scrubbed a hand over his face. "Deal."

* * * * *

"Well, maybe the reason you can't catch her in the act is because there's nothing to catch. Her hubby is probably mistaken."

Nick smirked. "He's not mistaken. He brought proof."

"Yeah?"

He stood. "I'll show you."

I watched him cross the room and dig in his desk drawer. The coffee and aspirin had morphed him into human form again. He looked semi-revived. An overnight bag, fresh clothes, and presto-chango, Nick the slick was up and functioning, back among the living.

We were discussing one of our cases—suspected adultery. While I was out of town the skeptical husband, a Mr. Todd Campbell, hired our firm to tail his wife, Denise, a real estate agent. She worked odd hours but of late the hours were a tad *too* odd. Four days of undercover work later, Nick surfaced bone dry.

He sat beside me. "Here."

I accepted a smallish envelope and dumped the contents in my hand. Photographs. Explicit photographs. Jaw dropping photographs. I took my time gawking. "Wow, I'm surprised."

"That this type of thing goes on?"

"No. At how small this one guy is here." I pointed.

"He looks about as tall as me."

"He is. I'm referring to his…um…well, his thingymajobber."

"His—" Nick let loose a deep belly laugh "—thingy-what?" he wheezed.

"Well, look at the size of his feet! I would never have suspected."

While he roared, the phone rang. "Can you get that?" Nick gasped.

I punched his shoulder, which felt like punching titanium, and answered the phone. A prospective client confirmed our business hours and after rattling off directions, I plopped beside the laughing hyena.

He gusted a happy sigh, wiped his eyes, and used an amused tone to comment, "You can calmly look at photos of heavy BDSM, but you can't say the word penis without blushing?"

"I didn't blush. And I can say…that word."

Slipping the pictures back inside the envelope, he turned to me with an evil twinkle glinting in his baby blues. "Say it."

My lips twisted. "Penis. There, happy now?"

"Ecstatic, thanks for the laugh."

"You're welcome but riddle me this, Sparky. If said husband has photos of his unfaithful wife, why does he need us?"

"In the pictures, what color hair did the woman have?"

"Blonde."

"His wife's a brunette, like you, and obviously one smart cookie. Notice how there's not a clear shot of her face?" I nodded. "He knows it's her, even has a divorce attorney lined up. They have three kids, though, and he wants bargaining power during custody negotiations."

"So he needs solid proof."

"And there's an extra five grand if we dig up full backgrounds on her partners by week's end."

I whistled. "How did hubby get his hands on those pictures?"

"Dropped by her office last week on the chance she'd be free for lunch. She was out; he had suspicions, so he searched her desk. Pilfered these goodies—" Nick waved the envelope "—from her bottom drawer. He doesn't think she'll discover their absence anytime soon. There was a mountain of double prints; he only swiped a few."

"Okay, run it by me again. Thursday, nine a.m. sharp, you tail her from home to office, where she sticks for three hours and leaves at noon…to go where again?"

"A couple showings. Strictly kosher. Carted around an elderly couple, took them to lunch, then drove back solo to her office and didn't leave again until six. She went straight home."

"That's a lot of office time. Real estate agents live out of their cars. Break down her building for me."

"Strip mall, corner of Crooks and Hamlin. Three agents, one receptionist, in a four-female-office sandwiched between a take-out Chinese restaurant that serves up a damn fine Szechwan chicken combo plate and a hair salon running back-to-school discounts. Parking in front with a back alley exit."

"Sure she's not shimmying out the rear, maybe using a different vehicle from there?"

He flashed a smile. "I'm sure. I put a trip wire relay on that exit."

I stood and paced. "And you said the rest of the week has been more of the same?"

Nick stretched his arms along the sofa's back. "The only break in routine occurred yesterday. All three agents manned an open house." He rubbed the back of his neck. "Dumpy part of town, too, over in Hazel Park."

"All three women? That's odd."

"Before you ask, yes, it was a legit open house. There's a for sale sign out front and except for one desk and chair, the house is empty."

I smirked. "Played peeping tom?"

"Prospective home buyer."

I stopped pacing. "You burnt your cover? You went inside? You met the women?"

"Yes, yes and yes."

"Why, why and why?"

"A hunch. The whole setup didn't feel right." Frustration crossed his face, lingered in a small crease between his brows. "My hunch turned flat. They gave me the grand tour, all five minutes of it, and ushered me out."

"Five minutes? That's quick. They flirt with you?"

"No."

"Sidelong glances?"

A smile played at his mouth. "Nope."

"Spot any drool on their chins?"

"Not a drop."

"Were these women alive?" He barked a laugh. "I'm serious," I said. "Three female real estate agents escort a blond Viking through an empty house and there's no wafting pheromones?"

"Not a whiff, but only two escorted me. The third was in the bathroom."

I shook my head. "Something smells fishy."

"Because nobody fainted at my feet? C'mon, Des."

I plopped beside him. "Cut the modesty. Your hunch wasn't flat, something's rotten in Denmark."

He smiled. "You mean in Hazel Park?"

"There, too."

"Well, we'll soon find out. During my tour, I bugged the house."

Chapter Three

While typing, I hummed a sonata off-key.

Beethoven, I believed, but for all I knew it belonged to any dead musician. I've always held the theory only old farts (sucking on fat cigars between sips of one-hundred-year-old brandy) listened to classical music. Until Armand. He listens to it and ingests neither brandy nor cigars. Blew my old fart theory to smithereens.

I seldom visit his home without hidden speakers oozing soft classical or jazz, the contrasting genres mirroring what I've always seen in him — a beguiling mix of refinement and deep sensuality. Rock and roll's much more my style, Motown too, but over time I've come to appreciate his musical tastes, although I won't soon admit it because I appreciate even more our spirited debates on the subject.

The ten o'clock sun lit two easterly windows and fell warm on my back as I crossed all the T's in the case file before me. The bell on the front door tinkled a jolly hello, interrupting my spirited humming, and I tried to veil a frown when Sam Bearns entered.

"Good morning, Desy." At my thunderous expression, he caught himself mid-smile and mid-bow. I disallowed them. Bows, not smiles.

"I'm just finishing something here," I said with a firm tone, the kind you use for door-to-door salesmen. "Have a seat and I'll be right with you."

"Thanks." He ambled to the couch.

Sam owns Club Wicked, a techno dance nightclub catering to the under-21 Goth crowd—also the site of a past investigation, my first mystical battle, and currently a basement haven for his small coven. Sam's a witch, and friendly but not friends, we both wanted something from the other. He wanted me (and Armand) to lead and expand his coven. I wanted him to leave me the hell alone.

See, the label High Priestess didn't sit well with me, nor did Sam's expectations. Both weighed thick and itchy, like a medieval hair shirt. Frankly, I still struggled with the entire concept of witchcraft and so to be thrust into a Wiccan power structure where I top the pecking order, well, thanks but no thanks. It was ludicrous. The idea of supernatural politics, hierarchy, and my holding dominion over it all was as absurd to me as trying to squeeze into a size three. It just wasn't gonna happen.

I tolerated Sam's perennial visits because he magically healed Armand once after battle. I felt indebted to Sam, but that didn't make me qualified to govern his coven. Govern-smovern. I had enough trouble just deciding what to wear each morning.

Eleven-ish, I was scheduled to rendezvous with Nick, who was off on another exciting day of shadowing Ms. Real Estate Agent. Unfortunately, Sam Bearns always ran a tad longwinded. It looked like I'd be late.

Smothering a sigh, I joined him on the couch; unaware this particular conversation would brew storm clouds on my personal horizon. Hindsight's a bitch.

"Thanks for seeing me." His mouth stretched into an apprehensive smile.

Viewing each subsequent visit as escalating Wiccan pressure, I began to wear curtness like Kevlar when around Sam and he in turn began to grovel, which irked me no end. Over time, I'd turned into a shrew and he, an anxious jellyfish. Neither mutation suited us.

I replied, "Sure, but let me hurry this along, shall I? Yes, it's a beautiful day. Yes, work has been going along mighty fine, thank you. Yes, Armand is doing well. Yes, I'm peachy keen, too, and no, I will not attend your next coven meeting."

He fiddled with his tie and invoked the bewildered expression of a kicked puppy. "We uh, generally meet on alternate Friday nights, but if that's inconvenient, we can gather any day that better suits your schedule."

"How about February 30?"

Sam swallowed hard and migrated south on the couch in a nervous shuffle. "We really need help, I'm afraid. There's a disturbing rumor."

"Yeah, I've heard it, too." I leaned toward him. "Elvis…is…still…alive."

He released a puff of uneasy laughter. "Seriously, it's not just my coven. All Michigan covens are under threat."

He sat before me trembling like a Chihuahua in a snowstorm. I wondered how high he'd jump if I suddenly yelled "Boo!" and summoned an award-winning portrayal of someone who gave a shit. "Okay, tell me what the problem is."

"Oh, thank you!" His stiff posture relaxed a degree. "It's Warren. He's due back this week."

"Okay, Warren is due back this week…and that's a problem because?"

"You do know who Warren is, don't you?"

"Haven't a clue."

"Oh, I thought Armand would have told you."

I stilled. "What does Armand have to do with this?"

In a nervous tug, Sam pulled on his goatee. "I...I went first to Armand about Warren because I know how, how reluctant you are about...all this."

"And Armand said?"

"He said he wouldn't present my case to you, that I needed to do it myself."

Smart man. "Who's Warren?"

"He's Michigan's High Priest."

Great. Employing power and birthright, witchcraft has its own governmental bodies within each state or country, reigned by a High Priest and/or High Priestess along with a High Council of thirteen. Decades ago my parents ruled in France. So coveted were their seats, they were murdered, then Armand and I were manipulated into a mystical battle over ownership of those seats not three months ago.

Wiccan politics are dangerous to your health. I wanted no part of them.

The wall clock above Sam read 10:30. My gaze fell to his fretful eyes of blue. "So, here's your spiel in a nutshell," I said, ticking the highlights off on my fingers. "Warren is a High Priest. He's returning from somewhere. That's a problem. There's a rumor. You feel threatened. Armand won't help coerce my involvement. *And* you believe I can straddle a flying broomstick, chant a merry spell, and somehow save the day." My lips pursed. "How am I doing so far?"

Sam flashed a weak smile. "Warren views the non-Wiccan populace as subservient. He devised some type of plan and took it before the Council. The rumor is they rejected it." He fiddled with his glasses and cleared his throat. "He'll return sometime this week displeased, and Warren displeased is cause for great concern. He's already called a mandatory meeting for this Friday."

"It's the High Council's job to keep him in line."

"But he can do a lot of damage before they act."

I sighed. "So what exactly do you need from me?"

He hunched toward me. "Covens believe your and Armand's presence at Friday's meeting will deter Warren."

I snorted. "Well, I believe our presence will only threaten him, and I've dealt before with a High Priest who felt threatened. It wasn't pretty." I stood and he followed me up. "I'm sorry, Sam. I won't be involved in this."

I ushered him toward the door that rapidly became swallowed by a huge shadow before swinging open. Sam and I stopped in our tracks as a mountain of a man ducked through the entryway. He had to be close to seven feet tall. I should know. At five-foot-two and one centimeter, I'm used to looking up at most people but with this one, I had to search the heavens for his face. I squinted up…and up.

Sam whispered, "Oh no, oh Desy."

I ignored him and greeted the giant. "Hi, may I help you?"

Said giant pulled off his sunglasses and smirked down at me. "You fat?"

The smirk was not wholly unexpected. Most people can't resist tittering at my last name. I've experienced a lifetime of juvenile amusement at my expense. Sam tugged on my sleeve and I batted his hand away. "That's P-h-a-t-t, Desdemona Phatt." I held out my hand. "And you are?"

"I called earlier." Tucking his glasses inside his breast pocket, he looked around the office with a negligent expression. "I need a moment of your time." My outstretched hand lingered in midair, wobbled, then fell to my side.

Beneath his breath Sam hissed, "Desy!" as I told the giant, "Of course. I'll be right with you." I prodded Sam through the open doorway.

Out on the hot concrete he spat a frantic whisper, "You don't understand."

"Sam, my answer is no. Now be a good little boy and run along home." The bell tinkled goodbye behind me as I approached my visitor. I motioned to a chair. "Please, have a seat." Curving my lips into a professional smile, I settled behind my desk. "How may I help you?"

Even seated, the man loomed so huge he no doubt registered on satellite imaging. A three-piece suit hung custom-made and expensive on his bulky frame. "Mr. Williams requests your presence in one hour." He handed me a business card. "A limousine will escort you there."

The card read *Mr. W. Williams, 37 Chalmers Place, Grosse Point North*. Expensive cardstock, off-white with raised black script. No phone number. Odd.

Right then would have been a dandy time for my brain to kick into high gear. I should have paid attention to Sam's fevered whisperings. Should have listened to my gut that said with a slow roll this request might be a good one to deny. Should have lingered a tad longer on Mr. Williams's first initial.

That morning's regretful oversights dawned the genesis in a long week of Should Haves.

I met the giant's impassive stare. "And this concerns?"

"A business proposal."

"Mr. Williams won't come to my office?"

He replied in a dry tone, "People go to Mr. Williams, he doesn't come to them."

My fingertips drummed the desk. Tap. Tap. Tap. "The earliest I can see him is one p.m. I'll use my own vehicle." Tap.

His eyes hardened as he unbuttoned his suit, slipped a hand inside. Unease prickled my neck, stiffened my spine. Gun, knife, rubber ducky—who knew what he would withdrawal. Cautious, I watched his steel gray eyes.

"Mr. Williams instructed me to give you this for inducement." He slid a small, folded sheet of paper across my desk.

I dwelled for a moment in the anticlimax before opening the paper. A check. My eyes widened at all the fat happy zeros.

"That's your consultation fee. Can he expect you in one hour?"

Pros and cons tussled in my brain. Cons won. I ignored them. "All right, but I didn't catch your name."

He stood, thereby eclipsing the sun. "I didn't throw it."

* * * * *

The anemic butler scored a nine on my personal freak-o-meter.

"This way, please."

I followed the limping albino from the foyer down a wide hallway. It wasn't his pale skin, pinkish eyes or limp that made me look askance, it was the blind monkey perched on his left shoulder.

Before sliding onto the waiting limo's Corinthian leather that morning, I'd done three things: One, I called Nick. Two, I searched the internet for Mr. W. Williams and discovered large quantities of zilch, which prompted number Three, arming myself with both a Taser and a Browning 9mm.

The concealed guns felt comforting as I trailed monkey man. Due to his pronounced limp, progress inched painfully slow. Feeling we might soon travel backward, I neared a lethargic trance—step, drag, shuffle…step, drag, shuffle—and so the primate's deafening squeal caught me unprepared. When my feet touched ground again, a nervous chortle preceded my query, "What's his name?"

"Nancy."

"You named him Nancy?"

"Her."

"Oh."

He lurched portside into a huge room. Acres of furniture, bookshelves, and obnoxious wealth met my eyes.

"Please be seated. Mr. Williams will see you soon."

"Thanks."

"Would you care for a refreshment?"

I eyed the ape. The possibility of monkey drool splattering in my iced tea arrested all thoughts of thirst. "No, thank you. No."

"Very well." The monkey's tail curled, swishing against the departing butler's back.

Still skittish from the primate's jungle call, I meandered over miles of plush Oriental rugs, eyeing curious knickknacks and collectibles, small sculptures, stopping now and then to regard oil paintings depicting the circus. In fact—I spun around—every decoration in the room was circus related. An odd theme.

Lifting a small statue of a crying clown, its porcelain form awash in agony, I wondered at the owner's fascination with the big top. Wondered, too, at that morning's surfeit of oddities—the giant in my office, the butler and his monkey, this very summons, and nape prickling, I suddenly knew someone stood behind me.

"That's one of my favorite pieces," a youthful voice mused soft and almost boyish.

Clown in hand, I turned to view a slender man, hovering five-seven-ish or so, with wide hazel eyes set in an amiable face beneath what Aunt P terms dirty dishwater hair, a muddy shade between dull brown and even duller blonde. In his mid-thirties or thereabout, his slight frame bore a crisp navy suit and his face, a slight smile. First impression? A nice, affable millionaire.

"What do you think?" he asked with a growing grin, then prompted to my blank stare, "About the statue."

"Oh!" I peered at the porcelain form clutched in my hand. "It's—" *disturbing, ugly, whacked* "—um, compelling." I returned it to the shelf.

"This room is in total balance," he informed, adjusting my placement of the clown a hairbreadth to the left. "There. Now we're back in chi."

Ooookay. "Mr. Williams?"

"Yes, and you're Desdemona." We shook hands. His smile shined so brightly I needed SPF30 protection. "It's certainly a pleasure. Please, let's sit."

"Thank you." We settled in facing black leather chairs. Very comfy. I began, "I've brought a history and referral sheet on my firm," and his quick reply, "That won't be necessary," staved an archeological dig in my briefcase. My relief showed in a polite smile. "How may Sage & Phatt Investigations be of help to you?"

"They can't."

"I'm afraid I don't understand."

"You're here not because I require a detective, but because I require a High Priestess."

Chapter Four

"I beg your pardon?" Shock hid behind my best poker face.

"That's the problem I'm talking about, right there." He gave a brisk nod.

"It is?"

"Yes. We shouldn't have to deny who we are. *They* certainly don't have to." He spat the word *they* like it reeked worse than month-old dirty laundry.

I wondered if I'd somehow blacked out and missed essential parts of the conversation. Beyond baffled I ventured, "They?"

Mr. Williams shot from his chair and began to pace in a clipped gait, slender hands stabbing the air to punctuate his fervid speech. "*They* can choose any vocation they wish, whereas we can only hide our true selves behind acceptable professions or they'll drown us...or burn us."

Growing comprehension swirled unhappily in my gut, not to mention the beginnings of motion sickness when he began to circle my chair.

"Even my own parents weren't able to accept me," Warren informed. "They and their church tried to *pray* magic out of me." He gave a mean little bark of laughter and my fingers curled into the chair's soft leather.

"Your parents?" I ventured.

"Non-Wiccans both. I'm adopted. They punished me each time I used magic, all because I was too young to understand control and sometimes I'd have an accident. A dish would float at the dinner table or—" he paced "— maybe the book they'd taken from me would reappear the next day. It was always something."

He spun toward me. "I tell you this to illustrate the persecution our kind has suffered for centuries continues still. We need to rise up a—"

"Parents taking a book from a child is persecution?"

He pierced me with a hard stare. "By the time I was twelve, they'd taken to locking me in a basement cage. I stopped that soon enough."

Stopped that soon enough, my mind slowly repeated. I didn't have to ask how; the answer shined in his eyes with a type of sick glow. I began to gnaw the inside of my mouth. I do that when I'm nervous, or around psychopaths.

Warren crossed his legs after he settled in the chair.

"After my parents were dealt with, I contacted my father's friend, Bill. Used to call him Uncle Bill." A fond smile slid across his face. "Bill was a circus roustabout and a drunk—easy enough to control. He arrived within the week and helped me—" his smile sharpened to grin "— clean up, so to speak. When it was time for him to return to work, I tagged along."

During his candid walk down memory lane his magic leaked, spilling on me in thick droplets of twisted power burning mighty, potent, and just plain wrong.

By then, the fierce beat of my heart would have won first place at any solo drum competition. Was there a reason, I pondered, why I attracted crazed witches? What was I—walking flypaper for freaks? Perhaps "Insanity Welcomed Here" was somehow magically tattooed on my forehead and could only be read by demented High Priests? Because that's what he was. Call me a little slow, but I'd finally pieced everything together and arrived at the sure, unwelcome knowledge I gawked at one Mr. Warren Williams. Sam Bearns' Warren. Warren of the dark rumors–Council declining–Friday mandatory meeting–very displeased variety.

"The circus," he said. "Ever been?"

"A couple times."

"It's spectacular, isn't it? I was amazed my first night there. Tricks and magic were performed freely. I knew I'd found a real home. Some required my guidance, of course, but soon everyone welcomed me. I traveled with them for years. Several members of my staff are past performers. Sam, my butler, used to be a front-lining act."

Imagine that. "And I'm here today because…"

"Because I'm finished trying to reason with the Council. They obviously must be made to listen. I've come to realize they'll always play it safe. They can't see the big picture. I've told you of my background so you will understand. With you by my side they'll approve my proposal, then our state will be the first to recognize and honor witchcraft." He leaned toward me. "Together, Desdemona, we'll bring witchcraft out of the closet, out of persecution, and I will be the leading force behind a worldwide movement. Magic won't be hidden, but revered."

I plastered a contrived smile on my face and though it felt as stiff as dried mud, I prayed it wouldn't crack. "And you think the general public is ready for that?"

"I don't care if they are or aren't. It doesn't concern me. We have all the power. Why do we hide it?"

I asked a question of my own. "Why would the Council accept your proposal with me by your side?"

"Your power. They'll have no recourse with our combined magic and if they attempt to refuse again, we'll weave a binding spell to control them."

I experienced a late attack of common sense and stood. "Sorry, you've got the wrong High Priestess. I like my closet." My sweaty palm latched onto my briefcase and I took one step in retreat.

"Stop." For some reason I did, stilling when I should have sprinted. Hindsight again. He cocked his head. "I'm afraid I must insist on your cooperation."

That didn't sound good, not good at all. Before I could burble a rejoinder, his power washed over me. Whatever it was that made me a witch lurched and flamed to life, answering in kind. Power lifted my hair in long curls of brown, prickling up my back, sliding inside me, anxious and strong and ready. Magic poured into me like a heady elixir.

I knew my brown eyes darkened to an unnatural black, knew a warm breeze circled the room humming with energy, knew, too, I stood in deep, dark smelly stuff.

"You'll go with me before the Council." His words pushed at me, powerful and suggestive, nudging against my mind.

Okay, so maybe my first impression of him was a tad off. I got one out of three, though; he was a millionaire all right, just not nice or affable. "No, I won't."

Confidence sparkled in his smile. "You will."

His power felt cold and vile prodding at my mind and in defense, my magic pressed back, arching with anger. "Get out of my head!"

My magic fought his, inexperienced against adept, and inside my skull his nudge turned to shove. Pain spiked. My left hand flew to my temple as power clawed through my head, forcing a low moan. I swung my right hand, which clutched my briefcase, and eight pounds of scuffed cheap leather collided with Warren's smiling face. Whap. He crumpled to the floor like a prom dress at a cheap motel.

Dizzy, head throbbing, I pivoted from his sprawled form and staggered through his lessening power to the doorway. Only problem, Goliath blocked it.

"You hit him," protested the giant I'd met in my office.

"Yeah mom, but he started it." Okay, I have a mouth on me, I admit, and under normal circumstances I'm usually able to contain it. Those weren't ordinary circumstances. Anger flamed in the giant's eyes and I backpedaled. "Anyone ever remark that if you stumbled in green paint, you could star in the next Hulk movie?" He advanced into the room and I dodged behind a sofa.

"I'm going to make you very sorry you hit him."

"Couldn't you just put me in time out?"

Growling, he charged. Magic leapt within me, swelling, and targeting it down my arm—heat sizzling beneath my skin—I flung it outward. A blue streak of soundless energy shot from my fingertips and hit the giant's chest. His eyes rolled back and he fell, breaking a small end table on his merry way down.

My heart and lungs labored alongside roiling power.

Mon chou, I'm on my way. Tell me you're all right.

Armand. In preparation of our last mystical battle, we performed a merging spell that combined our powers, strengthened us, and had as a dandy byproduct granted the ability to "mindspeak" with each other when we engaged our powers.

I'm fine. How'd you know I was in trouble?

Sam called me.

I looked around for my briefcase but made the delightful discovery two additional men, both sporting linebacker builds, had entered the room. Had Warren cleared out all the stock at Rent-a-Henchman?

One kneeled at the giant's side and the other man, the one who looked as if someone had emptied a whole can of ugly on him, charged me.

I yelled, "Shit!" Like that would help.

Hold on. I'll be there in five minutes.

I sprinted behind a recliner. *Three would be better.*

Ugly grabbed the chair and I barely managed to dodge as he fired it at me. It crashed into a lamp shaped like a Ferris wheel. Ceramic shattered.

Stay safe. Focus your power.

Armand's worried voice flowed in my mind as energy hurtled down my arm, hot and willful, to leap from my fingertips. Power zapped through the air like blue lightning but Ugly dived to his left and it sizzled past him to blow up an ottoman.

The intricate blacks and reds of Warren's Oriental rug rose to greet me as someone tackled me from behind. I struck the floor and all the air whooshed from my lungs, which were seconds later rendered completely useless when two hundred and fifty pounds of dumb muscle landed on me.

I groaned when he grabbed my hair, lifted my head and slammed my face back down. Thump. Sharp pain slapped my temple. That got my dander up, but good; I was absolutely fit to be framed.

Mon chou?

Sorry, kinda busy right now.

My hand searched my waist for my stun gun and as he yanked my hair again, lifted my head in a sharp tug, I jabbed his side with 625,000 volts of happy juice. An electrical seizure and two harsh moans later, he flailed off me.

I rolled over, gasping for air, just in time to view the sole on Ugly's size fourteen descend toward my face. A dirty wad of gum stuck in a blue lump to the bottom of his shoe. Ick.

An upholstered chair blocked my immediate left; I rolled to my right and found myself between his legs. How convenient. I shoved my Taser into his family jewels and zapped him a good one. Snap-Crackle-Pop.

He squealed like a jackal giving birth and keeled over backward. I smiled when the thud shook the entire room.

I need to hear your voice. Now.

Armand sounded torqued. I stood with a slight sway, nerves as stable as nitro. *Know how you keep making me practice my blue-gamma-ray-thingy power?* I asked.

Desy. My name sounded halfway between grateful prayer and murderous frustration. His sigh feathered through my mind. *The combust stream? Oui.*

Have I thanked you recently?

There's no need.

Oh, there's need all right. Thank you.

Thank me in person. I'm pulling onto Warren's property.

Even after a nice zap with my power, the giant attempted to rise. My motto? If at first you don't succeed, try try again. I kicked him a good one in the ribs — thought maybe I heard one crack. Yippee. It felt well worth the stinging pain that shot up my leg when he fell back to the floor in a sorry heap, like a bag of garbage tossed to the curb.

Just when I assumed everything appeared hunky-dory, power flooded the room anew, cold and maleficent, pebbling my skin and pushing against my mind. Shit. Warren.

I spun around and my heart leapt to my throat to find him so near. As a nifty keepsake, my briefcase left a reddened lump bulging high on his forehead. It looked nasty. He grabbed my upper arms in a vise grip and seared me with blazing eyes; I read royally ticked in their depths but when he jerked me flush against him I read otherwise and it opened up a whole new dimension of disgusting. "Please tell your pants it's not polite to point." A knee thrust in the problem area seemed a grand idea, but he neatly blocked my attempt.

"Your power is so very alluring," he breathed, capturing my hands in one wide, crushing palm. Warren had a surprising, meaty grip.

I tugged uselessly and then stilled with shock when his free hand cupped my breast. "Hey," I snarled, "Leggo my Eggo!"

My face turned aside when his mouth neared and he kissed the edge of my lips, my cheek. As far as an initial business meeting went, our appointment scored fairly high for exhilaration, the kind you feel when your parachute doesn't open while skydiving.

"We'll make quite a pair. You are absolutely magnificent."

"Gee, thanks, and you're, what's the word I'm searching for? Um…almost got it…*insane*."

Pressure spiked in my skull, I grew lightheaded and tried to yank free, but his hand squeezed mine with more force than a junkyard-crushing machine.

"You'll find, Desdemona, I always get what I want. And I want you." Encased in power, his words pushed at me in a silken web of coercion, weaving through my consciousness, pressing, compelling me to listen. "You will be at my side Friday night." Again he kissed my cheek. "And you'll stand with me against the Council. Say it. Say yes, Warren."

I shivered and ached. A fit of nausea gripped my gut in a tight queasy fist as pain beat at me in unrelenting waves. I felt as if I treaded thick water, cold and exhausted, while beneath me his power grasped my ankles and began to slowly pull me under until I finally…slipped…beneath…the surface.

"Yes, Warren," I whispered.

He smiled. "You want nothing more than to please me."

"Yes."

"Kiss me."

Mon chou, where are you?

I blinked.

Desy!

Swimming up through thick quelling power toward Armand's voice, I instructed, *Take the left corridor off the foyer.*

Warren released my hands when I kissed him and following his pleasure-filled hum; I bit into his bottom lip and pressed my Browning against his erection. Blood and fear filled my mouth; neither mine. He jerked, stilled, and within my mind his magic ebbed. Reluctantly, I released his lip.

"Tell me why I shouldn't empty my entire clip, Warren, because I have an eensie confession. I really, really want to."

Behind me came Armand's smooth voice. "I see you have everything in hand."

I stared into Warren's cautious eyes. "Armand, have you ever met Warren Williams the Witch?" It was a catchy name (but try to say it five times fast).

"*Non*, I've not had the displeasure."

"Well, that's probably a good thing. His hospitality blows." I dug the gun deeper into his dwindling erection, smiled when he paled. "He tried to get inside my mind."

"A binding spell." Armand's hand smoothed up my arm to linger on my shoulder.

Though never before under one myself, I'd seen firsthand the effects of such a spell, how it glazed the victim's eyes, subduing all freewill. "It was really quite unpleasant." My gaze continued to lock with Warren's. "Short of making you a eunuch, which by the way I find mighty tempting, I don't quite know what to do with you."

Armand said, "I have an idea."

"Yeah?"

"Lean a little to your left," he told me.

"Like this?"

"*Oui.*" Lightning fast, Armand's fist cracked into Warren's face. Blood spurted from his nose, and for the second time in that hour he toppled backward to sprawl unconscious on the floor.

Holstering my gun, I appreciated the fine view of Warren's expensive navy suit, wrinkled and spotted with blood, his pummeled face, bloody lip, the stain spreading dark and wet at his crotch.

I turned into Armand's waiting arms. God, he felt good, and he coupled his relieved whisper of "*Mon chou,*" with a bone-crushing hug; I didn't mind in the least my lack of oxygen. "Desy," he breathed, "you're not to do this ever again. I absolutely forbid it." He kissed me hard.

"You're right," I agreed when he allowed me air. "The next time a psychopath has me in his dastardly clutches, I'll tell him you absolutely forbid it."

"See that you do."

"Thanks for coming to my rescue."

Armand's gaze swept the room, taking in the four downed men, broken furniture, and the smoking ottoman. His brow arched. "You're welcome."

I grinned. "Let's hit the road."

While he located my briefcase, I retrieved my Taser from its just resting spot between Ugly's legs.

"During the ride, you'll tell me all about your exciting morning," Armand said.

My mouth brushed his in a soft caress and then because he tasted so damn good, once again. "Okeydokey. I'll begin my tale with shrieking Nancy, the blind monkey. Ready?"

"Always."

I followed him through the doorway. "It's a shame about the room."

"What about it?"

"It's no longer in chi."

Chapter Five

"So he's obviously a few peas short of a casserole," I said in conclusion, recapping to Armand that morning's titillating meeting with Warren.

Earlier on the phone Aunt P assured me she was fine, but rather than return to work I asked Armand to take me straight home to double-check on her. I wasn't overreacting. The last time I tangled with a sanity-impaired High Priest, he shanghaied my aunt. There'd be no encore.

We pulled up to my house and Armand turned to me in the car. "And that is precisely why we need to arrange a meeting with the ruling Council. Much as I'd like to deal with Warren myself, a formal complaint needs to be lodged."

Due to Warren, my foot had already stepped in a slimy magical quagmire; I certainly didn't want to jump in knee-deep by contacting the Council. "He'd have to be mad to tangle with us again."

Armand stroked my cheek. "From what you've just told me, he is exactly that."

"Shit," I sighed. "You're right but *dammit*, I know my math, Armand. You and me plus one demented High Priest equals one very large mess squared. I don't want to get involved."

"I know. You're still uneasy about magic, and even more so with other witches' expectations of you. I understand your reluctance, I do. You've had very little time to acclimate, but I'll not permit your misgivings to jeopardize your safety."

"You were moving along fine and dandy until you uttered *I'll not permit*. Those words really rub me the wrong way." Temper brewing, I stared unseeing out the car window.

"*Mon chou*…love, look at me, please."

Our gazes fused when my head turned. His eyes shone a dark, molten brown and he gave me *The Look*, the one that has the ability to double my heartbeat.

"I won't take risks. I can't. You are the most important thing in my life."

More and more of late Armand verbalized his feelings for me. The big four-letter "L" word had yet to be uttered, the delay of which I felt heartily grateful for. I just wasn't ready to hear it, though every time I looked into his eyes, something extra shined steady in their depths. I pretended it was indigestion.

He leaned toward me and over the stick shift I met him halfway in a brief kiss, almost chaste, then his tongue washed over the full curve of my bottom lip, captured it between his teeth for a tender nip. My lips parted and in heady answer to the invitation, his tongue pushed inside.

It didn't matter if that was our fiftieth kiss or our five-hundredth; somehow it always felt like our first. Each time his lips meet mine, flurries of excitement swirl hot and dizzy in my tummy, my heartbeat lurches to a brisk pace, a flush scorches my skin, and the crotch of my panties dampens.

I moaned and his hands moved, one to cup the back of my head, the other to cup my breast, sending hot tingles of pleasure pulsing to my womb. I wiggled in torment, rubbed my legs together.

The midday sun glared as we sat parked in front of my house, hardly an appropriate site for what I thought about. But think about it I did. Sizzling images swam behind my closed eyes. Images of straddling his lap, releasing his cock, winding my fingers around its stiff girth, long thick flesh, and sliding down its length in a slow, wet glide to swallow him whole. He would fill me, stretch me, undo me. I would drink down his hot groan, relish it, as I slicked up and down, moving with a tempo that would begin slow and sensual only to speed to frantic rutting until we came and the scent of satisfaction filled the car.

At the intoxicating thought of being filled first with long inches of Armand, then with hot spurts of cream, thick frothy eruptions, a helpless little moan slipped free.

He tore his lips away and with large hands cradling my face, pressed his forehead gently to mine. "If it weren't for your neighbors," he said after a moment, "I'd throw you in the backseat and have my wicked way with you."

"If it weren't for the neighbors, I'd let you." I kissed him again, a slow needy buss, whispering against his soft lips, "Let's go inside now because I'm one second away from saying to hell with the neighbors."

"I'm half a second away."

I opened the car door and grinned at him. "You're no help."

"*Non*, not when you kiss me like that."

I stepped out, peered back inside. "Coming?"

With a wry twist of lips, he gestured to the huge bulge straining his zipper. "Give me a moment?"

My grin widened. I waited for him on the sidewalk, running my gaze over my house, a rambling Victorian sandwiched between an English Tudor—owned by Ted, currently divorced, in the throes of a midlife crisis, and brand new member of a hair club for men—and to my right, a darling cape cod bustling with an energetic family of six, two toy poodles and one pet iguana named Miss Lucy.

It's a pretty street dotted with thick mature trees, nice green lawns, and vintage homes hearkening back to the era of silent films.

Aunt P never met a color she didn't like and as testimony one need only glance (or wince, as the case may be) at the neon rainbow of shades highlighting the Victorian's peaks, trim and front door. The brash nerve of my house forces a squint.

I turned when Armand's hand trailed along my back. "All recovered?"

"For the moment." His mouth curved in a slight smile.

Unsuspecting, we went inside and to my complete stupefaction found a giggling Aunt P on the living room's loveseat snuggling barely the width of a limp spaghetti noodle from an elderly stranger. A man. They looked cozy.

In retrospect I should have followed Armand's lead—acted refined, perhaps slightly amused. Don't snicker. I can drum up "polished and elegant" if the need arises. I can even arch my brow now nearly as high as he can. (I've been practicing.)

But all that effort takes forethought and therein lays the problem. Seeing my aunt with a man felt like a blow to the head and the resulting concussion swept away all coherent thought. Left with only dumbfounded bewilderment and shock, shock that stole my breath and then my manners, I demanded, "What the hell is going on?"

The couple on the couch looked up. My aunt's eyes sparkled. "Sweetie pie!"

Aunt P uses a large assortment of pet names for me. Sweetie pie tops the list. She also uses a large assortment of expressions and the one on her face at that particular moment told me to be a good girl, act polite, wear clean underwear, and stand up straight.

The gentleman beside her so resembled Kentucky's dearly departed Colonel, I glanced at his hand expecting to see him clutching a finger lickin' good drumstick, extra crispy. He stood and spoke with a wide flash of dentures. "Why, you must be Desdemona. I've heard so much about you. I'm Franklin Crenshaw."

I eyed his extended hand. Crenshaw. Crenshaw. The name rang a distant bell.

Armand cleared his throat.

Brow furrowing, I shook the offered hand and motioned to Armand. "This is Armand Bellamy."

As they shook hands, Franklin ventured, "The beau from France, right?"

Armand smiled. "*Oui.*"

"Armand," Aunt P said, wearing a wide smile and a sleeveless frock in an eye-popping purple and orange stripe. "Would you care for some iced tea and gingersnaps? Desy dear, would you?" We declined. "Well, everyone sit, please."

With my brain whirring faster than a tornado in a trailer park, I settled on the couch beside Armand, straight across from the two cooing lovebirds. I'd never before seen my aunt with a man; the sight was unnerving. I couldn't seem to wrap my mind around the concept. "Mr. Crenshaw," I said, clearing my clogged throat. "Your name is somehow familiar to me."

"You've probably heard mention of my wife, Sally."

My right brow inched up my forehead. "Your wife?"

Aunt P hastened, "Franklin's a widower, Desy. Sally passed away in March. She used to play Wednesday night bridge with the girls."

For centuries Aunt P has played weekly cards with the neighborhood ladies. I remembered talk of Sally Crenshaw, who as I recalled owned a ribald sense of humor and a blue ribbon apple pie recipe before a car accident stole her life.

"My condolences on your loss, Mr. Crenshaw," Armand said, and I mechanically echoed the consolatory words.

"Thank you both. Sally was a great gal. I miss her."

Aunt P clasped his hand. "We all do."

I looked at their entwined hands, their private smiles, and something inside me clutched.

* * * * *

I fell for his spiel so fast, I almost shouted timber.

It went something along the lines of my aunt was fine, she was with a friend, strong protective spells guarded her, yada, yada. As spiels went, it wasn't such a bad one and it got Armand exactly what he wanted—a lunch date with me before I returned to work.

I chose a little hole-in-the-wall diner downtown at Second and Lafayette. I'd eaten there countless times but it would be a first for Armand. Truth to tell, it gave me a secret kick to see my suave Frenchman sitting in a booth upholstered in duct-taped, worn blue vinyl.

Culture, polish and money ooze from Armand's very pores, though he's not a priss by any means. Refinement is just an innate quality of his being, and so it tickled my funny bone no end to see his Armani suit lean where a sticky toddler undoubtedly pressed his wad of Juicy Fruit.

Tiny, the diner is staffed by one cook and two waitresses. We sat in Mabel's section, though in retrospect we should have plopped in Lois's, who would have served us our food with a smile and at most some polite talk of weather. But *no*, still reeling from the disturbing sight of Mr. Crenshaw's beefy paws on Aunt P, I heedlessly chose a Mabel booth. She's a real firecracker, that Mabel. In her late sixties, standing shorter than I do even beneath four inches of teased blue hair, she doles out free side orders of unsolicited advice with each plateful of food.

My stomach growled as a list of that day's specials swam before my wide greedy eyes. "Mind if I order the entire left hand side of the menu?" It was Armand's turn to pay. At my insistence, we alternated restaurant tabs.

"Order the right hand side as well," he said. "We'll share."

Mabel sidled up to our booth and I winced when she gave Armand a low whistle. By sitting in her section I expected some good-natured ribbing, but on that particular lunch date I got much more than witty repartee.

"You won't need dessert with this one," Mabel commented. "He looks good enough to eat."

Armand's gaze flicked to her nametag. "I'm flattered, Mabel. What would you recommend for lunch?"

She tapped her order pad with a chewed pencil. "Good looking *and* fancy accent. Hmmm. You a meat and potato man?"

"*Oui*, yes."

"Our Sam makes a mean meatloaf."

"Mashed potatoes and gravy?" Armand asked.

"Does it come any other way?"

"I'll have some then, and coffee, please."

A salad, I thought, I should have a small salad with lo-fat dressing on the side. One crouton.

"You?" Mabel asked of me.

"I'll have what he ordered."

She scribbled on her pad. "So, this serious between you two?"

I suddenly found the tabletop's chipped Formica incredibly interesting.

Without hesitation he answered, "Very." My gaze lifted to meet his hot stare. "Very serious."

"Well, handsome," Mabel countered, "there's very, and then there's *very*. I don't see a shiny ring on her finger. What's the holdup?"

Fight or flight hit me and I briefly eyed a nearby fire exit. "Mabel," I said in an aggrieved tone, "we've only known each other three short months. Can I have a diet cola instead?" With the amount of sugar I dump in coffee, the cola would shave a hundred easy calories off my plateful of sin.

"Love is love," she said. "My Harry proposed after the first date. We've been together now thirty-seven happy years."

"A diet cola?" I pleaded. "Please?"

When Armand said, "You and I are of the same mind, Mabel," I broke out in a nervous sweat. The entire subject gave me heartburn. My hand pushed through my hair and I bleated, "How 'bout those Red Wings! I hear they've already started mini-camp."

Mabel tucked her pencil behind her ear. "Then what's the delay?" she asked Armand. "This one's a real doll. You better grab her up before someone else does."

He said, "I agree, but there's a small problem."

I considered just slinking beneath the booth's table, huddling there in the dark, subsisting on dropped crumbs and spilled drinks. No one would be the wiser, I was sure of it. Instead I wheezed, "I hear tomorrow's forecast calls for rain. Yep, puddles...driving hail...swarms of locusts."

"What's the problem?" Mabel asked Armand. "Maybe I can help."

"Maybe you can. Desy, here, is a little...skittish...about commitment."

Was I so obvious, then? It was probably the white knuckles that gave me away. I released both my clench of the table's chipped edge and an unsteady breath.

Mabel nodded. "Ah, one of those."

Armand gave her a small agreeing hum and accommodating shrug of shoulder. "I have to move very carefully so I don't scare her."

Mabel nodded again. "My advice?"

I broke in, "Mabel, I've changed my mind. Bring me a double chocolate malt. You have those, don't you? The double chocolate kind? Topped with whipped cream?" I held my hands wide apart. "About this big?"

"Don't move too carefully," she counseled him. "She may just need a good push."

"Excellent advice. I've been thinking along those same lines myself of late."

She tapped the table with her pad. "I'll be right back with your drinks." Her head tilted my way. "Diet cola, Desy?"

I sighed. "Yeah."

She left a wheezy chuckle in her wake.

Armand's warm gaze roamed my face. "Your cheeks are pink."

"It's heartburn."

White, even teeth flashed with his quick grin. "Rings, commitment, marriage, all fascinating subjects, *mon chou*. I'd like to continue this line of conversation," he needled. "Would you?"

"I'd rather be tied up and forced to listen to Barry Manilow."

"Hmmm. You tied up makes an intriguing picture."

My smile matched his. "Pervert."

He slid his palm toward me along the tabletop. "Meeting Mr. Crenshaw upset you."

I tucked a stray curl behind my ear (who am I kidding? All my curls are stray—think Shirley Temple meets Medusa) before slipping my hand in his. "He seems like a nice man." With the comment I aimed for generous and mature and adult (which were three laudable emotions I wasn't actually experiencing at that precise moment).

"*Oui*, he does." His fingers lightly squeezed mine. "Talk to me."

I gave a little sigh. "It just kind of threw me, I guess. It's obvious they know each other fairly well, but that's the first time I've met him."

"Are you worried about Penelope?"

"A little. It's more…it's just…" At a loss for words, I sighed again.

"You feel unsettled, betrayed and guilty. You've had her to yourself, but now you have to share her—that's unsettling. And because she didn't speak of him to you, you feel betrayed. Then over such selfish thoughts, you feel guilt."

That was exactly how I felt. Tension eased. "How'd you know?"

His thumb brushed my knuckles. "Because I've experienced those same feelings myself. After my mother's death, my father waited three years before dating. I'm afraid the first woman he brought home met a very hostile young man."

"How old were you?"

"Seventeen."

I cocked my head. "Tell me about it."

Over plates of thirty-five greasy, glorious grams of fat, he did.

Chapter Six

Once upon a time, I had normal dreams. Common ones.

The kind where you either morph back to high school and stand panicked in front of your locker because you've suddenly forgotten the combination, or you're mingling in a roomful of people, only to glance down and discover you're completely nude. Nonsensical, ordinary dreams.

Not so anymore. Not since Armand, anyway. Now the landscape of most nights is a lush, erotic one brimming with both reality and illusion. Magic. No longer solitary visions, my dreams, I share them with Armand. Only High Priests and Priestesses are bestowed this gift, and then only if they wish to accept.

I admit the phenomenon still unsettles me a tad.

That Monday, late afternoon yawned into evening while I relieved Nick in surveillance of Mrs. Campbell. I sat outside 853 Westin, a truly nasty part of Hazel Park, for endless hours whistling Dixie. Whatever the ladies did inside the house for sale, they did quietly. Too quietly. And it involved the male species.

Throughout that morning and early afternoon, Nick captured on film a spattering of men coming and going, one after the other. Half a sheet of paper filled with his scribblings of license plate numbers. I continued surveillance and caught the last gentleman, a short, balding specimen, entering the residence at eight p.m. He didn't leave until nine-thirty. Some house tour, huh?

Two close friends—my laptop and research—helped pass the time. It bugged me I had been unable to dig up no more than the bare basics on Mr. Warren Williams the witch. The fact he'd traveled a number of years with the circus didn't help matters. I dug deeper. His parents couldn't have just disappeared without someone taking notice.

I gnawed a pencil nearly in half skimming endless newspaper archives online until a small article on suspected arson caught my eye. It told of a house burning to the ground and the tragic death of John and Margaret Petersburg, regular churchgoers and adoptive parents of a boy, age thirteen. I grinned, reading the son's name. B-i-n-g-o and Warren was his name-o.

All was not sunshine and mirth in the Petersburg household, though. There was a history of abuse and regular visits by Child Services. Reports the teen had been home schooled and never ventured from the house. Odd people, the neighbors had said.

My adoptive parents and their church tried to "pray" magic out of me. What must Warren have lived through to end up in a basement cage? He hadn't just slipped over the edge— he'd been pushed.

There was no mention of murder in the article, nor could arson be confirmed. My take on it? Warren had used magic, covered his tracks well and then changed his last name. The police were hoping to question the Petersburg teen but speculated he'd joined the ever-growing number of Detroit runaways.

I penciled a note to follow up on Warren's past. Adoption records are usually sealed, though, and the arson case was over twenty years old, so I wasn't too optimistic on finding much.

Mrs. Campbell drove home at ten.

And me? After tailing three car lengths behind her, watching as her house lights flicked off one by one, I moseyed home and after the news' nightly telecast of worldwide mayhem, tumbled bone-tired into bed.

Soon after I found myself immersed in a nighttime fantasy and up to my neck in water. Soothing and tranquil, it enveloped me in a warm caress as it lapped against the pool's edge. I was nude and knew right away it was a dream. (Armand had yet to coax me to swim buck-naked. What about the neighbors? I always protested.)

I realized, too, it was Armand's dream I shared, as his were always of a more romantic nature than mine. An example? For that night's illusion the pool not only glowed under the brilliant light of a full moon, but as well by the soft flicker of two dozen fat, white candles scattered about the deck. The candles were a nice touch and one I certainly would not have dreamt up.

Diving beneath the water, I surfaced several feet away feeling mellow, relaxed and curious. Where was he? An awe-inspiring stroke, the only one I know—a modified dog paddle (thrash-kick-thrash)—took me to the pool stairs and on the fourth step, halfway up, a splash sounded behind me. I looked back.

A large shadow glided toward me beneath the water's surface. Armand. Nude.

Hot waves of anticipation infused me, one traveling from the tips of my toes and rolling up my thighs, the other from the top of my head, flaming down past my breasts. They converged in a scorching wet pulse between my legs.

The water purled when he broke its surface, and I watched as Armand flung back his long hair, smoothed it with both hands, and moved purposefully toward me. I took one step down intending to greet him properly, having in mind a scorching kiss.

"Stay there," he ordered. "Don't move."

Accent pronounced, his voice held an intoxicating blend of lust and need, firm command, and it ran through me in a burning caress, pooling molten and urgent low in my belly. My heart raced even as my breath slowed, thickening with anticipation.

On the shallow-end steps I stilled, wet hands gripping the steel handrails, one leg bent on a higher stair, open to him, revealed, with nipples pebbling in the night air and warm water lapping mid-thigh.

Armand caressed my calves. "*Mon chou*," he whispered. "You are lovely, like a sea nymph."

"More like a drowned rat," I heard myself say. Often I make half-jesting remarks about myself, flippant observations, but his words, his actions, always calmly, firmly, push them aside.

"*Non*." Underwater his hands slid up to tickle the backs of my knees, playing there softly before curving around my thighs. "You're beautiful, always."

Peering down at him over my shoulder, seeing that look in his eyes I know so well—passion, hunger, greedy lust—incited my own wants to twitch and flame. His eyes turned scalding black the longer we stared.

Armand's tongue traced the curve of my rear. "Do you know what I'd like to do?" he whispered.

His tone sent my stomach on a wild spin; my eyes drifted shut. "What?"

"I'd like to eat you up." His teeth latched onto the meaty part of my ass and he bore down until he reached the slim border between pleasure and pain.

I moaned. Rich. Needy. Excited. And wanting more.

His tongue swirled wet and slow on my stinging flesh, trailing upwards. "Eat up every inch."

My breasts grew heavier, the nipples two aching points, as his tongue edged along the cleft of my ass to settle in a wet coil in the small of my back.

Goosebumps danced on my flesh when he whispered, "All of you."

His right hand covered mine and he climbed two stairs, pressing flush against me in a hot crush. The long length of his cock rested against my cheeks, and just as my heart settled into a fast puttering thrum, his broad thumb and forefinger tugged my nipple. I pushed back against him with a slow hip grind.

He ground back, rumbled, "Christ," and swept his tongue along the curve of my ear. "I want to consume you so I don't know where you begin...and I end."

My entire body was one big throb.

Armand rubbed against me the way large cats greet one another—face rubbing face—so that I felt his cheek glance against mine, his nose trail softly over my temple, nudging against my ear, in my wet hair, to the back of my skull, my nape, all the while he still toyed with my breasts, my nipples, our hips meshing and circling, until I gathered tight and my body surprised me with one long climax.

I inhaled sharp and fast, the breath expelling on a broken moan when his teeth fixed on the tender skin between my neck and shoulder. I leaned into his bite, pushing my gyrating hips back into his, feeling the thick outline of his erection, his balls, their full roundness, the masculine prickle of thatch, while his palm cupped my mound, fingers curling into wet hair, supple folds, pulsing need.

I whimpered.

He hummed.

"Move up one more step," he coaxed in a low whisper, rubbing his free hand along my left thigh. He kissed my nape, swirled his tongue there, ministering to his mark, as I moved my leg to the next stair, opening myself wider for him. "*Bon, bebe.*" His leg echoed mine, moving up one tread. "Guide me inside." God, that voice. His soft dictate, riven by dark hunger, drugged my system further and pulled me under.

I tangled my hand with his between my legs, finger sliding against finger inside myself, brushing together through juicy swollen lips until our thick panting filled the air and I could withstand not another second's tease.

Reaching beyond I grabbed his cock, thrilling at his raw, deep grunt.

He licked a hot swath between my shoulder blades. "Show me the way." We both leaned, accommodating, and I brought his cock to my entrance, hard meeting soft. "That's it, love."

His hips shifted and inch by incomparable inch, pinching pressure scalded as his cock tunneled up inside. In a smooth thrust, his full length sank home, completely submerging between my legs.

"Armand," I whispered as he crooned, "So good. So damn good."

His splayed hand heated my lower belly, my mound, and with a light press, tilted my pelvis so his cock slid up, lodging higher. My hand reached back to flare over the wet, rigid column of his upper thigh and gliding farther north, discovered the enticing curve of his ass. Squeezing it felt like grasping warm steel and my fingers just slid along skin, dipping into the slight hollow of his cheek.

"Look left," he coaxed. "Tell me what you see."

My gaze swept over the outdoor kitchen, deck chairs and huge potted plants before landing on our reflection in the glass patio door. Candlelight flickered over our bodies, displaying a soft dreamy image of Armand's large frame joined to me from behind.

I had never seen a more erotic sight.

The glow of moon and candle fell on planes and curves, the strong dips and swells of his profile, highlighting the powerful length of his bent leg, the firm swell of buttock beneath my hand, outlining the shadow of waist, the sheen of back, and caressed in a soft glow the meaty arch of shoulder down his muscular arm.

All male, he draped over me with banded muscle and wet, smooth skin while his hair, long and dripping, slicked back from his face to fall past his broad shoulders. Of myself sheltered within his shadow I saw only the high thrust of breasts, pointed nipples, my hair brushing his where he leaned his head against mine, and the reflection of my stormy eyes meeting his black gaze.

"God," I breathed.

His kiss scorched my shoulder. "Watch."

My hand fell to my side when he leaned back. The patio door's mirror image displayed his cock withdrawing long and rigid and glistening, its wide head still within me, only to slip forward and disappear between my legs.

A breathy sound left my mouth at the carnal silhouette and the thrilling, tight plunge of Armand up inside me. Water droplets rolled from him onto me.

His hand swallowed my breast, cupping and squeezing, fingers pinching my nipple, while his hips began a steamy rhythm, rocking his broad length slowly back and forth as we watched.

My breast plumped high in his circling squeeze and I dipped my head, sucked his middle finger deep inside my mouth, pushed my hips back against him in a slow, needy orbit.

Armand hummed during open-mouthed kisses pressed hot along my shoulder, and began a faster tempo between my legs. He steered my hand downward and our fingers brushed, nudging against my stiff clitoris. Sharp, prickling tingles roamed my body in a coiling, fiery wash, spiking as his pelvis rapped against my ass with each forceful lunge. His cock filled me, burrowing up inside, and I watched it withdraw inch by wet inch, thick and straining, only to return in a swift thrust, tunneling home again and again.

An orgasm neared just seconds away, and my hands tightened, one on the steel handrail and the other against Armand's fingers in the plump, saturated folds where we played. My eyes drifted shut.

And then he disappeared. His hand, his body, his cock all left me. A soft sound of protest escaped me, and my eyes flew open. Armand kneeled behind me—water sloshed with his movements—and his hands grasped my hips with a firm hold, thumbs spread me wide the same second his tongue plunged, wiggling wet and pliant.

One sharp gasp later, I came in a scalding rush, splintering around his tongue with hot, resonating contractions. Armand drove his tongue inside me over and over, laving up to my anus, plunging inside, flicking in and out, causing the climax to spike and roll me under again. My spine bowed and my wild cry filled the night as my legs wobbled, then gave way.

"I've got you," he said, looping his arms around my waist. My back pressed against his chest as he eased us into the water, and Armand whispered, "When you come, you make a little noise in the back of your throat and the sound rips my gut out every time."

Turning, I wound myself around him. "And when you look at me like that," I said, searching his dark eyes, curving my hand against his cheek. "I want you all over again."

He brushed his nose along mine. We whirled in the shallow end, gazes locked, and he pressed my back against the pool's edge, grasped my rear, and I reached between us to guide his cock where we both needed it most—thick and hot up inside me again. In one wet, sizzling plunge, he slid home.

Armand groaned and I cradled the back of his head, pressing wanton kisses along his strong jawline before capturing his earlobe between my teeth. He grunted when I bit, and then shoved his cock higher, lodging it tight.

The water rippled as he moved with powerful digs, pinning me against the pool's lip while plowing between my thighs. Our lips met in a scorching kiss, tongues swirling in bold, eager strokes, and his hand dipped below the water to finger my clit.

I trembled during my steady climb toward another peak and gripped him with inner muscles, plunging in counterpart, deepening his every stroke with a volleying thrust.

My clitoris sang when he pinched it, and on his very next lunge, I flew over and burst with a soft cry against his lips.

"That's it, *bebe*," he crooned, sliding in and out with maddening strokes. Armand's hips churned one moment, stilled the next, and following a breathless pause, he groaned, spraying thick jets of cream.

"That's it, *bebe*," I said, returning his words, and after a moment, received a playful nip on my chin.

"Was it good for you?" His words surprised a laugh from me.

"Wise-ass." I'd once mentioned a college boyfriend who always asked that question after sex. Armand had replied with a shake of his head, "If a man knows what he's doing, that question need never be asked."

My hands still framed his face and I smiled into his dark, laughing eyes. The moment stretched long and quiet, turned serious, and a thoughtful stare slowly replaced our smiles. My heart began to pound faster than it had the entire past hour because I knew what he thought, what those incredible eyes of his said. Their quiet, heated message flashed as bright as a neon sign.

Armand's mouth parted but I pressed shaky fingers to his lips, began to trace their firm shape, lingering on his full, lower lip. His tongue dipped out to tease my fingertips and I leaned toward him with a kiss tasting sweet and deep and fine.

I shivered and he moved us into deeper water, submerging my shoulders beneath the water's warmth. Arms and legs still wrapped around him, his cock still hard and buried high, stretching me, I threaded my fingers through his wet, shiny hair as our mouths met over and over.

Mindspeak is a very intimate form of communication and not only can it be used when both our powers are engaged, but also when our subconscious hold rule in the netherworld of dreams. He used it in a question that took me by surprise.

Tell me a secret, mon chou, your most hidden sexual fantasy. My lips broke from his and our gazes met. *Tell me,* he urged.

His voice was a drug and his gaze absolutely mesmerizing. Even so, I put up a token resistance knowing he expected from me no less. *Fantasies are awfully private things.*

He rubbed his nose along mine. *Oui...tell me.*

We're talking mad monkey sex? Hoochie coochie? Swinging from the chandelier?

Exactement. A sensual smile curved his mouth while his tongue traced my lips.

Mmmm...you first, I stalled.

With a twist of his mouth he complied. *I want to take you, make love with you somewhere semi-public, where our every moan might be overheard, somewhere unexpected where we risk being discovered.*

Having sex with Armand with people somehow nearby? My breath hitched at the revealing tone of his fantasy. I kissed him, pressed my breasts tighter against his broad chest, wound my arms around his neck. *I love your fantasy*, I said. *It excites me.*

A good thing, oui?

Oui.

And now, mon chou?

And now what? I further stalled.

Tell me your fantasy.

My fingers found his ear and I traced its rim before opening my mouth wide with a stupid, glib joke I still deeply regret. The pain in his eyes that trailed my words, the bruised look that swept his face stung sharp and palpable. My preceding smile must have hurt him even more.

A threesome, I whispered. *That's what I'd like. You, me, and another man all tangled together in one sweaty pile on your bed.*

His hands tightened, bit into my skin, and his eyes, oh his eyes, they blanked and turned a dead matte black. *A ménage à trois?* The ever-present richness of his voice, the lush resonance that never failed to thrill me, fell, weighted beneath a raw tone. *You would have another man touch you? This is something you yearn for?* His brow furrowed into a disquiet line and he raised one hand to cup my cheek. *Christ, Desy.* His hand tightened. *Jesus Christ, I'll not share you with anyone. Ever. You're mine...mine alone, and I – fuck.* He stole a deep breath and on his exhale, closed his eyes.

I stammered, *No...no-no-no! I was just kidding. You know my sense of humor – sometimes it's a little lame.* His eyes remained closed, twisting my heart. *Okay, a lot lame. Hugely lame. God, Armand, look at me, please.* "Please."

His eyes opened and their pain knifed through me.

"I'm so very, very sorry." I placed my hand over his on my cheek. His features blurred. "It was a joke and I'm such an ass. An idiot. A complete jerk. I should live out on the streets, alone and dirty, eating out of garbage cans to avoid inflicting myself on others. I'm a menace. I should be flayed alive, then shot. Say you forgive m—"

"Shhh," he soothed, kissing my hand, wiping my wet cheeks. He forgave me by way of a slow, sensuous kiss, one that sped my heart and curled my toes. One that I didn't deserve.

At its finish I held him close, so very close, wrapping myself tight around him in the water, and while candles flickered around us, right before the dream faded to an end, I whispered in his ear my true sexual fantasy.

I'll never forget his slow smile.

Chapter Seven

Tuesday morning I awoke not to the happy song of chirping birds but to a deafening roar springing from the very depths of hell itself, or my backyard.

I rolled out of bed, staggered to the window. An industrious Mr. Sandman worked overtime that night and I rubbed an excess of sleep from my tired eyes, trying to focus on the racket below.

Beneath shiny orange hard hats, a crew of burly men stomped about my yard and my neighbor Ted's. They fed long branches into a hungry tree chipper that relished each new limb with a bellowing whine.

The elm they hacked into itty bitty pieces stood in Ted's yard. It had long since died, but I remember it once stood proud with long, thick arms stretching over the fence in welcome, hanging just low enough for neighborhood kids to scrabble up on.

Ted shouted trivial conversation with a beefy worker, whose left boot lodged impolitely in my petunia patch, and my smiling aunt moved among the men, serving coffee along with muffins the size of bowling balls.

One worker's spiked boots cut into bark as he climbed high in the elm, looped a thick rope around a branch near the trunk's vee and pulled up a chainsaw. Within seconds, its roar joined the piercing whine of the tree chipper.

Figured the one day I could sleep in and not think about work until a midmorning appointment, men would serenade me at eight a.m. with dulcet tones of heavy machinery.

My sigh held mild displeasure and no suspicion whatsoever that in the very next minute I'd madly sprint outside in my wrinkled superman jammies. Panicked shouts reached me mid-yawn and I gaped below to witness everyone on the ground looking up at the worker who wobbled precariously on a branch.

Oh, slap my ass! I thought—he was going to fall, and the same second I gasped, he plunged.

A split second can last an eternity, or at least it seemed to that morning. The man fell in a kind of slow motion—midair spin, limbs akimbo, hard hat falling off—and I watched the chain saw follow him down with the sure knowledge the mishap's end wouldn't be a pretty one. Not unless I did something about it.

I called my power, felt it surge through me from head to toe, spoke one word—*Stop*—and everything did. Like flipping off a switch, total silence replaced the whir of chipper, the whine of saw, and every alarmed voice below. Not one bird cooed, not one dog yapped. Nothing breathed.

With one simple word, time stood still.

I sprinted outside and walked among the frozen crowd. Aunt P stood off by herself with tilted head, hand covering her open mouth. Shock puckered Ted's face in a tight wince, and the tree trimming crew stood in various states of a frozen mad dash toward the falling man. Fifteen–twenty feet stood between his head and the hard ground.

Pressing question—how was I to save him? I considered and dismissed several options, all the while speculating on how far my weird cosmic freeze ray truly stretched. Perhaps three-four houses down, everyone within might be unaffected and with one casual glance outside a startled family of four could see me in my creased jammies standing near flattened petunias and frozen human beings. Just how would I explain that? Smoke and mirrors?

If a speech bubble floated above my head that very second, it would have overflowed with question marks, @ signs, and points of exclamation. I gnawed on the inside of my mouth, deliberating on how to fix this mess in a way the backyard spectators would find believable.

My gaze swept the scene again. The falling chainsaw hung from a long rope and if the other end somehow secured from tree to Mr. Tumbling Tree Trimmer, a happy ending might be had by all.

I *could* somehow shimmy up a ladder, all the while pretending I wasn't hysterically afraid of heights, or I could use my magic again, which was not as easy a choice as one might think. I've only practiced witchcraft for three months; I'm not that great at it. There're layers and nuances I've yet to figure out, spells and incantations still to try, power untapped. But on that particular morning, I had no better option.

Power reawakened in me, sliding around strong and eager, and with steady concentration I willed the rope to move. It coiled and jumped, climbing to a sturdy branch where I directed it to circle the limb in a knot, then snake down to Tumbling Tom's ankle.

The plan was to make it appear as if he'd luckily tangled in the rope, thus saving his sorry hide. The worker would swing free of the elm, stop a foot or two from the ground, and everyone would be so gosh darn relieved they wouldn't stop to ponder the why's and how's.

That was the plan, and if only the damn rope had proved more obliging, or my magic more proficient, I would have managed it fine and dandy. But it felt like threading a needle to get the rope to knot around his ankle and a worse seamstress than I you can't find.

Pressure clamped my jaw as I tried over and over to make the rope obey, only to watch it slip off his boot each time and just for spite, snag on his spikes. My chest rose and fell in agitation, my hair began to whip rather than waft, and narrow-eyed I glared at the rope, tapped one bare foot against dewy grass, trying to recall where I'd last seen the damn stepladder—basement or garage—when dumb luck struck. Rope and tree trimmer's ankle married in a tight, happy union. Hallelujah.

After an attempt at calmness (breathe in, breath out), I pilfered a muffin as I dashed by Aunt P on my way back inside the house.

The kitchen window afforded a clear view of the frozen scene. With fingers crossed and just one word— *Go*—the air shimmered, voices shouted, and life resumed in my suburban backyard.

One end of the rope snagged the worker's ankle, halting his plummet, and the other end safely swung the whining chain saw aloft. The crew rushed to release him while relief replaced tension in my backyard.

Grinning, I bit into the muffin.

* * * * *

"I didn't expect to see you until later. What are you doing here so early?"

"Well good morning to you, too." My hands landed on my hips.

Nick stood near the coffeemaker swirling a spoon in his cup and flashed a sheepish grin. "Sorry. Rewind. Morning, Desy, don't you look nice."

I took a quick glance down at my cream pantsuit before meeting his gaze. "You think?"

"I think." He leaned against the table, coffee cup in hand.

"How many years have we known each other?"

"Is that a trick question?"

"You never give me compliments." I plopped on the couch. "So this one is mighty suspect. You hitting me up for a loan? Time off? The secret to cold fusion?"

"None of the above. Want some coffee?"

My lip curled. Nick doesn't make coffee. He percolates tar. Best described as a rich blend of formaldehyde and asphalt, it burns so acidic you actually feel your stomach lining melt. I liken it to the intensity of swilling a Molotov cocktail, only worse, and stressed, "Not in this lifetime."

"Still boycotting my coffee?"

"Uh — *yeah*. Duh."

Grinning, he pulled a diet cola from our small office fridge and handed it to me before settling on the opposite couch. Beside him perched a plump bed pillow, sporting a small patch of drool on its green case. He obviously spent the night there. Again.

I drew a deep breath and plunged. "You slept on the couch?"

The moment stretched; he sighed. "Yeah…hey, do you remember a Paul Snider?"

Nice dodge. "Should I?"

"He lived here for a year or so, either seventh or eighth grade. Dark brown hair, thick glasses, perpetual runny nose."

A quick image glimmered of a new kid back in Mrs. Travis's class, eighth grade. He was as Nick described, possessing the warm personal charm of a dead fish. "Wasn't he that nondescript future janitor of a boy who mumbled to himself in the halls?"

"You're a mean one, Des."

"Sorry." I pulled the tab on the can and listened to its fizzy salutation. "It's just that he kinda sorta made fun of my last name."

Nick released a quick gust of air. "Name one kid who didn't."

"Got me there."

"A small obit in yesterday's paper caught my eye. Paul Snider, 27, visiting family in the area, died from a drug overdose a couple days ago."

"Now I feel like a real heel."

"And so you should," he said with a grin.

"So tell me, Charlie Brown, since when do you read the obituaries?"

"Since I couldn't sleep last night."

"And we tie in neatly with my original question." I chugged pop for courage, although diet cola in the morning is not my idea of adequate caffeine. "You've been sleeping on this couch so long it's starting to sag. Ha-ha." No smile from Nick. "Ha." I squirmed on the couch. "Are you and Anita okay?" I looked into eyes so blue they bordered turquoise and waited for his response.

And waited.

And waited.

He ran a hand over his face and I noticed a patch of white skin circling his ring finger. "No, we're not okay."

At last—the conversation he'd avoided for years. I took a calming breath and a shot in the dark. "If you're arguing about work or long hours, we can shuffle the caseload around to get you home earlier each night."

"That's not the problem."

"Oh, okay. Look, I'm no Ann Landers, but maybe I can help."

"Doubtful."

"Thanks for the vote of confidence."

"Des," he said after a moment, "we argued about you."

"What about me?" My chest was one big knot.

"Anita thinks...well, it's just that..."

"It's just that?" I took another sip of pop while his second sigh floated across the room.

"Anita thinks I'm in love with you."

Cola sprayed from my nose. Nick lunged, pounded my back while I coughed up a lung.

"You okay?" he asked, settling beside me.

My pantsuit was ruined. I wheezed, "Shit!" and grabbed the tissues he offered, dabbing the mess while my nose burned and fizzed. "Don't even *think* about the cussing bowl unless you fancy wearing it," I threatened.

Behind the office's Bunn a fishbowl lies in wait, dunning one dollar bill for each muttered curse word. We call it the cussing bowl and it nearly overflows with greenbacks...mostly mine. Often salty, at times holding more brine than a pickle jar, my speech needs cleaning up, and Nick appointed himself head curse cop to police the problem.

I asked, "Has she lost her mind?"

Nick sat stiff and awkward beside me, his body language shouting discomfort. I could have ended the conversation right then and there, perhaps saving us heartache. Perhaps. But I plugged onward, completely unaware I cruised toward a large pothole in the winding road of life.

"If that's what this is all about—" I motioned to the bed pillow "—then just sit her down and explain we're only friends." Communication and testosterone, the odd couple. I shook my head at Nick, thinking men are often unfathomable, like crop circles.

"I can't do that."

"Why not?" I wiped my thigh. Dab-dab-dab.

"Because I think she may be right."

Dab...dab...dab. My hand clenched the tissues. "What are you saying?" I turned toward him.

"I'm saying..." He grabbed my free hand in a firm hold. "I'm saying Anita and I have separated, and I have feelings for you."

A large man and his brother sat on my chest.

"Feelings?" I squeaked. "Mushy ones?"

"Like Cream of Wheat."

"Since when?"

Nick wore a slight smile and his eyes warmed the longer they stayed on me. "Do you remember the time you kicked me in the shin and called me a crybaby?"

"Last Monday?"

"No, before that."

"Yeah, we were six years old."

"Well, since then."

Dumbfounded, speechless, staring at my best friend, a man I've known forever, I wanted nothing more than to find an oven and stick my head inside.

His smile faded. "Des, you should see your face."

"Hell, Nick."

"You didn't have a clue?"

"Nary a one."

"Is it really such awful news?"

He used a hurt tone and empathy swept away some of my shock. I squeezed his hand. "No, it's not awful. I'm just a little unsettled and, and confused."

"That makes two of us."

* * * * *

The cordless phone sat pinched between my ear and shoulder while I steeped in the warm familiarity of stubborn denial. Pretending all was right in my small corner of the universe (when in fact it was anything but) is a specialty of mine. Like when your aunt is getting all cozy with a neighbor, denial can be your chum. Or when you endure a run-in with the local High Priest (plus have a niggling suspicion it won't be the last time you set eyes on him), denial soothes the soul. And best friend's shocking confessionals? Denial. Works every time.

Mrs. Denise Campbell was off on another busy day in the exciting world of real estate and Nick once again shouldered babysitting detail. I was scheduled to relieve him after my ten a.m. appointment, but in the meantime, I had the office all to myself. Taking advantage of the time, I called Armand and waited on hold long enough for me to doodle two smiley faces, one lopsided geometric pattern and his full name three times. With hearts.

"Desy?"

"Hi. Am I interrupting something?"

"Nothing as important as you. What's wrong?"

"Nothing's wrong."

"*Mon chou.*" His voice traveled over airwaves to curl smooth and sexy in my gut. "You seldom initiate our phone conversations and your voice sounds...off. Something's wrong."

The man was too good at reading me. "I've had a challenging morning, no big deal really. I'm calling to ask you out on a date." Dead silence. "Armand?"

"A date."

"Yes, a date. There's a jazz festival running for the next two nights down at Hart Plaza. Interested?"

"You hate jazz."

"No, I like jazz."

"You said it all sounds the same, *you said* it belongs only in elevators."

"And the last time we gorged on pizza I also said I'd never eat another piece again as long as I lived. Did you actually believe me? Look," I said, "I like jazz. I just like razzing you about it better."

"You've never initiated a date. What's this all about?"

"Crow. And you're going to make me choke on it, aren't you? I'm sorry about my joke last night. I'm sorry I upset you. And I just thought I'd make up for it a little bit by taking you out somewhere. So—" I sniffed " —jazz festival. Yes-no-maybe so?"

I heard the smile in his voice. "*Oui.* Tonight. I'll pick you up at seven."

"Oooh. You make me go all gooey when you take charge like that. But I asked *you* out. We'll use my Jeep."

The office door opened and in walked my ten o'clock appointment wrapped in a dark three-piece suit. With humidity already inching toward three digits that morning, more than one damp spot must have dotted his Fruit of the Looms. I held up a finger and with a polite smile, motioned to a chair.

Armand said, "I'd rather make you go all gooey by other means, and unless you intend to tie me up and drug me, we'll take my car."

I watched my visitor wipe the chair and then sit.

"C'mon, my Jeep isn't that bad." I huffed at Armand's snicker. He was right, my Jeep had seen better days. It now boasted a new rattle that vibrated with every left turn, and something sharp kept poking me in the back, which meant the seat was either possessed by evil spirits or a spring had fought its way through the worn upholstery. "Okay, you win. I'll see you at seven."

"Good, and *mon chou*?"

"Yes?"

"You're very sweet."

Heat climbed up my neck and I cleared my throat. "Um, you too. Bye." I hung up on his chuckle.

Chapter Eight

A dead furry rodent perched atop his head.

Even though the office's air conditioning blasted on high, his upper lip glistened with sweat. The poor man sat roasting beneath both his suit and the roadkill that masqueraded as a toupee.

"Sorry to keep you waiting," I said. "Mr. Beckman, right?" He accepted my hand in a weak clasp.

"Yes, from Townsend Investigative Services."

"Desdemona Phatt. You mentioned on the phone yesterday an overflow case?"

In the vast ocean of private detective agencies, Nick and I are small fish, say a guppy or flounder; Townsend Investigative Services is a large humpback whale. On occasion, they toss us a worm when their belly is full.

Beckman said, "Yes. Will your partner be present for the initial overview?"

"No. He'll be out of the office for most of the day."

"Hmmm. A pity."

I gave him a plastic smile. "I'm sure I can handle whatever you throw our way. Before we begin, though, would you care for a beverage?"

"Coffee please."

I got up and as the dark brew inched up the cup, cautioned, "As a professional courtesy, I have to warn you my partner made this pot. Cream, sugar?"

"Just black."

I set the cup in front of him. "Sometimes it can be on the strong side."

"I'm sure it will be fine." He slid a thin legal-sized folder across my desk. "Here is your case file and contact. The client is the Billmark Hotel down on the riverfront. A number of guests have complained about missing valuables, jewelry and the like. Management suspects one or more employees but hotel security has been unable to discover anything."

I scanned the folder's contents. "Says here no listening devices or cameras can be used in the investigation?"

"Strictly against their privacy policy. All it would take is one guest to stumble on a hidden camera or microphone and a lawsuit would ensue." I flipped a page, humming in agreement when he added, "They want this handled quickly and with discretion."

My gaze met his. "Quick and discreet, that's me."

"Good. This will be the standard 60-40 cut." He sipped the coffee and his eyes bulged wide as it slid down his gullet. "This tastes like—"

"Embalming fluid? I know."

* * * * *

Aunt P clucked when she saw my cola-splattered suit and I whipped up a hand. "I know, I know—it's unlikely to come out, but I had a brainstorm on the way here. Let's tie-dye it and I'll wear the suit to my next Halloween party. I can wrap a scarf around my forehead and pretend to be a hippie."

She smiled when I flashed the peace sign. "Desy dear," she said, eyeing the stain. "How did you manage that?"

"Well, I thought it would be a nifty idea to squirt cola through my nose."

"A nifty idea?"

"Yeah." I followed her into the kitchen. "And for the record, should you ever attempt this yourself, don't try it when you're wearing your spanking new Donna Karan knockoff you budgeted two and a half weeks for."

"Duly noted." She pulled a platter of cold cuts from the fridge. "Would you like to join us for lunch, sweetie pie?"

I looked past her to the table set for two. "Us?"

"Frankie will be here in a few minutes. We're having turkey sandwiches and potato salad." Aunt P set down the platter and fiddled with the placemats. "I made peach cobbler for desert."

"Frankie? Mr. Crenshaw is coming for lunch?"

"Mm-mm. There's plenty to go around."

"Thanks, but sorry, don't have time. I only stopped by to change clothes. Nick's waiting for me."

"And how is our Nicky?"

Our Nicky's up to his eyeballs in matrimonial crisis, drools on the office couch each night, and claims to have Cream of Wheat feelings for me. "Same ol'." I kissed her cheek. "Gotta throw something else on and run. Enjoy your lunch."

Her hand fixed on my shoulder. "We haven't had a good talk yet about Frankie. Are you okay about him?" Concern whispered in her words and soft brown eyes. More than anything, I wanted her to be happy.

I kissed her cheek again. "One hundred percent okay." Liar, liar, pants on fire.

She beamed and then tapped her palm to her forehead. "Silly me! I forgot to tell you about the flowers. They came for you this morning. I put them in a vase on the living room table." My eyebrows shot up. "There's a card," she added, eyes all a-twinkle. "Didn't he mention anything?"

Armand? "Not a thing," I said before excited curiosity took me to a vase of two dozen long-stemmed roses. Pink. I sniffed, smiled and opened the card. My heart dropped faster than a ship's anchor. *See you this Friday*, the card said. *Warren*. "Drop dead," I whispered through tight lips.

I took the flowers upstairs, threw them in the trash, and a short ten minutes later sat behind the wheel in a genial yellow sundress driving to meet Nick. Lunch traffic chugged moderately. I made good time and parked beside his 'vette in the strip mall's busy lot.

I slipped in his passenger side. "Howdy, partner. What's the scoop?"

"Hey, Des. The scoop is I'm starving. Had lunch yet?" He smiled when my stomach chose that precise moment to rumble with all the gusto of a passing Amtrak. "Chinese sound good?"

An enthusiastic yes left my lips just as Mrs. Campbell stepped from her office and headed toward her car. I breathed, "Shit," waving a mental goodbye to my little white carton of Moo Shu heaven.

I studied Campbell. Hair in a short, no-nonsense bob. Conservative suit, low heels. Drove a sedate Ford. The average person would never suspect what really lurked behind her boring bank clerk look.

Nick straightened in his seat while we watched her fumble around in her trunk, and my elbow stabbed his side when a woman pulled in front of us and climbed from her car yodeling Denise's name. They waved to each other and Denise began to walk our way.

"Hell, she's going to make me," Nick snapped.

He turned toward me and we listed into each other's arms in a choreographed sway, one we'd used many times before. The casual observer sees a couple going at it hot and heavy—arms entangled (conveniently obscuring our faces), bodies wrapped tight, lips locked—but in reality I snuggle next to his mouth in the vicinity of chin and cheek. Sometimes I pass the time there with a whispered dirty joke while we wait. If it's a really good one, Nick will pinch my elbow.

His confession that morning shocked me all the way down to my Revlon-red toenails, but what he did next astounded me. On my way to his cheek, he angled my head for a straight-on collision and pressed his lips to mine.

I stiffened and he whispered, "They're watching," before deepening the kiss.

He kissed me. Nick. Kissed me not as a friend kisses another friend, but as a man kisses a woman. Nick's lips rubbed against mine, the same lips that pursed, blowing bubbles with me when we were nine, and Nick's large hands dug in my hair, Nick's hands, the same hands that reeled in my runaway kite on windy days in spring.

I kissed my best friend. My married best friend. And in that moment I felt more confused than ever before in my entire life.

"They're getting in the car, probably going out to lunch together." His breathing sounded choppy. "You okay?"

"Um, yeah...yeah." I eased from his arms. "I've got to go. Tail them. Go and tail them. You'll relieve me at six?" I opened the car door.

"Six's fine. Des?"

I swung my legs out and looked back. "Yes?"

He shook his head after a moment's stare. "Nothing. Be careful."

The ladies separated after lunching at an upscale Italian restaurant. Mrs. Campbell topped off her fettuccine alfredo with a busy afternoon showing identical tiny row houses to a young couple with a wailing newborn. And the dazed women staring off into space a tad too often while parked near each subsequent showing? That was me.

Traffic delayed Nick that evening and I reached home a good half-hour late to find Armand's black Jag already parked at the curb.

Private investigation causes tardiness, which fortunately never seems to ruffle Armand. Detective work also causes one to be a voyeur but more often, an eavesdropper. Eavesdropping for the job is one thing, but eavesdropping at home was something I never pictured myself doing. Ever. It's sneaky and underhanded, and somehow I found myself wearing both adjectives when my feet stilled just short of the small library. I was the main topic within.

"Most young couples live together nowadays," I heard my aunt say.

"She's still skittish about spending the night. Asking her to live with me is premature. She's not ready."

My heart skipped a beat.

"You're not concerned?" she asked.

"*Non*, Desy will come around, but in her own time. She'll one day accept what I've known from the start."

I rolled my eyes. His words rang arrogant but Armand would just smile if I said so and tell me no, they were merely confident.

Aunt P sighed. "Well, I think it's my fault. She had only me growing up. Why, the closest she came to seeing a good marriage was with Nick's parents."

"You can't fault yourself for that. And her reticence has more to do with magic than anything else, I believe."

My heart skipped two beats.

Aunt P questioned, "What do you mean?"

"I brought magic to her. It's a commonality that binds us. She may feel that to embrace a future with me, she has to fully accept witchcraft."

"And she's not ready to do that?"

"*Non.*"

"Magic is such a gift," my aunt sighed. "I don't quite understand Desy's misgivings. My sister absolutely loved being a witch."

"It's the short time frame. Her mother grew up with the craft. I've spent my entire life around magic as well." Aunt P made a soft sound of agreement. "I do think if she wasn't a High Priestess with all that entails, she would be more accepting."

"Well," my aunt said, "we mustn't also forget stubbornness runs in the family and Desy has more than her fair share of the stuff."

"It's just one of the many things I adore about her."

My heart skipped three beats.

"Me too." Aunt P agreed, a smile in her voice. "But let it be our little secret. Otherwise, she'd be even more incorrigible."

He said, "My lips are sealed."

I inched down the hallway shouldering a new medical discovery—eavesdropping causes heart murmurs.

With the loud slam of the front door I announced my homecoming in a strong falsetto. Aunt P and Armand met me in the foyer.

"Sweetie pie, it must be a hot one today. You're flushed. "

Guilt, I assumed, painted me pimento-red because even my ears burned. "A hot one, yep."

Armand fingered the thin straps of my sundress. "You look lovely."

With a heavy conscience and the taste of another man still on my lips, I rose to meet his mouth. The kiss was brief, but potent, and he ran this thumb over my chin. "Are you ready?"

"As I'll ever be."

We said our goodbyes and drove south through the dreary, antiquated skyline that belongs to downtown Detroit. Hart Plaza is on the riverfront in the very bowels of the city. In winter it has an open ice-skating rink and hosts popular venues for the remaining three seasons. On that balmy summer's day it held happy people enjoying outdoor jazz, a juried art fair, and a woman scarfing down a hotdog because she'd missed lunch.

"I hesitate to get too close, *mon chou*. You might miss and accidentally gnaw off my arm."

I managed a grin with a full mouth and talked around my food. "It wouldn't be an accident—you're tasty." I surfaced for air after a large swallow. "I know I'm being an oinker but I didn't get lunch today." My ravenous gaze fell to his half-eaten hotdog. "You going to finish that?"

With a finely arched brow, he handed it over and we sat at the end of a long bench amid waxing notes of keyboard, drums and sax. A three-man band stood on stage playing improvisational jazz.

We listened for a while before Armand said, "On the phone today, you mentioned your challenging morning. Tell me about it."

I thought immediately of Nick, my mind blanked then coughed up the image of the tree trimming crew. I filled Armand in.

"How does it feel to know you most likely saved a man's life today?"

"Supercalifragilistic."

He grinned. "And that you couldn't have done so without the use of magic."

I popped the last of his hotdog down, licked mustard off my thumb. "I know where you're going with this, don't think for a minute I don't."

"You missed a spot." He grabbed my hand.

I watched my thumb disappear into his mouth, felt his wet tongue swirl around it. My gaze swept up and met brown eyes glowing with such intense heat, I felt dizzy.

"Jeez, Armand, I don't know how you do this to me every time." I wondered if there was a bed nearby...or a sofa...a threadbare rug, a small patch of grass...anything.

Clapping broke out and a new song was introduced on stage.

He released my hand and slid an arm around my shoulders, pulling me closer. A white tee shirt clung to his chest and khaki shorts sat low on his hips. I snuggled into his side, ran my hand along his thigh, plucking at the dark hair. "Tell me what you did today," I invited.

"What I did today...I woke up and thought of you. Held three overseas phone conferences before lunch. Thought of you. Lodged a complaint about Warren with the High Council. Thought of you. Talked to my sister, who by the way says hi, and one more thing, what was it? Oh yes, I thought of you."

I grasped a handful of his hair and tugged to bring his mouth in range, planting a loud wet one on his kisser. He grinned. "Except for the Warren moment," I said, "your day sounds swell."

"It was. It is. Care to hear what the Council had to say?"

"Sure," I said, nose crinkling with distaste. "In five or six dog years."

Armand shook his head. "Ignoring it won't make it go away, *mon chou.*"

I singsonged "Hello?" and waved my hand. "You're talking to a card-carrying member of Denial Anonymous. It's a ten-step program."

"They'll meet with us this coming Monday to discuss our grievance. I wanted an earlier appointment but they cited a full calendar."

I resisted the urge to plug my ears and chant "Lalalalalala"; instead, I stuck out my bottom lip in a pout worthy of a first-grader snubbing broccoli. "You're raining on my parade."

He briefly fingered my pouting bottom lip. "We all get wet now and then, but I agree, now's not the time." He kissed my forehead. "Feel like browsing art? We can still hear the music over there."

"Sounds good. I wonder if the hotdog vendor is still open."

We stood and Armand said, "You can't be serious."

"You're right, I'm not. I'd much rather have a burger."

Chapter Nine

People pressed wall-to-wall.

That's not exactly true, there were no walls, but you get the point. Summertime. Outdoor art fair. Free jazz. A crush of Homo sapiens moving inch by inch. It was so crowded Armand and I couldn't walk side by side. He stood behind me as we pointed at, viewed and discussed everything from pottery to paintings.

The artists displayed their creations in tents and open booths along a rolling, grassy knoll. Live jazz mixed with the crowd's voice, stirring the air, the sun beat down in dense fat rays, and from tent to tent I led Armand, whose hands never left me—a caress at my elbow, a brush of my shoulder, a glide at my waist—until I felt ripe and mellow.

We stopped to admire an artist's oil rendering of a landscape; Armand pressed close behind me. A sea of people swam around us but the moment felt as if it belonged to just us two.

The painting whispered in soft, muted pastels. "Do you like it?" I asked.

His hand played along my nape. "Mmm. You have such pretty hair. Did you know the sun reveals all its shades? Cinnamon, dark honey, cocoa."

"You sound like Betty Crocker. Do you like the painting?"

"Not as much as your hair."

I first felt his lips in my curls, then a swell of lust wash through me, settling deep in my bones. My hand reached back between us and cupped his crotch. The very fact so many people milled about enabled me to touch him unnoticed.

Near my ear he whispered, "You seem to have misplaced your hand."

"Nope. It's right where I want it." His cock stirred beneath my palm.

"Desy."

"What do you think of the artist's use of light and shadow?" His cock lurched.

"Your hand is on my dick. You expect me to think?"

I laughed, squeezed his growing erection.

"Desy."

"That's my name, don't wear it out. I've got a question for you."

"Would it have anything to do with how many ways I'm going to make you pay for this torture?"

I made a buzzing noise. "Wrong. See the tent to our left?"

His hand slid along my waist. "*Oui*."

"Did you happen to notice the little red sign on the flap?" It took him a moment.

"It says he'll be back in—" Armand checked his Rolex "—twenty minutes."

"Yep. I figure if we hurry, we can make it in just under that."

"You've lost me."

I grinned. "Consider yourself found." I led him to the tent, unzipped it, and drew him inside. The two-sided zipper refastened with ease.

Armand's voice held caution. "Desy, what are you doing?"

I reached beneath my hem and stepped out of flesh-toned, lace undies. He stared at me. "Semi-public," I said, smoothing my finger along his parted lips. "Where we might be overheard…somewhere unexpected…where we risk being discovered." I held the panties high, dropped them on the grass. "Ring a bell?"

His eyes glazed over. "Jesus."

"And guess what?" I went to work on his khakis.

"Guessing involves a functioning brain."

He stepped out of his shorts and underwear and I tossed them beside my panties. I grabbed his stiff cock—he sucked in a breath—and I guided his hand under my dress. "I'm already dripping for you."

When his fingers beneath mine slid through saturated hair, wet plump folds, Armand's eyes slid shut. The very next second is still a blurry patch in my mind. One moment we stood there, hands delving in very interesting areas, and the next I found myself sprawled over an emptied display table. Two paintings and small easels lay on the grass, my dress bunched high around my waist, and Armand was on me like peanut butter on jelly.

His cock plunged as his hand cupped briefly over my mouth, quieting my cry. He felt enormous from behind, pushing through the tight pinch of muscles, pausing only when his pelvis smacked my ass. "Christ," he breathed.

Shadows moved along the tent's yellow canvas. People's voices buzzed. Jazz slid through the air. And Armand began to plow between my legs.

"Harder," I whispered. The legs of the table started to wobble with his wild lunges. Armand's hand splayed on the tabletop near my shoulder, shoring his bent position above me, and my fingers followed the strong column of his arm, digging into muscle. "Harder, Armand."

His cock slid deep and high with each fierce thrust, stretching me, our panting rose above the wet sounds of my arousal, and knowing each lunge granted his fantasy — feeling his wild arousal — I felt myself climb.

Someone scraped the canvas, brushing against the tent with a loud whizzing sound, but Armand's hips never faltered. He rasped my name and I mewled louder with each upstroke. "Shhh, *bebe*." The back of his hand stroked my hot cheek before palming my ass, rubbing my anus.

I bit my lip to prevent the next moan, thrust back against him, and the moment turned surreal when two women beside the tent began to haggle over an artist's piece.

Fierce tingles pulled taut around his cock and a singeing flush swept across my breasts, prickling my nipples. A keening wail wanted nothing more than to burst from my mouth, but it would be heard, we'd be discovered, it wouldn't be a smart thing to— "Oh My God!" I cried. Muscles clamped in a tight rhythm around his cock, Armand's hand fastened over my mouth—his pounding hips stilled—and he poured into me, spurting long streams of seed over a hushed moan.

He lay on me then, cock still buried high, and nuzzled my nape, licking the hot skin there. His breath beat against my skin with hard bursts. We stayed joined for a long, full moment, luxuriating in the aftershocks, and he whispered in a thick accent, "I am so damn crazy about you."

A smile curved my mouth. "Ditto."

All the feelings I wasn't ready to fully acknowledge whirled inside the hot tent with us that summer's eve, saxophone curled through the air, hundreds of noisy people milled about, my dress was one big wrinkle, and I'd never felt happier.

A small moan slipped free when his cock left me in a long, wet drag. He turned me around, kissed me, shook his head with a bemused smile, kissed me again, and kneeled at my feet. I held my dress up and he eased on my panties, his teeth nibbling my mound the whole while before concealing it behind stretchy lace. He'd just kissed me again, buttoned his shorts, when the tent's zipper whined.

A squat man entered carrying a Styrofoam plate piled high with fried foods and he stopped short when his rounded gaze found us. "What the—?"

"Forgive us," Armand said. "My wife had to see more of your work, you know how women are, and I'm afraid she's never been that sure-footed." Armand looked down at the paintings strewn on the grass and shrugged. "She stumbled."

The man's face turned magenta, his three chins wobbled, and he plunked his plate on a stool. "Now just a minute h—"

"We'll take them, by the way."

"Take them?" he sputtered.

Armand whipped out his wallet, flashing a thick wad of green. "*Oui.* Those two on the ground and also the large oil outside, the landscape. My wife is specially taken with that one."

"Oh...oh, well okay then," the artist stammered. "I'll just wrap those up for you."

Armand barely acknowledged the mean little pinch I gave his butt.

* * * * *

"Yuan is not a word," I huffed.

Armand flashed a killer grin. "Challenge me, then."

I scowled at the Scrabble board, and Mr. Crenshaw — Frank — to my left cleared his throat. My gaze lifted and he gave a slight shake of his head.

"Desy," Aunt P said. "Did you notice Armand's on a triple word score?"

"Are you trying to be helpful or give me apoplexy?" I hated nothing worse than losing. Armand grinned again, that familiar wicked glint sparked in his eyes, the one that says *I dare you*, and my competitive spirit soared, getting the best of me. The dictionary lay clutched in my hand. "Challenge," I confirmed, rifling through its pages.

Armand's grin widened.

Mr. Crenshaw noted, "Yuan is currency in China," just as my finger landed on the word and my eyes narrowed.

I muttered, "Hell."

"Desy — your language," Aunt P scolded.

"I believe I've won," Armand said. "Shall we tally up the points?"

"Sure," I snarled, "if you want to leave in a body bag."

Mr. Crenshaw trumpeted a laugh just as my cell phone rang. ID said Nick. "Perfect timing," I answered. "You just saved me from going postal."

"What's wrong?"

"Armand just won in Scrabble."

"And he's still alive?"

"There are witnesses."

"Ah. Got a minute?"

"Sure, hang on." I stood, glanced at Armand. "You mind if I take this in the library?"

He stood and kissed me. "It's fine."

"I'll make it quick."

I made my way there and turned on a lamp before settling in my favorite chair. "Okay, Nick, shoot."

"Denise Campbell—days of nothing and tonight it finally clicked."

Anticipation made my heart jump up and do the jitterbug. "I'm all ears."

"Remember one of the ladies was in the bathroom during my house tour?"

"Uh, yep. Two of them showed you around while one was indisposed."

"I viewed a first floor bathroom during my tour and in the basement when I tried a locked door they told me it was a second bathroom."

"Okay—turning gray here—what's the punch line?"

"City plans show that house has only one john."

My mind shot off, jumped through hoops, then backtracked. "Previous owners could have added a second bathroom without a permit."

"Thought of that, but there's no exterior piping."

"Son of a b...gun," I breathed. "So there's a room in the basement."

"Uh huh."

"A room you couldn't bug because it's locked."

"Keep going."

"And men coming and going into the evening...and incriminating pictures."

"Almost there," he encouraged.

My mind dribbled down the court, shot and swished. "Well shit—that's no open house. The trio's running a 'tie-me-up-I've-been-a-bad-girl' service and using the real estate business as a front."

Joy swam in his thick laugh. "And the lady wins a kewpie doll."

"Hells-bells! I can't believe we missed this for so long."

"Hey, I'm not beating myself up, they've got a great cover. I'll set up some PV squares tonight. Thursday at the latest, we should wrap up this case."

PV squares are one-inch wireless cameras with pinhole lenses that conceal just about anywhere. They have full video and sound capabilities. Neat little things. Nick would have no trouble picking locks and planting the devices but I wanted to be sure. "You need help tonight?"

"Thanks, I can handle it. And you've got...company over."

"Okay."

"Des, it's serious, isn't it? Between you and him."

Since the very first time our eyes met. My hand squeezed the phone. "Yeah...yeah, it is."

Silence, then, "I'm not going to apologize for our kiss."

"I'm not asking you to."

"Does he know?"

The conversation turned sour, curdling in my gut. That particular topic pricked uncomfortably enough without Armand in the very next room. I could hear his laughter in the kitchen and the warm sound twisted with burning guilt inside me.

"Des?"

"No, he doesn't know. I've got to go."

Another pause. "Tomorrow's the start of the hotel case?"

"Yep."

"Check in with me when you can."

"Sure, night."

"By the way—cussing bowl—two bucks. Night, shadow."

I slid my cell in my pocket and closed my eyes. Whatever he did, wherever he went, I used to tag along, like a shadow. Nick hadn't called me that nickname in years. It felt bittersweet now, and manipulative. He'd spoken it to bring to mind all we've shared, a lifetime of memories. It wasn't fair, but fairness hadn't been his point.

I yawned, released a heavy sigh thinking of him trying to bunk down on a couch that on a conservative estimate fell three feet short. I thought of his wife, Anita, and how we cordially disliked each other. It didn't mean I felt any better about the entire situation, but deep down,

I've always held the notion Nick got a raw deal when he married her. Not talking looks, Anita is stunning. Tall. Slim. Blonde. Her cheekbones are sharp enough to cut steel; modeling paid her college tuition. It's what runs through her veins — undiluted liquid nitrogen — I objected to. She seems one cold fish.

Damn, what a mess. I yawned again.

Had I ever thought of *being* with Nick? you might ask. The whole man–woman thing? Yeah, and more than once. So sue me, I'm human and he is one stunning man. But the musings were always short-lived, just transitory flights of fancy, and as we matured they settled into a type of abstract admiration for his beauty, never blossoming into anything remotely close to how I feel around a certain Frenchman.

"Des?"

My eyes slowly opened, settling on Armand crouched beside my chair. "Sorry. Must have dozed off for a sec." Some hot date I was.

He ran his hand through my hair, lingering to play in the curls. "Losing at Scrabble must've hit you hard. Frank just left." He kissed my brow. "He said to tell you goodnight." Armand's lips brushed my nose. "I should go."

"You missed a spot," I complained.

A slight smile curved his mouth. "Where?"

"Come here," I said, grabbing his hair. "I'll show you."

I brought his mouth to mine and rubbed, nibbled, and the second I slipped my tongue inside, my stomach dipped, rolling with a smooth wave of lust. My hands slid deeper in his hair, cradling his head close to mine, and as his body heat, his scent washed over me, I felt a peculiar, fanciful need to crawl inside him and lose myself. Hide.

"Mmm," he hummed. "I'm leaving, *mon chou*. If I stay another minute, you risk being thrown over my shoulder and carried upstairs. The sight would shock poor Penelope."

I snorted. "Poor Penelope, my ass. She'd sell tickets."

He kissed me again, looked deep into my eyes. "Dream of me."

And then he left.

I padded around the house turning off lights and found my aunt on the sunroom's couch. She looked miniscule against its mutant, purple flowers. Pink lipstick lay smudged beyond her lip line. I didn't want to contemplate how it came to be that way. "I thought you were already in bed," I said. "It's after eleven."

She stood. "I'm heading that way now." She took my hand and we walked down the hall. "He's a very good man, you know. Reminds me of your father at times."

What did Mr. Crenshaw, a retired accountant, have in common with a murdered High Priest from France? "I know you're fond of him."

"Very much so, and he loves you."

I knew she wanted me to like Frank but that was pushing things a bit. My feet turned sluggish. "That's a far stretch, don't you think?"

She sighed. "No at all, it's obvious. You just don't want to see it."

We paused at the foot of the stairs. "Look," I said. "He's a nice man, I like him, but we've just met."

"He's more than just nice." My aunt's voice climbed. "He's absolutely perfect for you."

"Use your indoor voice," I said, staring at her like she belonged in a white, padded room. "And what in the world are you talking about?"

"I'm talking about the pitter patter of little feet. I'd like to hear them soon and I'm not getting any younger, you know." A long lecture readied on her face; I knew all the signs.

"Did you swallow mouthwash this morning? Forget your four o'clock pill?" I leaned down and searched her eyes. "Are you really an alien imposter—a pod person?" I yelped, "Shit!" when she yanked my hair.

Aunt P tsked and began to climb the stairs. I had no choice but to follow as she still held possession of my hand. "I admit perhaps I'm a little overeager," she said, "but I've lived a lot of years—know a good thing when I see it—and contrary to what you seem to believe, Armand's patience isn't limitless."

We stood outside her bedroom. "Armand," I said. "You're talking about Armand."

"Of course I am. Is there another man in your life?"

That seemed a tricky question. "Sorry." I gave an easy grin. "I guess I'm more tired than I thought." I kissed her forehead, wished her goodnight, and halfway down the hall called over my shoulder, "By the way, if you yearn to hear the pitter patter of little feet, I suggest putting tiny tap shoes on the cat."

Her loud snort widened my grin and I plopped in bed minutes later with a happy sigh. The backyard phlox waved in full bloom and their sweet perfume rode every gentle breeze. My eyes closed, my mind wandered, and just as I slipped under for some much-needed REM, fifteen pounds of Repulsive landed on my gut.

A surprised grunt burst from me and I blinked at the monstrosity kneading my stomach. An impudent, green-eyed gaze met my hard stare. Stringy white fur (completely resistant to brushing), crooked tail kinked in two spots, a ragged stub masquerading as a right ear, Repulsive, my familiar, meowed, settling in for the night with all the feline pretension of mutual favor when in reality our relationship strained dubious at best.

To attend and guard their witch is the familiar's prime duty. Since his arrival three months past, all Repulsive has managed to do is lick our floors clean and whiz in my shoes. When he began to upchuck on my bedspread, we came to a tacit agreement. I would stop threatening him with the Humane Society and he would stop depositing various bodily secretions on everything I owned.

An uneasy alliance, I admit, but one that worked.

I sighed—which proved difficult because Repulsive lay partially on my lungs— and tumbled into unquiet sleep.

Chapter Ten

The dream sprang into my subconscious so quickly, I felt perhaps I missed the opening scene.

The room felt familiar, though I'd seen it before only once. A large bed, soft lighting, generic prints on the walls; one desk, one chair, one dresser. My gaze swept over the common, universal theme of the modern hotel room. A case last year pulled me east into the guts of New York City and I stayed alone in that particular room one chilly October eve. The room itself wasn't memorable, but my first crisp bite of the big apple had been. The crowds, the noise, the frantic pace had all left a lasting impression.

Aglow in starlight and neon, the balcony overlooked a still-bustling street. People walked below, cabs raced by, and the brilliant yellow, red and orange of sidewalk trees gleamed beneath dirty street lamps. Here the sweet scent of summer phlox didn't waft, but rather the acrid bite of exhaust fumes and lingering amalgamate of grease and spice from the all-night diner down the street. The air nipped my nose.

A familiar squeak sounded behind me—its owner, the bathroom door—and I turned to watch Armand enter the room. A white swathe of thick hotel towel wound low on his hips and he ran a second towel vigorously through his wet hair. Steam swirled in his wake.

"*Mon chou,*" he said, spotting me. "You look rested."

"Um…thanks?"

"You've been asleep for awhile."

One of the bed pillows held a dent. "Why would I dream of taking a nap?"

A smile accompanied his shrug. "And why dream of this particular hotel room?"

"Best guess?" I said with an answering shrug. "Yesterday I drove by a thin sapling already turning color and I thought of fall, and then fall memories, and voila, here we are."

Dark hair sprouted from the hollow beneath his arm and rounded biceps jumped with each brisk movement of his toweled hand. "Would you like some room service?"

He crossed to me and I watched his every step with hot anticipation thrumming through my bloodstream along with quiet astonishment such a man, such a devastatingly handsome, sexy, wonderful man, found me interesting and attractive. "No, I'm fine. You?"

"Fine as well." The balcony doors closed with a wave of his hand and his fingertips stroked my cheek. "I watched you sleep."

"TV not working?"

His lips twitched. "I watched you sleep, *mon chou*, and thought how very lucky I am."

"That my mouth wasn't running?" I smiled when he tugged my hair. "I've always wondered, do I snore?"

"*Non*, although twice you gave a quiet little purr."

"Is purr your gallant way of saying drooly snort?"

His brow arched. "Would I fall for a woman capable of drooly snorts?"

I laughed and a big grin lingered, tugging on my mouth. "Good point. You're much too suave to stoop."

"*Exactement.*"

We stared at each other and into the long moment I murmured, "Fair warning. I'm going to explode if you don't kiss me soon. Think of the mess."

A slow smile tilted his mouth. "Not to mention I'd be forced to take another shower. I'll kiss you in the name of water conservation."

I nodded. "I commend your environmental inclination."

He dropped the towel, used both hands to frame my face, and our gazes held for a hot second before he sank into my mouth. The intoxicating taste of him threw me into a realm where only emotions dwelled, flooding me with a plethora of feelings—wonder, arousal, hope, need, arousal, captivation, longing…and did I mention arousal? I wanted nothing more than to jump his bones.

Mmmm, I hummed, enjoying his tongue rolling along mine. *You missed a back molar.*

His amusement floated through my mind in a warm chuckle as his tongue swept deeper, using bolder strokes. I felt my eyes roll back inside my skull and knew any moment my head would blow off in a messy splatter. By my standards he wore too much clothing and my hands whipped off the towel from his hips before filling with very enthusiastic lower anatomy.

Armand grunted, rocked his hips.

I'll be right back, I said.

Non, he grated…*I don't think so. I want to kiss you till morning.*

I nipped his bottom lip. *Trust me, you'll like my trip. I'm taking the scenic route downtown.* My mouth laved from one flat nipple to the next, leaving two wet, pointed nubs in my wake as my teeth nibbled along his ridged abs. Muscles jumped against my lips and his cock bucked in my sliding palm when I slid to my knees, burrowing my tongue inside his navel.

The hotel soap left an unfamiliar scent on his skin and I ate it up, swirling my tongue over warm flesh, soft, soft hair, on my way to lower things.

Nestled beneath his thick erection, a tightly drawn sac bulged high and full, and Armand moaned when I pulled gently, rolling my tongue along its curves before following a thick vein up long inches of cock. Near its head I looked up to meet his sweltering gaze. *I love the way you taste*, I said, dipping my tongue into his wet slit.

His eyes went supernova. *Mon Dieu* skittered inside my mind, and his hands cradled my head against his erection. *And I love watching you suck me.*

A sopping throb found a home between my thighs as I took his velvet cap into my mouth, drinking his pool of musky arousal. My mouth slid down farther on him while my hand's firm grip chased my lips up and down his cock.

Armand's hips thrust forward with every plunge of my mouth and we settled into a slow, sensual rhythm.

The broad feel of him in my hands, thick against my tongue, gliding to the back of my mouth, the sucking sounds mingling with his pleasure-filled hums, made me dizzy and wet with need.

My left hand gave a farewell, tugging squeeze to his balls before traveling between his legs. Armand groaned, widened his stance, and I rimmed his anus with my forefinger before slipping inside to my first knuckle. Tight muscles squeezed, thrilling me, as I rubbed sensitive nerves, sliding my finger up, wiggling deeper with shallow thrusts until it buried fully inside him.

Against my tongue his cock leapt high, thrusting harder, faster, a new sense of urgency pulsing with each powerful lunge, while my finger slid inside his tight ass, rubbing firmly along the solid bulge of his small, sensitive gland.

His hoarse cry drew up the muscles in my belly, knotting them in a thick searing pinch, and as his cock pushed even deeper into my mouth with frantic, wild drives, I squeezed my thighs together to quiet the relentless scream of my clitoris.

Armand's guttural *Jesus Christ* sliced through my mind, his hands fisted in my hair, anus clamped down on my finger, his frenzied, churning hips stilled, and his cock jerked with explosive contractions. Come spurted thick and creamy, plentiful, down my throat in streaming bursts, and I hummed as I drank him down.

His cock glistened clean and he made a low sound as my finger slowly left him, before drawing me to my feet, pressing his lips against mine in a scorching kiss — tongue swirling against tongue — and waving a hand over my sweater and jeans. They disappeared, lingerie as well, and we tumbled nude and eager to the bed.

The second my legs spread, he plunged his still spike-hard cock, knocking against my clit. I cried out, coming in long, liquid pulls so delicious, so overwhelming, the edges of the room blurred. The orgasm consumed me, and as my skin tingled in lush waves, my heart pounded an unsteady rhythm, roaring in my ears. Gravity left and I floated in pure sensation.

Armand began to pump into my tight, drenched core. Each roll of his hips dug his cock higher, pushing muscled thighs against mine in a teasing, crisp tickle of hair. Needing an anchor, desperate for one, my hands latched onto the meaty part of his shoulders and held on.

He'd just emptied himself down my throat so we enjoyed a prolonged, wondrous ride together that seemed boundless, with no beginning or end, time in which soft whispers were exchanged, smooth moans hummed and echoed, and heated gazes locked before tension rose anew.

Armand's mouth drew on my breast, eliciting an exquisite pain when his teeth raked my nipple, and because he knows my body so well, he began stroking my stiff clitoris to speed my steady climb.

Delectable waves of tingling warmth sharpened to lashes of white-hot lightning and my orgasm hovered at the threshold, gathered force and volume, before soaring high and bursting in hard, searing contractions.

Armand crooned *That's it*, and with a series of powerful lunges that rapped against my ass, shoved me inch by inch up the bed, a broken moan escaped his mouth while he came, jetting a second load of dense, hot seed.

That moan he gives, the one that bursts from him when he comes, hides nothing. It's a guttural sound, deep and raw, pulling up from his very soles, and the fact I'm in part its cause never fails to amaze me. With my ears still ringing from his loud release, his full weight settled on me and my hands slid through his damp hair. Every vertebrae I owned melted into the sheets.

I hummed when he laved my neck, very aware his cock still lodged completely rigid inside me. *Are you finished?* I asked. *Because if you're not, I'll have to be put in traction.*

He spoke as he nibbled my throat. *Am I finished? Non, not yet.*

You can't be serious.

Can't I? He pressed kisses along my jaw line, rose to his elbows and met my gaze. *I'm going to fulfill your fantasy now. All you have to do is lie here and enjoy it.*

* * * * *

Hairless. Bald. Shorn. That was my sexual fantasy.

I am the owner of a black belt in karate, three guns and some pretty neato magical powers. I'm no wuss, but the idea of ripping hot wax from my nether region or swiping any sharp object way down below turns me pasty green, like a bruised avocado. Somehow though, the thought of Armand between my legs, in any capacity, invokes the opposite effect.

"Hey, I didn't sign up for all of this." I eyed the full mystery bag he produced.

"Just some supplies I need."

"Supplies? One razor, Armand." I wiggled one finger. "One tiny razor—preferably dull—that's the only thing you need."

His brow rose to a lofty height. "*Mon chou*, there's a vast difference between doing something, and doing it well." He dumped the bag's contents on the bed where I sprawled nude on a thick towel.

My eyes widened.

We'd ventured from bed earlier for a shower where I'd rubbed soap over his wet body. It was as I fondled his hard, soapy butt that he pivoted, pinned me against the ceramic tiles, and shoved his cock high. Within minutes he had me screaming like an opera singer on steroids.

And so I lolled without muscle or bone on the bed, blinking wide-eyed at the menagerie of dispensers, razors, creams and lotions he'd spilled beside me.

"Those all look...interesting. What's that small silver thingy?"

"Shaving cream warmer."

"Huh, nice. You really need all that stuff, though? Planning to shave a harem tonight?"

He smiled, pulled the items closer to him. "It pays to be prepared. We'll experiment, see which lotion you like best."

"I'm all for experimentation."

"Good. Spread your legs."

"You sweet talker, you." I shifted on the bed and he scooted closer, settling nude in a sitting position between my sprawled knees. I gathered from his growing erection he was happy to be there. "Hey," I complained, pointing. "Put your wildebeest away. You'll get distracted and nick me."

He blinked. "What did you call it?"

His stunned expression pulled a chuckle from me. "Seriously, Armand." I eyed his growing cock. "How are you going to work around that monster?"

"You never cease to surprise me," he said, shaking his head. "Trust me, Des?" He smiled at my instant yes. "Then don't worry."

I glanced at the ceiling. "Don't worry he says." I looked at him, sighed. "All right, I'm one with the

mattress. I'll worry no more. You can tar and feather me—
"

"Which is as unlikely as you actually relaxing while I do this." With a smile still curving his sensual mouth, Armand lifted the warmer and pumped cream into his palm. "Incoming."

"What?"

His hand swooped, swirled warm shaving cream over my mound, and I hummed, easing from my elbows to lay flat.

The whole shebang ended in a matter of minutes. The razor rasped along my delicate skin, Armand's gentle fingers played over my inner thighs, my folds, and before I knew it, I gleamed so shiny and bald down there I could almost see my reflection.

I rose to my elbows for a better look-see. "Wonderful job, my fine Frenchman. What's next?" He stared between my legs and I snapped my fingers. "Yoo-hoo?"

Armand palmed my newly revealed skin, whispered, "Mine," and ran his gaze up my body, lingering on my breasts before lifting to my face. The heat in his eyes seared through me. "You're so damn pretty," he said, trailing his hand down my thigh to my knee.

He set the small water basin and extra towels aside, motioned to the pile of tubes and jars. "Oil or cream?"

Oil sounded messy. "Cream."

He chose a slim tube and rubbed the contents with small, circular motions into my bare mound and lower, drawing a soft hum from me. Now that he no longer wielded a razor, hidden tension seeped from me and I luxuriated in his touch. God, his touch.

"It feels cold…tingly."

"Like it?"

"Absolutely." I sniffed. "Peppermint?"

"*Oui*, and now this." Into a small jar of reddish cream he dipped his finger, rubbed it along my slit and clitoris.

My breath thickened, turned choppy. It didn't help matters his gaze locked with mine in blistering fusion or that his cock reached toward the heavens in a mile-high salute. He blew on my tingly crotch and my eyes nearly crossed.

"That red cream, it…it stings a little," I breathed.

"Cinnamon. Air releases its heat."

Chills pricked my mound and vulva but inside, especially around my clit, heat stung and throbbed, commingling into one needy pulse. I squirmed, dug my fingers and heels into the mattress, and squirmed some more.

"There's an interesting feature about the creams I chose."

Armand's smooth voice curled inside me, my sight went blurry, and I wheezed, "They cause permanent blindness?"

"*Non*, they're edible." He buried his face between my thighs and I let loose a cry not unlike the late night howl of a cat in high heat.

Was it the creams? Newly shaved skin? The sexathon we seemed to be having? Perhaps a sudden fetish for bland hotel furniture? Who knew? But in rapid succession I came twice with just the wet slide of his tongue along my folds. Every touch, however slight, seemed magnified on my sensitized flesh.

His tongue plunged, wiggled, licked up to nudge my rigid, throbbing clit, and he smoothed his hands up my stomach and ribs to fill them with my breasts. I gasped, arched into his touch when he squeezed, and came again.

I caught my breath and moaned. "Sweet mother of all that's holy, you're killing me. How are you going to explain to Aunt P I died from sex?"

He surfaced from my crotch to laughingly murmur, "Not a great time to mention Aunt P, love," before diving back to work.

My giggle turned to howl and I shoved my throbbing core into his face. Insanity neared and I helped it along by circling my hips and pressing his hands harder against my breasts.

Could one be fucked to death? I wondered, as I climbed toward another release. Armand slurped me up, enjoying what seemed like liters of creamy arousal seeping from me like I was a large chocolate-covered cherry and he'd just taken a bite. I began to pray the dream wouldn't end before he got around to shoving his cock inside me again. I wanted desperately to be filled.

It neared then, that twisting, tingling pull, the Big One where you feel as if you put your wet finger in a light socket—the Mt. Everest of orgasms, so huge it electrifies you from head to toe, and as it snapped inside me, my back bowed off the mattress, a rush of cream gushed from me, and I let loose the high bleating caterwaul of a dying buffalo.

White bursts of light exploded behind my closed eyelids, my entire body spasmed, and I turned light and weightless, as if undergoing an out-of-body experience. Hell, I thought, you could be fucked to death.

"I'm dead now, aren't I?"

His cock began to inch inside me. "Feel that?" Thickness pushed in and in and in.

"Yes," I breathed on a moan. He felt enormous.

"Then you're not dead." Over my weak laugh he grated, "You feel so good." He buried his cock, filling me with stiff pressure, and his curly thatch lodged against my shorn mound, igniting fiery prickles.

Armand eased my near-limp body up, rocked backward, and arranged us sitting face to face in the middle of the bed. My thighs draped over his and his long cock joined us in a tight union, one I never wanted to end. His eyes blazed a stormy black, filled with wanton promises, and his hair had dried except for the very tips. My hands buried in the rich mass.

"That last one knocked my socks off," I said, still trying to catch my wayward breath.

"You're not wearing socks."

"Exactly." I smiled and ran a finger down his glistening chin. "Mr. Bellamy, you're a little messy."

His large hands caressed my hips and pulled me closer, lodging his cock even higher. "Spoils of victory," he whispered, humming as I began to lick him clean.

My tongue washed over his chin and lips, and his tongue came out to play with mine in the inch of air between our mouths, flirting, swirling, before he sank into me with a sweeping, lusty kiss.

Sex seeped everywhere, the sheets, the air, on our flesh, in our mouths, sliding thick and scented in our lungs.

My mouth coasted off his to press kisses on his eyes, nose, jaw, and then into his ear I whispered, "I love everything you do to me. Everything."

The corner of my eye took in the closed door over Armand's shoulder and something seemed to move within the dark corner. I stared in that direction when Armand flexed his hips, his cock, and my eyes closed briefly as overwhelming pleasure flooded me.

He rasped my name, smoothed my hair behind my ear and nibbled my lobe, something he knows I adore, and just as goosebumps covered my left side in a tingly blanket, a shadow shifted again in the room's darkened corner.

I stilled and stared; considered the real possibility Armand fucked me so hard I was having visions. Any minute I'd begin prophesying. His tongue tunneled in my ear and I made him groan when I squirmed on his cock, wrapped myself tighter around him, squishing my breasts against his broad chest.

"I love your scent," he whispered in my wet ear, bringing a smile to my mouth. "Your skin."

I stiffened. There. Right there. It moved again. Big, dark. "There's something there, Armand. Something big just moved."

He flexed his cock. "You're just now noticing?"

I pulled his face from where it burrowed in my nape and met his laughing eyes. "Behind you, near the door. Something moved." His eyes searched mine and I assured, "I'm not joking."

Concern emptied his face, and in one smooth move he withdrew from me, spun on the bed and stood facing the door.

"Fuck!" He turned to me. "What the hell have you done?"

Chapter Eleven

"Me? Me! I've done nothing." Sadness, happiness, humor, lust — these emotions I've seen before on his face — but never what blazed there at that moment. I pulled on the sheet, clutched it to my breasts, and looked into his hard eyes. "I've done nothing," I repeated. "Is something really there? What is it?"

For a long moment Armand held my gaze, searching, and then he glanced back at the dark corner. "Fuck!" The anger, the fury in his voice clawed my heart. He shoved a careless hand through his hair, dragged it over his face. It lay in a fist then at his side. "You can't see who that is?" he shot at me, his face tight, fierce.

"It's dark, just a shadow. What's going on? Tell me."

"Dammit, Des. Goddammit."

He disappeared. The second he left, I jackknifed up with a soft cry in my small bedroom. Repulsive spit an annoyed meow and jumped down from the foot of the bed. He strutted through a patch of moonlight on his way to the hall.

My chest rose and fell in short, fast bursts. What in the hell just happened? Emotions blocked the way, obstructing my every attempt to understand the dream's end. Armand was furious. It hurt he directed his anger at me, hurt he left without explaining.

Hurt. It also royally pissed me off. The alarm clock glowed four a.m., casting a lighted swath of green on my cell phone. I snatched it up, punched in Armand's number.

He answered with a curt, "*Oui?*"

"You're ticked—I got that. But don't you think you owe me the courtesy of explaining why?"

"Courtesy?" A spat of air. "And if someone stabbed you in the heart, would you then offer them a towel to clean their knife?"

"What the *fuck* does that mean?"

He growled my name and after a short pause, a sigh, whispered it. "I can't talk about this now. We'll discuss it later."

"Fine. When?" No answer. "Armand?"

He'd hung up.

I squeezed my cell so hard that if it were a piece of fruit, pulp would have splattered the walls. A vicious toss sent it bouncing with a loud clatter along my bedside table. Sleep was out of the question. Air hitched from my lungs as I threw the sheet from me and stalked to the bathroom.

While water poured from the showerhead, my camisole thumped on the tiled floor and I yanked down my boxers, inhaling fast. My mound shone smooth and hairless.

Memories rode on the tail of that discovery—the look in Armand's warm eyes as he told of watching me sleep, his mesmerizing touch veering from feather-light to rough in the hours of love play, the slick soapy feel of him as he took me against wet ceramic in the hotel shower stall, nuances of his every intoxicating kiss.

And with those memories my anger channeled into something different, something that stung my eyes, blurred my sight.

It was allergies.

* * * * *

"Mr. Adams, the speediest manner to catch your employee is for me to book a room, set up surveillance and plant some jewelry."

"Our own security suggested that, but hidden cameras violate hotel policy."

Frustration hid behind courteous professionalism on my face. "Here's an alternative," I proposed. "You meet with housekeeping every morning, nine o'clock, correct?"

"Yes. I review their assigned floors and any unexpected staffing shortages."

"I'd like you to introduce me this morning as Susan Chalmers, your latest trainee."

Mr. Adams, general manager of the Billmark Hotel, unbuttoned his pinstriped suit coat and sat back in his chair. Brown eyes sharpened behind gold-rimmed glasses that pinched his wide flared nose, and he assessed me over the steeple of his clasped hands. Skin the color of coffee, a rich dark roast, conjured a wistful yearning for more caffeine. I'd had only one cup since four a.m.

"Which floor do you want to be assigned to first?"

Jewelry had been lifted from only the top two floors, which were cleaned by a staff of four. They alternated floors biweekly. I'd already reviewed a current schedule along with the maids' files and had a ready answer. "The tenth. I'd like to begin my training with—" I shuffled through the files on my lap "—Rebecca Carlton."

He nodded. "I'll find you a uniform."

Four hours later, I had swathed myself in the mauve and cream of hotel housekeeping, slipped into serviceable beige shoes, stored my belongings in a basement employee locker, attended my first staff meeting, and found myself staring down at a pubic hair curled dark upon white porcelain. It was not the first one I'd encountered that morning.

"Almost done in there, Susan?" Rebecca called.

"Another minute." She'd given me bathroom duty. Ick. I despised cleaning my own bathroom, much less a stranger's. I stabbed at the toilet rim with my long-handled brush, flushed the offending foreign follicle in a blue swirl of cleaner, and folded the end of the toiler paper into a neat pointless point.

I cast an eye over the eighth bathroom I'd cleaned that morning and gave a little shuddering sigh; silently admitting perhaps that morning's brainstorm had not been one of my best. Rebecca—"Call me Becca, all my friends do"—Carlton could, with a deft hand, relieve any valuable she fancied while I mucked knee deep in each room's tiled bowel, squeezing an industrial-sized bottle of Tidy Bowl.

People were pigs, a rash generalization I'd arrived at five toilets ago.

"Looks good," Becca said behind me. "Ready?"

I turned, mustered a smile. "Yep."

"After lunch, I'll start you on beds."

Thank you God. I never thought dirty sheets and dust mites could sound so appealing. "Great, lead on."

Rebecca Carlton was a tall, thin woman with a brassy laugh that sounded like the whinny of a startled swaybacked horse, two inches of brown roots glaring atop her Clairol Nice 'n Easy head, and an annoying habit of snapping gum between her teeth.

I found her surprisingly likeable.

Of the four maids in question, she was the only single female and as such topped my short list of suspects. I just couldn't picture a married woman with 2.1 children going home to cook up some Hamburger Helper with stolen jewelry in her pocket. Didn't fit.

Sheets, vacuums, towels, dusting, toilets, blankets, toiletries, garbage bags—throw all that together and you get several hours crawling by in endless monotony. The last room, number 1030, loomed.

Becca's pocket rang and she sighed, pulled a cell phone from its depths. "Yeah?" A pause. "Well, what do you expect me to do, drop everything right now? I got another room to do." I pulled garbage bags from the cart's bottom shelf, knowing three were needed, and caught the exasperated roll of her eyes. "Mom, you're gonna havta wait. I—Mom?"

Becca glared at her cell. "Jesus Christ on a pogo stick. That woman is gonna kill me." She shoved the phone back in her pocket.

"Problem?"

"My mom—she's sick. Got cancer. Can't even go to the bathroom without help now." She pushed the cart farther down the hall; I followed like a lost sheep. Baa. "Anyway, I leave a bedpan for her but she won't go in it for some goddamn reason."

Becca's face twisted with frustrated self-pity and guilt while she parked the housekeeping cart outside our last scheduled room.

I said, "I'm sorry about your mom. Listen, why don't you go home now?" My hand motioned to the room. "I can handle this."

"Oh no, I couldn't. It's your first day and all."

"Hey, I've been trained by the best. Go home. It's fine."

A tentative smile wreathed her mouth. "You sure?"

"Yep." I tapped the cart. "I park this monster in the basement?"

"Right outside the lockers. Thanks Susan."

"Sure. See you tomorrow."

"Eight thirty," she said with a wave.

I rapped on 1030's door, yelled "Housekeeping," carded in and yelled it again. The guest sat at the sparse desk, writing on hotel stationery and we startled each other. "Oh, I'm sorry. Should I come back later?"

He was a large, round man wrapped in a burgundy robe, which was an unexpected sight. The robe, not his size. It was four p.m. I noted his greasy hair and bleary eyes.

"It's fine." He waved me in. "I need more towels."

From his appearance, it looked as if he hadn't used any to begin with. "I'll just be a minute, sir."

I walked back to my cart with sore feet and no suspicion whatsoever that in less than one minute my elbow would snap his nose, shattering bone cartilage. On purpose.

Laden with towels and supplies, I made my way to his bathroom, the worst yet. He'd missed the toilet more than once, resulting in a yellow stagnant pool on the tiled floor. Dismay and disgust wrinkled my nose. A mountain of wet towels sat in the corner. Toiletries were strewn about. I noticed three extra large jars of petroleum jelly and couldn't begin to contemplate why.

The toilet seat closed with a snap. I set down my supplies and my next breath came in a startled gasp against the bathroom wall where I was shoved hard and pinned.

His body stood as a meaty wall behind me, his hands large forceful paws holding my face, twisting one arm.

"Scream—fight me—I'll hurt you," he said with a shove.

His grip squeezed hard, flushing me with pain and anger. He'd obviously never before tangled with underpaid housekeeping staff. My free hand reached up, grabbed his greasy hair and yanked, as if pulling down a steer in a rodeo, while my heel jabbed back against his shin. It snapped. He roared as he fell, taking me down with him, and my elbow found a nifty resting spot in his face.

Scared would come later. Alarm too. At that moment, though, my back pressing into his beefy chest, I felt only anger. He still struggled with me, ripped the sleeve of my new uniform, and I raced with quantum speed straight to boiling fury.

My foot snapped his kneecap as my elbow plowed into his face a second time, breaking his nose. Over his bellow I yelled, "Let go you fricking toad!"

The air shimmered and I no longer lay on a robed man; I lolled on cold bathroom tile. Dirty, sticky bathroom tile. Ick.

I scrambled up, turned, and he no longer sprawled there. Poof. But something else did, and it croaked at me. Air wheezed from my lungs like an asthmatic's.

A toad. Somehow the bastard was now a brown, slimy toad. A fat one, too, with big bulging eyes. This couldn't be happening, I thought. No-no-no! My hands whipped up and covered my mouth as I stared down at it, shaking my head.

One of the many problems of being a witch is the occupation doesn't come with a Witchcraft for Dummies manual. I had no idea I was capable of turning one thing into something completely different, much less how to undo it. "Shit-shit-shit!"

The toad began to hop toward the dark safety of the bed's underbelly, and I grabbed the squirming thing up— ew—and spun around the room with arms outstretched, searching for a place to contain it. The empty wastebasket near the dresser caught my eye and as I placed the toad inside, it made a wet, unpleasant toady sound. "Back at you," I snapped.

I sank down on the corner of the bed with various body parts throbbing from where he'd shoved me against the wall, my elbow screaming an endless rap song, and the beginnings of thick denial.

My eyes closed. This wasn't happening. In reality, I sipped mimosas delivered by Buff, the cabana boy, on a sandy beach beneath a tropical sun. My skin slowly toasted to perfection, holding a tan so golden the swarm of freckles peppering my body blended together into one homogeneous shade. I must have fallen asleep, lulled by the heat, the rolling waves, and the call of hungry seagulls.

The toad croaked, belching a loud protest. My eyes flew open. Hell. This was just crap-tastic.

The cell phone lay clutched in my hand, Armand's number punched in, before I remembered he was ticked off at me for some mysterious no good reason. He would help me anyway, I had no doubt.

All he did was answer, "*Oui*," and my rapid heartbeat slowed.

"I'm in trouble."

"Where?"

"Billmark Hotel, room 1030."

"Twenty minutes," he said.

"It's a half hour drive."

"Twenty minutes. Stay safe for me."

He rang off and I stared down at the phone in my hand. I *was* safe—the biggest threat I currently faced was contracting warts from that damn toad.

My sore feet protested as I paced the room.

Chapter Twelve

"And so the dipwad tries to maul me and I tanned his hide a good one."

Armand looked down at the toad in the wastebasket. "You certainly did, *mon chou*. His hide is now officially tanned." He held out his arms. "Come here, you're shaking."

I hugged myself. "I'm fine."

"And stubborn. Come here."

I went into his arms, spoke against his chest. "Thought you were pissed at me."

His arms wrapped around me, holding me close and I felt his lips press in my hair. "I'm upset, but that's for another time. We'll deal with it later. Right now, I just need to hold you." One of his hands swept up and buried in my hair. "He bruised your cheek," Armand whispered. "Where else do you hurt?"

All over. "I'm fine. How do we change him back?"

"Why would we want to?"

My laugh gusted in a muffled snort against his chest. "Spending the rest of his life with four legs is a bit harsh just for being a sick bastard. Besides, he might have a wife, kids."

"Let's find out."

"How?"

"We'll start with his wallet."

I looked up at him. "When did you get so smart?"

"Since I started hanging around a frisky P.I."

I smiled, he kissed me on the nose, and we began our search, all thirty seconds of it. A thick black wallet sat under scattered papers on the small desk.

"Ooh—jackpot." I dug out three different forms of ID. "He's either Mr. Richard LeBlanc from Grand Rapids, Michigan…uh, a Sam Clarkston from Las Vegas…or by way of the sunshine state, Wayne Douglas Roper. No family photos."

Armand held a wrinkled sheet of paper. "Mr. LeBlanc had a court date today."

"Say why?"

"*Non.*" He glanced at his Rolex. "But it was scheduled to begin three hours ago."

I flashed a mean smile. "I say we make a phone call or two."

"You do that and I'll ready the spell."

Hotel security would require more personal involvement than I felt comfortable giving. I made an anonymous tip to the police using the hotel phone and my best Madonna impression.

"Ready?" Armand asked.

"Yeah." I crossed to where he stood beside the wastebasket. "What's that?"

"I wrote down the spell for you. Here." He handed me a small paper. Bold slashes of inked rhyme flowed along its surface.

I shook my head and spoke in a mournful tone. "Do spells always have to rhyme?"

"*Oui.* It's simple."

"As long division." I met his gaze. "Armand, I was born without a rhyming gene."

His fingers gently touched my sore cheek. "You'll do fine."

I sighed and as I began to read, magic prickled up my spine. "*Change back this toad to human form now, no memory of today or how. And should he think to harm again, let him feel pain of triple his sin.*"

The air turned warm, shimmered, and the toad was no more. Sick bastard stood before us, one foot lodged in the wastebasket.

His face bore a thunderous expression and the pulpy damage from my elbow. A tight line of anger and pain pulled at his brow. "Who the hell are you?"

Armand's face twisted and he answered by way of a flashing fist plowing into the man's beefy face. Richard — or Sam — or Douglas (I'll just stick with sick bastard) jerked back hard and with his foot planted inside the wastebasket, stumbled around, arms flapping like a Three Stooges' comedy sketch before falling.

He thudded onto the blue hotel carpet with his robe open, displaying a small, sorry sight hanging beneath the mountain of his gut. Anger flushed his face red and he spat blood, rolled to his knees to get up.

I breathed, "Hell," envisioning a nasty fight and stepped forward, but Armand caught my arm.

"Wait."

The enraged look on sick bastard's ugly mug abruptly changed to one of intense pain, then morphed into downright illness. A putrid white, the color of soured milk, replaced the red flush on his face and he groaned, clutched his stomach.

An intent Armand, with a face empty of all emotion, stood watching the man. My gaze fell to sick bastard and I caught the white rolling flash of his eyes before he toppled sideways, sprawling unconscious on the carpet with a tidy thump.

"Wow. Your little rhyming ditty did the trick."

"He deserves far worse," Armand said in a voice too calm.

"Hey," I ventured, moving in front of him. "You okay?"

His eyes shone unnaturally black, filled with magic. "He touched you." His jaw flexed. "Hurt you."

Slow to realize that beneath his calm lay anger and fear, concern for me, I lifted Armand's hand—the same one he'd used on bastard's nose—and ran my thumb over the reddened knuckles. "Yeah, but he didn't know I have a handsome Frenchman with a mean right cross." Armand's unsmiling face stared down into mine, and I cupped his cheek. "I'm all right. Really. And as soon as I clean up this mess, we'll be on our merry way. I'll even let you buy me a snack; I've a hankering for a Snickers."

Armand first pressed my hand to his lips, then waved his free hand in a wide arc. The room turned clean in a nanosecond, nearly sparkling, and a moan spouted from my gaping mouth. "Shit. You mean I didn't actually have to clean twenty toilets today?"

"*Amoureux*-sweetheart, you always think of your magic as a last resort instead of a first solution." He kissed me lightly. "It's who you are. Use it."

"Shit," I repeated. "Let's hit the road."

Armand walked by my side as I pushed the cart down the hall. By the elevators he said, "*Mon chou?*"

I punched the down button. "Yeah?"

A warm light returned to his eyes and he purred, "I like that uniform on you very much. Wear it tonight?"

* * * * *

"Hey squirt, how's the hotel business?"

I snorted. "If I never again see another dirty hotel room, I'll die a happy girl."

After Armand and I parted ways following a five-minute toe-tingling kiss in the hotel's parking structure, I made a stop at work to pick up some files, never expecting to encounter Nick.

I shuffled through three phone messages—one from Warren I'll-never-leave-you-alone Williams. He'd called early that morning.

Nick walked around his desk to meet me. "Make any headway?"

I thought of the toad and frowned. "Not really." I waved the pink message slip. "This all he said—see you Friday?"

At Nick's nod I smothered a sigh and crumpled the message. It gave a faint ping hitting the trashcan's rim before falling inside. Two points. "How is our real estate agent doing today?"

"At the house since two. Cameras are working fine."

"Yeah? Any scintillating action?"

He hummed a distracted, "Uh-huh," and touched high on my cheek. "Gonna have a shiner there, Des. What happened?"

Nick stands a couple inches taller than Armand, with an overall heavier build. I've always felt like a munchkin from Oz beside him, never more so than that moment when our eyes met. Looking up, the start of a crick stabbed my neck. "Would you believe I walked into a wall?"

"If you believe I train anteaters to sing in my spare time." He shook his head. "Try again."

I told him everything...minus the magical bits and pieces. Throughout my short narration, he stared down at me, cupping my cheek, rubbing his thumb along my bruised skin.

His eyes darkened to a stormy ocean blue by my finish. "Used to be when you had a problem, you'd call *me*."

I whispered, "Used to be."

His left hand mirrored his right, cupping my face, and he slowly leaned down to press his lips to mine. A sweet kiss at first brush, it slowly unfurled into confusion, forcing me to once again see there was a man beneath my best friend.

"Wait. Stop." My hands clutched his massive shoulders. "This isn't a good idea."

Nick smoothed his hands into my curls and whispered, "It's just me, Des. You've known me forever." I said his name in one quick plea and he whispered, "Honey, it's okay." And he sank back into me, this time pushing his tongue inside.

Freshman year of high school, we played spin the bottle with a small group of friends at a party. Nick sat beside me in the circle of teens, and Tommy Moore, who I had a secret crush on, sat to my right. I remember feeling the flutters of nerves dance inside my stomach when it came my turn, praying the bottle wouldn't stop across from me on Peter Haynes because he was such a world-class doofus, and then the rush of shock that flushed me when the bottle pointed to Nick.

He led me in silence to the kissing closet, closed us inside behind the dark, wooden door. "How long should we wait?" I asked in a relieved whisper. It felt stuffy inside, hot, smelling of wool and dust.

In the blackness Nick's hands found my arms, my shoulders, my face, and he whispered, "It's just me, Des," before pressing his mouth to mine. I jerked when his tongue touched my lips and he gave a breathy chuckle. "It's okay, just a French kiss. It won't hurt. Open your mouth more."

I obeyed without question, knowing Nick so well, trusting him, and his tongue slipped inside my mouth in a warm awakening. My first French kiss, an inaugural lurch toward adulthood.

His tongue twirled with mine in our office, the firm we run each day together, and one of his large hands swept down to rest on my shoulder. I jerked back with a soft cry and he took his hands from me, meeting my gaze with a troubled expression. "He hurt you there?"

"Yeah." I took a step back. "Just a little sore. No big deal."

Concern creased his brow. "Des, I know you're tough but maybe I should take you to a doctor."

"I'm fine, really." He took a step toward me and I took another back, shooting up my hand. "I've got to go." Armand expected me at his house in about an hour. "Do you have that list of car licenses? I thought I'd start on them tonight if I had time."

He sighed after a moment's stare, brushed a hand through his short, blond hair. "I'll handle it. Have dinner with me tonight."

I took a shallow breath. "I'm having dinner with Armand."

"Tomorrow night then."

"That night as well."

He shoved his hands in his pockets, balled them into fists. I saw their tight roundness push against his slacks, and his frustration settled around my heart.

"Lunch," he urged. "Have lunch with me."

"Are you paying?"

"Yeah, Mexican—your favorite."

"A big fat burrito?"

"With extra sour cream, just the way you like it."

"Sure. We'll catch up on our caseload. Talk about our schedule."

"Among other things."

"Yeah...okay." I edged toward the rear door. "Meet you here around—"

"Whenever, Des. I'm here. I'll wait for you as long as it takes."

I had the feeling he referred to more than just lunch and I gave a choppy Queen Elizabeth wave on my fast exit through the door.

The situation with Nick clung messy, but since his Tuesday confessional I'd gained some objectivity through the unique distance only denial granted.

When you're an expert at the sublime state of denial like I am, pesky problems get pushed to the back burner and simmer there. Sometimes they bubble and froth and smoke from long inattention, developing into an even peskier problem than you started with. But sometimes denial allows needed time and distance for abstract reflection.

Through the mess, the confusion of the past day with Nick, I arrived at a belief: he was taking the easy way out, the only path that felt familiar. Since day one Nick's life has sailed along with an easy glide—sports, school, women, even his profession came with an established firm and his name already on the sign out front.

"Easy" recently left his life and floundering in the midst of a failing marriage, he latched onto a familiar, simple way out of grief. Me. Nick had channeled his pain into something that truly didn't exist between us.

My take? You can have as a best friend a person of the opposite sex. You can view that person as sexually attractive. You can even love that person. But it doesn't mean you're *in* love.

That's where I think Nick took a left turn, an easy detour around full-out heartache.

He'd eventually discover this on his own, I believed. Time was his answer, and patience, mine. Trouble was, just a few hours down the road an angry Frenchman would tell me I didn't have any time.

I called Armand while my Jeep bravely vibrated through rush hour traffic.

"*Bonjour.*"

"Hi there. I'm calling about two things."

"Number one?"

"I'm *starving*. I hope you're making enough for an army."

A smile warmed his voice. "An army eats less than you. Number two?"

"Very funny. Would you mind if I'm a smidgen late? I'm desperate for a shower."

"Shower here."

"But then I'll be stuck with the same clothes."

"I have clothes for you."

"I left clothes there?" I didn't remember doing so.

"*Non.* I bought some."

"You bought me clothes?" I said slowly, like I had an inner ear infection.

"And lacy lingerie."

"Why?"

"Because lacey's your favorite kind, and mine."

"I'm not talking about lacey underwear. Why did you buy me clothes?"

"So you couldn't use the lack of them again for not spending the night."

"Ah." If I had no clean clothes to change into for work, I couldn't very well spend the night, not if he didn't want me to have to rise before roosters did and race home first, or so my pretext went. He'd found a way to zap my best excuse. "You have a very devious mind."

"A very determined one. I want you in my bed tonight. All night."

"Hmmm, so let me get this straight, Snowflake. There's this unbelievably sexy Frenchman cooking me a mouthwatering meal, who just bought me clothes, wants me to use his decadent shower with ten—count 'em *ten*—pulsating spray heads, and demands I spend the entire night in his arms? God, this is all such a *chore*, Armand. I suppose you'll want to have sex, too?"

He murmured, "It crossed my mind a time or two."

"It crossed mine three or four. See you in twenty."

"I'm waiting."

I made it there in fifteen minutes flat, still wearing a dopey grin when Catalina opened the door. "Miss Desy, please come in. Like the weather today?"

She closed the door behind me. "It's beautiful. But did you hear the forecast for tomorrow?"

"No." She looked at my pained expression. "And now I'm afraid to ask."

I patted her arm. "It's best you don't know. You'll sleep better tonight."

"That bad?"

"Uh-huh." I sniffed some kind of delicate cream sauce, clasped my hands over my heart, and pretended I'd never before heard the word cholesterol. "Tell me I'm smelling my dinner."

Catalina's nose crinkled with her laugh. "You're smelling your dinner, some kind of pasta dish. They're waiting for you in the great room. Would you like a beverage?"

"Love a diet cola, thanks." I began my stroll over the foyer's acre of marble and stopped short. "Wait a minute. They?"

"They."

I didn't want a "they", I wanted only a "him". "Who's here?"

"A gentleman."

"Named?"

"I'll just get that cola for you now, Ms. Desy."

She scrambled off over my huff and I moseyed to the back of the house. My feet pulsed, my entire body throbbed, hell, even my eyeballs hurt, and I wanted a boiling shower, a pile of pasta doing the backstroke in my tummy, and a sexy Frenchman on top of me. In that order. Making happy with a gentleman sounded as appealing to me as burping bowls at a Tupperware party, and so I entered the great room with a dark storm cloud brewing above my head.

"Desy, hello." Sam Bearns launched from the couch and began a bow.

"Stop! No goddamn bowing, Sam." My gaze snapped to Armand, who worked at veiling a smile as he crossed to me. Not even that sensual stride of his could lighten my disintegrating mood.

He touched my bruised cheek, lightly kissed my mouth. "This will only take a minute, *mon chou*."

Sam sidled beside me so that I stood between the two men, like creamy filling in a cookie.

"What the hell is going on, and wait—" my hand whipped up "—before you answer, know I have a fully loaded gun."

Catalina entered with my drink and Armand instructed her to place it on the table before wishing her a good evening.

I hissed, "What is he doing here?" as Sam went to lock the door.

"I invited him." Armand stroked a hand over my hair and I silently fumed, trying in vain to recapture my good mood. "Did you know when you're upset," he ran his fingers over my temple, "a small vein throbs right—"

I batted his hand away and Sam returned just as a fierce scowl began to pucker my face. I was acting bitchy...I knew it...and I didn't care.

"Maybe we should postpone this," Sam said, edging around me.

"*Non.*"

"Postpone what?" I nearly growled. "What's going on? Is this about Warren or the Council? Because if it is, I've got a couple words for both of you, and they start with—"

Armand pressed his finger to my mouth briefly and those unbelievable eyes of his met mine. "*Mon chou,* you've had an exhausting day. You're tired and bruised. Sam is here to help you." My eyes blazed. "And you're going to let him."

Sam's special talent is magical healing, which is all good and fine, but I didn't want to be indebted to him much less have his hands on me in any capacity. My gaze shifted to the cautious witch, catching his expression of a man awaiting a blindfold and cigarette. "You can go, Sam."

"Stay," Armand countered. "Begin."

Sam pulled on his goatee, cleared his throat twice, no doubt choking on a thick wad of fright, and I gifted the men with a blistering look before turning to leave.

Armand's hands curled around my shoulders from behind and he spoke low in my ear. "You'll want to feel your best for the argument we're going to have later."

My eyebrows jumped and I slowly spun to face him. "We're going to argue later?"

He motioned to Sam, who promptly moved behind me. "*Oui*, and using one of your favorite expressions, I expect it to be a doozie."

Chapter Thirteen

I felt soothing heat along my back, penetrating deep into my muscles as I stared into Armand's expressive eyes. "A doozie? About what?"

"Many things," he said, taming wild curls behind my left ear. "But the worst of it will center around our last dream and…your shadow."

Heat pulsed along my skin, revitalizing energy, and the pain throbbing from head to toe began to ease. "My shadow? That thing's somehow mine?"

Armand's lips tightened, his gaze intensified, searching my eyes for answers to questions yet unasked. "*Oui.*"

"But—"

"I'm finished," Sam cut in, and I realized Armand had distracted me just enough for Sam to perform his hocus-pocus.

I felt terrific. And embarrassed. I sighed, gave Armand a contrite shake of my head, and turned to Sam. "I've been a class A schmuck, and I'm sorry. Thanks for helping me."

He smiled, performed half a bow. "It was an honor." Magnified by glasses, his eyes shone a dark, solid black, emboldened with magic, and he shifted his gaze to Armand. "You'll call me tomorrow?"

"Around ten."

"I look forward to it." He left after another small bow.

I waited to hear the front door close before I pounced. "Why are you calling him? What—" Armand kissed me. And kissed me some more. Long delicious minutes later, after every inch of my flesh buzzed a happy tune, I breathed, "Um…wow."

A slow, sexy smile curved his mouth, and those lips of his, those gorgeous lips I'd just spent room-spinning minutes tasting, spread wider the longer my stare continued. The flash of his teeth jerked me from a cataleptic state. "Armand, what am I going to do with you?"

"I have some suggestions, ones we'll discuss after dinner." He turned me around and swatted my butt.

"Ow!"

"Go take your shower. I'll finish dinner."

I made sloppy kissing noises, then sashayed from the room.

The shower washed away the first twelve hours of my day, swirling unpleasant memories of Billmark's tenth floor down the drain along with a fair portion of Armand's imported bath products.

The master bath connects to a separate clothes area and it was to this room I padded nude, intrigued to find a note taped to the far-left bank of closets. Two words lay in a bold masculine scrawl across the note's linen surface: *For you.*

Behind the doors clothes of every color, for every occasion, met my fast-widening eyes, all carrying true, honest-to-god designer labels. Ye-gods! I'd died and gone to heaven (where I'm sure only the very best couture is worn). Hangers skated along the closet rod as I ran my hands over each new surprise, the sheen of satin, the slide of silk, the warmth of cotton and wool and every blend in between.

And ooh—I breathed in deep, closing my eyes. Could there *be* a more delicious, incomparable scent than that of new Versace?

My knees wobbled when I spied my weakness—lingerie—hung in every hue. Even thong undies intermixed among the choices and I fingered them in curiosity, never quite understanding why anyone would voluntarily walk around with a wedgie all day.

I made my selection, primped a bit—all right, a lot—then found my very own French chef slicing and dicing in the kitchen.

He looked up when I entered, gave a low appreciative whistle. "I knew." He twirled a finger in the air and my slow spin gave a full view of the dark blue silk, designer concoction, complete with plunging neckline. "Beautiful," he said, wiping his hands on a towel. "Come here." I went there. His arms enfolded me and he hummed, slid his big hands all over my back, palms pressing silk-clad skin, my butt, giving the rounded globes a languid squeeze. He used a hot whisper. "Tell me what's underneath, what color...the blue, red, maybe the black?"

And I whispered back, "It's top secret." He tried to peek but I batted his hand away. "None of that, I'm yet unfed, but tell me the truth." I plucked at the silk. "This cost more than a third-world country, didn't it?"

He grinned, squeezed my butt, and moved to the middle island. "*Non*," he denied, lifting a bowl, "more like a small Balkan island." His grin widened with my snort.

"You're pretty wonderful," I sighed. "Clothes. Sam. Dinner. The hotel earlier. Thank you."

"You're welcome, *mon chou*." He hefted a huge chunk of Parmesan and shaved some curls onto the salad. "Almost ready here."

I watched him work, skating my gaze over his kitchen that never fails to amaze me. "You know, you could park a 747 in here."

He shrugged. "I like to cook."

"What a happy coincidence, I like to eat."

"Then you won't mind helping." He nodded to the stove, the one that has more burners than my closet has shoes. "Add a pinch of salt to that front pot?"

A pinch? Was that more or less than a dash? And pray tell what exactly was a scant? "Sorry," I said, holding up both palms. "I haven't cooked since I blew up my easy bake oven."

* * * * *

"Are we going to argue now?"

"That's the third time you've asked," he said. "After the lesson would be best, *non*?"

"I suppose."

Armand would prefer to teach me something new about magic everyday, but because I am a less than enthusiastic student, we eventually compromised on a couple lessons per week.

Pain free, wearing new clothes and feeling divine calories settling nicely in my tummy, I felt amenable to just about anything.

Magical items and supplies hide in their own locked room in his home's lower level and after dinner we ventured downstairs to play school.

He slid a large, shallow bowl toward me and I watched as he filled it with water. "The hotel case involves stolen jewelry, valuables, *oui*? And you need to discover the guilty employee."

I used my best truck driver twang. "That's a 10-4 good buddy."

"Scrying will help you with your case." He continued his explanation, sliding his hand up and down my thigh. Armand always touches me, and I secretly revel in each caress, suspecting his constant fondling more innate than conscious. Whatever the cause, it must be contagious because I can't be in a room with him and *not* touch him back. "You can scry over a map for lost items, sometimes even lost people, mirrors work well too, but I find water to be the most useful tool. Common witches need to consecrate the water first by exposing it to the light of a waning moon, but with your power, plain tap water will do."

With an anxious wiggle to my hips, I raised my hand to ask a question and he smiled, pulled it down to his mouth for a quick nip of my knuckles. "*Oui?*"

"Does this involve rhyming?"

He pressed a kiss to my palm. "*Non*. Call your power, look into the water, concentrate on what you want to see."

"Okay. Can I have my hand back?"

He kissed it again. "If you insist."

I grinned, scooted closer to the bowl. Magic answered my call with a fast tingle of skin, a warm breeze circling the room, and an eager power, large and hungry, shifting inside me. Energy swelled like a rising tide.

The water's surface began to ripple as I thought of the components in my case — the missing items, Billmark's ninth and tenth floors, the four employees under suspicion—and a hazy image appeared of my top suspect, Rebecca Carlton.

She finished making a bed, pulled the hotel's flowered comforter in place, and shot a furtive glance around the room before opening the nightstand's drawer. Something silver glittered and I squinted at the water, wishing the image appeared clearer.

Warm air shimmered, whispered against my face, and the water's surface cleared, displaying a distinct picture. I breathed, "Cool," and saw a dainty bracelet clutched in Becca's hand. She quickly shoved it inside her bra.

"Shit."

"Problem, *mon chou*?"

"Not really." Waving a hand over the water, I concentrated on closing my magic, binding it down, which after months of practice I still found a sometimes-challenging proposition, and leaned back into the couch.

Armand's large hand rested on my thigh. "Was it helpful?"

"Yeah, that was pretty darn neat. I was just hoping I was wrong and it wouldn't be Becca." I shifted toward him. "She took a bracelet, but there isn't one noted on the list of stolen items."

His finger began to draw small circles on my leg, setting off a rushing horde of chill bumps to scamper up my side. Armand smiled when I quivered. "The vision can be anywhere from past tense to future. Perhaps she hasn't taken it yet." His finger moseyed north, tracing tighter circles up my inner thigh.

I hummed my answer, squirmed on the couch.

"Or perhaps the owner never filed a complaint." His finger edged higher, circling and circling, coming close, so very close to where an urgent, wet heat throbbed.

I dug my hands into the couch.

"Tell me something," he breathed in a dark, husky whisper, his voice alone an aphrodisiac.

"Anything," I panted, wiggling toward his hand, and he asked softly, "What color lingerie are you wearing?"

I nuzzled near his ear with my own soft whisper. "Nice try."

With a gust of laughter, he tackled me on the couch and began tickling my sides. I began to fight him off, scream for mercy, when he swooped down and kissed me senseless. My hands buried to their wrists in the dark satin of his hair.

Years later against my wet, swollen lips he murmured, "It's time, *mon chou*."

"Thank god." I eased my hand along his straining zipper.

"For our argument."

"Aw crap."

* * * * *

"It's almost like you penciled this in with me for seven o'clock. I don't see how you can be so relaxed," I grumbled.

"I'm not relaxed—not at all—but I've taken the time to calm down. And having a blowup isn't going to get me what I want."

"And what's that?"

"You."

"Oh."

We sat together on an endless moss green sectional in his living room. The whoosh of air conditioning droned quietly in the background and a bamboo tray on the footstool held an aged French red in thin wineglasses, yet untouched.

"Any ground rules?" I asked. "Like no kicking, spitting, or biting but the odd scratch or two is allowed?"

"Desy."

I settled back into the lush cushions with a dramatic sigh. "Okay. Begin."

"Warren," he said, and I scowled. "Sam has told me more of his past rulings, his current leadership, and I can't allow him to continue here as High Priest."

"That's not your decision, and I already said I'd go with you on Monday to the Council."

"Monday's appointment stands, but as to Warren, he made it my decision when he touched you. I won't wait any longer. Witches here are unsafe."

"What are you saying exactly?"

"That if the Council doesn't act fast enough, I will. And once Warren is dealt with, you'll rule by my side."

I chewed the inside of my mouth before spitting an answer that began calmly enough but ended somewhat shrill. "I am *not* going to get involved. N-O spells *ain't no frigging way!*"

Armand's lips tightened. "I'd like to give you more time, I'd planned on it, but there isn't any. You'll accept the responsibility that comes with your power."

"Can you hear yourself?" I felt like pulling my hair...or his. "You sound so damn arrogant. I know what I need and it doesn't involve Wiccan politics." Anger pulsed through me where just minutes earlier arousal had.

"Monday we'll tell the Council of our plan."

I swatted a pillow. "Are you deaf?"

"And now that that's resolved, let's discuss Nick."

My jaw fell slack. "Wh-what does Nick have to do with anything?" I knew I wasn't going to like his answer because Armand's entire face hardened, the sensuous planes pulling into a tight mask. Tempered anger lay beneath.

He swiped an impatient hand through his hair. "That's something you'll have to explain to me. Your feelings for him have changed."

My heart tried to leap from my chest. Luckily, my ribs were in the way. "I...that's not true. My feelings are the same; his have changed, kind of. I just found out yesterday. How did you know?" Armand's jaw ticked the longer he stared. "Figure fifty or so," I snapped.

"Pardon?"

"You're staring at my face so long I assumed you were counting freckles."

He leaned, pinned me in place by planting his arms beside my shoulders. Reigned anger laced his eyes and words. "I don't need to count them. Do you think I don't know where every freckle is on your entire body? That I haven't tasted every one?" He gave me a hard, unexpected kiss. "You're mine, *mine*. What does he think he's doing? He's married."

I swallowed. "He's, ah, he's separated now."

Armand's eyes blazed. "Sonofabitch." He launched himself from my side, began to pace, and his long legs ate up the hardwood floor. "Sonofabitch!" He spoke in a stream of French, each syllable slicing the air in a blistering torrent, each foreign phrase unraveling my composure.

He sucked in a large breath; let it out slowly as his pacing slowed to a stop. "When were you going to tell me this?"

I released the pulpy bruise of my bottom lip, having nearly chewed it off. "It's a mess, Armand. I planned to wait until it blew over, two-three weeks, maybe a month, and then tell you kind of after the fact."

His brow knit. "Nick's marriage will be reconciled within the month?"

"No. Well, maybe. God, I don't know." I shifted on the couch. "He's confused right now. That's going to clear up soon."

"You're making no sense."

Emotions burned dark and dry in his eyes, but the one that stung my heart was his pain. It was obvious, and I had put it there. The knowledge cut clean through me; shaky legs took me to his side. "Nick thinks he feels for me something more than friendship, but I know him. He's just hurt and confused right now. In time —"

"There is no time." Armand grabbed my upper arms. "Do you think I'll be content to sit back and let this play out?" A humorless laugh gusted from him. "*Non.* End this right now — tomorrow. Talk to him tomorrow and explain very clearly you belong to me, or —" He released my arms, still staring down at me.

"Or what?" My heart beat so fierce, it would explode.

"Or do nothing, *mon chou.* Do nothing and throw us away."

With a sharp inhale I took a step backward, bumping into the ottoman. Glasses clinked, toppled over, spilling wine in a cascade of red. Alcohol splattered on the tray, the ottoman, the floor.

I swore in a thick voice, knelt to pick up the glasses and Armand left the room, returning with napkins that sopped up most of the mess. Hands on my elbows, he eased me upright.

"Shh," he soothed, wiping my wet cheeks. "It kills me to see you cry. Shh."

"I'm not crying. This is an allergy."

He shook his head, a very slight movement, and swiped his thumbs along my jaw, my lips. "It's all right. I don't care about the stain."

"I'm not having allergies over the goddamn stain!"

A slight smile began to curve his lips and his brown eyes further darkened, spearing me with their blend of anger and tenderness. "Jesus, Des, what you do to me." He leaned down, taking my lips with such devastating, stark emotion—sweetness and lust and anger and hot need—that more tears spilled down my cheeks.

I broke from him, met his dark gaze. "Red, Armand…the lacey red ones."

Chapter Fourteen

Two staircases wind the curving, opposite walls of the foyer, and it was to the left one he carried me, leading straight to the master suite. Surefooted, he stared into my eyes the entire way, sometimes pausing to kiss or murmur sweet words against my lips, before gently laying me on the large island of his bed.

I began to unbutton my top but his words stilled my hands.

"*Non*, let me." His finger traced a centerline in the middle of my forehead, down my nose, over my lips—I nipped at the fleshy pad—before it smoothed over the contour of my chin. In his eyes heat blazed.

His finger played in the hollow of my throat with tiny circles then slipped beneath blue silk, sliding inside my tight cleavage. The curves of my breasts hugged his finger, and the stroking tease, the warmth, hardened my nipples beneath lace and silk. They throbbed, tingled, ached.

"It was the hair of course," he murmured, trailing his finger along the swells of my breasts, "that first caught my eye." He unbuttoned the top button, glanced at the wild spray of my hair spread about the pillow. "All those long curls. We hadn't even been introduced yet and I wanted to bury my hands in them to see if they could possibly be as soft as they looked."

The corners of his mouth tilted up. "They're even softer," he assured, working at the next button. "And then the eyes—your big brown eyes, so pretty—they stared boldly, right through me. I felt like I'd been punched." Armand smiled, shook his head and undid the next button. "By the time I noticed your freckles, I already fought a hard-on."

"Armand."

He pressed his finger against my lips. "Shh. You'll hear me tonight."

The last two buttons slipped free and he opened my top. "The red looks good on you, *mon chou*." His hands filled with my lace-covered breasts and I arched into his palms, feeling heat lance straight to my center.

"I've always thought of myself as a leg man," he murmured, unhooking the bra's front closure. "And you have lovely legs, but these are just—" he peeled the bra from my breasts "—so...damn...beautiful."

He took the mounds of my breasts into his hands again, squeezed, and plucked my hard nipples.

I shuddered, squirmed along the mattress, feeling hot and needy and eager, having sprinted far past mere "ready" back on the stairs. In one prolonged seduction, he moved foreplay so slowly I felt I would burst into flames even before he removed my pants. My hands bunched in the sheets.

"I knew of you from those letters, the ones Penelope wrote to my father." His hands slid to my waist where one finger slipped beneath the silk, dipped into my navel. I flexed my hips. "She wrote of a smart child, precocious, always curious and getting into mischief, who grew into a bold, loving woman." His hands tangled around the waist of my pants and pulled the silk down my legs. "You're that, but so much more."

The panties stretched in see-through, scarlet lace across my hips, the cut a boyshort, riding high on my thighs. "Very nice," he said, splaying his hand over intricate lace, low on my belly. Lust churned beneath his large palm, hunger, the needy craving for his touch so intense I grew wetter, soaking the crotch of my panties with liquid desire.

"You view yourself as patient, but you're one of the most impatient people I've ever known." He trailed his tongue in a moist path along my thigh, toward my bent knee. Confusion furrowed my brow. "You're stubborn, *mon chou*, so goddamn stubborn, and you procrastinate, shy away at first from anything you find too emotional." Armand nibbled on my knee, teased the hollow behind with delicate brushes of his fingertips.

"If this is your idea of sexy bed talk, I have to tell you, Kumquat, it's sorely lacking," I shot, smarting from his comments.

With a slight smile he said of me, "Cheeky, often caustic, too," before moving down my leg with nibbles and licks and kisses. He reached my foot, danced his fingers along the high curve of my arch, sucked my big toe into his mouth. It slicked wet and tingly by the time he moved to my other foot.

"You have a temper, and it's very short," he murmured against my toes, licking between each one. "Independence is something you value too much, although you're learning to share more of your burdens with me each day."

I tried concentrating on his words but he'd hit a particularly ticklish spot. I began to squirm the longer he played. "Armand."

His wet tongue slid to my anklebone. "Don't trust easily, but humor," he whispered with a slight smile. "That one surprised me. Strong-willed, courageous, at times so fearless it's frightening." With languorous movements, he meandered up my leg. That mouth, that wicked tongue, those large hands of his that seemed to know just where to touch, how light, how hard, turned me into one quivering mass of nerves, aching for more.

A wild, wet pulse thrummed in my center and as his mouth neared, I whimpered softly, dying to be filled, and my heart raced with anticipation, but he moved past my body's most urgent need, dipped his tongue into my navel.

I sat up, tore off my open top and bra, tossed them to the floor, and fisted handfuls of his hair, cradling him against me as he moved up, took one pointed nipple into his mouth. I moaned.

Desire, building frustration, whipped through me. The man would drive me insane, I thought. A white jacket would soon adorn me, tightly strapped, and I'd babble incoherently before he'd get around to shoving his cock where desperation throbbed.

By the time he'd moved to my other breast, drew it into his mouth and bathed the puckered crest with his tongue, stroking round and round, fever lashed my skin, flushing me a rosy pink.

Wherever his hands went, his lips soon followed. If there was a spot on my body he'd never touched before, he found it that night.

A raspy, broken moan spilled from my mouth. Please, I thought. Now.

The bed dipped as he shifted and straightened, so that we stared into each other's eyes, our hands buried in the other's hair, me completely nude, every inch of skin throbbing, he still clothed. "Strong and smart and caring," he whispered. "I know you, Desdemona. I see all of you." He slid his hands down to cup my face, and my heart rocketed to the moon at the message burning in his eyes. "I want every part. You're mine, by God you're mine," he breathed in a fierce tone, "and I mean for you to have no doubt after tonight."

His gaze incinerated, my lungs stuttered to a stop, and he spoke in a thick accent, the fabric of his voice woven with passion and sweet dark honey. "I love you."

My entire body gave one large shuddering sigh.

He blurred before me and Armand kissed my eyes closed. "Your allergies are acting up again, *mon chou*." I garbled a hiccupping laugh, blinked my eyes clear. "You'll need time. I don't need the words returned now. I've already seen them in your pretty doe eyes." He traced a slow finger along my mouth. "Tasted them here on these unbelievable lips." He dropped his hand, brushed the back of his fingers along my bare shoulder. "And here, you're so soft, I've felt them here on this skin each time we touch."

I couldn't swallow.

"It's something I want. Need. But your words can wait."

He kissed me then, the sweetest kiss I've ever known and my shaky hands began to work on his clothes, fumbling with buttons. Soon we were laughing softly, sitting on the bed, untangling him from the mess I'd made of his shirt, his pants, and I spoke in a breathy tone. "You missed a spot earlier." A pile of clothes lay on the floor, Armand finely nude, a sight that never failed to melt my brain neurons.

His lips curved against my throat. "Did I?"

"'Fraid so, Chief."

"Here?" Hot lips pressed against my shoulder.

"No...cold."

"Here, then?" His hand moved down, fondling my left breast.

"Gosh that's nice, but you're still cold."

Against my waist, my navel, his hand caressed. "Here?"

"Warm," I breathed, nibbling on his ear. "You're getting very warm."

One tapered finger drew circles below my navel, traveling south. "Here, *mon chou*? Did I miss this spot?"

I wiggled closer. "Hot. You're hot now."

"Maybe here?" he asked, sliding his finger where each heartbeat echoed between wet, supple lips. "God, yes," I moaned. "You're so close."

"How remiss of me to have missed this very spot." Into tight cream he pushed three fingers, circling his thumb around the base of my clit.

I bucked, exploded, the climax raking in blistering waves so fierce, clamping and releasing in a relentless rhythm around his fingers, no sound could leave my lips. Armand moaned for me, began to slide his fingers in and out, in and out, and the familiar sounds of arousal—wet, squishy, slick—rose above our panting. When his baby finger slid along my anus, rubbing the sensitive pucker with each tempered thrust of his hand, tension clenched, broke again, and a second mind-altering orgasm pounded through me.

He kissed me, spoke in a harsh whisper. "Lie back, *amoureux*, I've got to taste you."

Falling backward was easy — the orgasms had melted my spine.

His hands slid beneath my butt, palming my cheeks, spreading them wide, and before my head settled on the pillow, his tongue plunged. With two sighing syllables, his name left my lips.

With no sheltering hair between my legs, I felt each lick of his tongue, each nibble of teeth, every slippery finger stroke, even the burrowing of his nose with keen intensity. The long silk of his hair tickled my inner thighs and the soft, bare pad of my mound.

"You're close." The words tingled across my drenched lips.

My heels dug into the mattress while I held my breath, circled my hips, and rode his tongue, his fingers, and clawing tension.

If I broke into shards, I wondered, would he pick me up? Reassemble me?

He caught my hard little shaft between his teeth and tongued it furiously.

I screamed, bowed off the bed, and burst...and burst...and burst. A singeing flush scalded its way up my body, and Armand's tongue rooted deeper along with a wet, masculine moan.

Contractions eased, tapering to pulsing swells, ebbing then to lazy ripples, and I felt Armand's soft kiss against my still-throbbing center.

The top sheet shifted in a tangled mess, the fitted one swam loose on the bed, and I sprawled among the twisted cotton believing myself completely wrung of all energy. The Frenchman soon proved me wrong.

"I love the taste of you," he murmured, and my eyes slowly opened, catching him straightening to his knees. His large hand, still glistening from my juices, wound around his hard cock and pumped.

The sight was unbelievably erotic — the tight squeeze of his fingers, the slapping sound he made with each tug — and as I watched, a warm wave of pleasure unfurled, rolling in my stomach. My hips began to waft to and fro.

His eyes closed briefly, his nostrils flared, and he leaned forward, planting his flanged head inside me. I lay beneath his heavy-lidded stare, and his hands clasped my legs, straightening them so my ankles rested near his shoulders.

The bare skin of my mound was reddened slightly from his fingers and teeth, but redder still flushed the long stretch of his erection. With muscular thighs braced, hips rocking in shallow thrusts, large hands gripping my thighs, he worked himself inside me.

"You're always so tight, *mon dieu*, so damn hot," he said, his gaze intense, possessive, and all male. The slight movement of his pelvis was a circling tease instead of heavy thrusts, so that I felt a subtle shifting of pressure inside me instead of pounding friction. He felt immense.

The gentle caress gave way to blinding pleasure when his hips began to rock. Sticky and glistening, his cock shuttled back and forth in hard digs, and each time it buried high, Armand would grind his hips, flexing within me rigid inches of hot flesh.

My teeth caught my lower lip as he hardened his pace, rutting with commanding thrusts, and my stunning Frenchman began to lean his body forward, push my legs toward my chest, slowly, carefully, letting me feel each shift in sensation until his mouth met mine and he slid his tongue inside, wet and hot and wild, all the while still flexing his hips, driving his cock between my legs.

Hair, face, shoulders, arms—I touched these, caressed his flesh with eager hands, before he eased back and began to rock his finger on my engorged clit. A wave of molten pressure built, surfing high, then higher, the sensation one of gliding through gentle waters, feeling the surface begin to ripple, then surge, carrying you away faster and faster, your heart pounding, until you hit unexpected rapids.

I cried out while every muscle went taut…then lax.

Armand rode me harder, plowing in the wet core between my thighs, and his features knotted with pleasure before turning to a grimace of pure ecstasy as he climaxed, spurting dense streams of come that filled me with thick, wet heat. I felt every hot splash.

Sex thickened the air, perfuming it with sweet musk and sweat, and as the setting sun left the room, darkness grew in its wake, casting long shadows. The lamps throughout the bedroom lit with one wave of his hand, and my feet touched the tangled sheets as he eased his weight down upon me, resting on his forearms.

Armand rubbed his nose along mine, nudging me in a silent caress, and so I could better see his eyes, I smoothed back his long, glossy hair. "Hi," I whispered.

He smiled, kissed my nose. "Hi."

His cock flexed, still rock hard, and my eyebrows rose. "Houston, we have a problem."

Gentle teeth nibbled along my jaw. "Problem?" he murmured between bites.

"A really big one. You keep ignoring sexual protocol. Rule 437.1 clearly states after you bang someone silly—Armand—hey, are you listening?"

"Mum-hum."

"Well afterward, you're supposed to...*go*...*soft*."

He circled his hips, sliding his cock higher and I gave a deep moan. "But that would ruin my plan, *mon chou*."

"Plan?" Curiosity spiked. "Top secret or can you share?"

"It's shareable."

"Oh goody. Spill."

The lips he kissed me with curved in a slight smile. "My plan is to enjoy you all night long. And later, much later, if you should fall asleep, I'll find wherever your dream takes you and love you there. Then *amoureux*, early in the morning, I'll wake you with my tongue. You'll ride me in the shower next—maybe we'll try the long bench in there. And just before you leave me, when you dress for work, I'll bend you over," he said, kissing me again, "and fuck you from behind."

He always uses the phrase "make love", so hearing the F-word emerge from my polished Frenchman spun my head. "I...I've got just one question."

"*Oui?*"

"After this plan, will I be able to walk?"

"Hmm," he purred, thinking it over. "Probably not."

He began to pump.

Chapter Fifteen

In the quiescent predawn before the day takes its first breath, we wallowed in the sweet aftermath of gluttonous sex. I lay spent in his arms, sheltered by his tight embrace and the long muscular leg he'd curled around my hip to pull me even closer. Replete, we slept like the dead.

In the fanciful world of his emerging dream, however, I strolled toward him along an unfamiliar moonlit path. Trees stood in silhouette like mute sentinels, their thick canopies swaying gently in the soft summer breeze, leafed arms reaching for the stars.

Armand watched my approach, standing tall and casually stunning several feet ahead. A blue ribbed shirt stretched across his wide chest, outlining the strength that lay beneath. Worn jeans rode low and sexy on his hips, outlining his thighs.

"Hey," I called out. "You look kinda familiar. Aren't you the same guy who just boinked me for over four hours straight?"

A flash of perfect white teeth. "*Non*," he returned. "I'm the guy who made love to you until you begged for a defibrillator."

"Which you never supplied."

He walked the last few steps to meet me and took my hands to his mouth, pressed soft kisses along my knuckles. "I let you sleep instead."

"How kind," I smirked.

"You look beautiful."

A long slinky nightgown hugged my curves in bold red. I glanced down, raised an eyebrow over the healthy show of cleavage. "Ever notice, Armand, you usually dream yourself in modest clothes but put me in—" I pinched the scarlet fabric " —this type of thing?"

He flashed a thousand-watt smile that could be seen from Mars. "I have definitely noticed, *oui*."

As I snorted, he slid an arm around my shoulders and we began to walk.

"Going to tell me where we are?"

"We summered here, my family." He dropped a kiss on my head. "After school let out, we'd pack up and stay until mid-August. I have many fond memories." Warm nostalgia glossed his words, and he pointed to the left. "Giselle and I used to climb that tree."

A swing hung from a thick lower limb and I steered us that way. "So this is France?"

"Southern France, Arles, in Provence."

"It's lovely." I tried to shimmy onto the swing, aiming for a manner of decorum and ladylike grace—one smooth glide—but the nightgown bunched and snagged. After a few ripe words and some wrestling, I managed to flail myself onto the swing. Armand chewed his lower lip, struggled not to laugh, and I fixed him with a penetrating stare, the piercing effect, I feared, ruined by poor light. "Not one word," I huffed.

He choked, "Not one, *mon chou*."

"Smart man." I dug my bare feet into the sparse grass—cool blades against my soles—and launched myself in motion. "Except for once the first week we met, you haven't dreamt of home."

He leaned against the tree, watching me swing with a small curve to his lips. "My home is with you."

I smiled, thinking he had a swell way with words, and began to swing higher. The night air, thick with the sweet scent of flowers, rose and lilac among them, and the song of all manner of small French beasties chirping underfoot, whispered against my skin as the swing carried me back and forth. Untamed curls brushed my shoulders and face with each pump of my legs.

"My cottage is just up this path," he said with an impossibly sexy smile and voice. I resisted the urge to melt into a pile of mindless goo. "There's an antique bed inside," he added in a coaxing purr. "Iron. And a mattress stuffed with down and feathers. You'll like it."

"Oh really?" I swung higher. He sounded cocky, which of late I somehow found to be just another facet of his charm.

"The bed is small, but we'll make do."

"That's all fine and dandy, but there's just one eensie problem, my fine Frenchman."

"And that would be?"

On a high back lift I challenged, "You'll have to catch me first." As the swing flew forward, I sailed off and hit the ground running.

His laughing curse spurred me on.

Galloping in a full-length nightgown is not as easy as one might think. Instead of my legs taking the ground in urgent gulps, they had to settle for shallow sips. I raced past trees, bushy grasses and flowers, dodging to and fro with the steady thump of masculine feet behind me.

Happy excitement accompanied every footfall and panting squeals escaped my mouth each time I looked back and saw how quickly he gained. A thicket edged a small open field, lit by the golden yellow of moon and star. It was there Armand caught my arm and laughingly scooped me up.

Twirling in his arms, I grew dizzy, or perhaps the sight of his handsome face, enrapt and filled with tenderness, caused my lightheaded haze. He carried me to the middle of the field and we lay flat on the soft grass beside each other, holding hands, looking up at the twinkling night sky. Our breathing began to slow.

"I love you," he said in a voice rich and full, and my heart fluttered in a soft caress, as if he'd wrapped careful hands around the muscle and stroked.

I hitched my gown to mid-thigh, rolled, and straddled his hips, casting my silhouette on his face. Though shaded, I still saw what blazed there and I met his mouth, told unspoken secrets with my lips, my tongue, my hands. A scarlet gown soon tumbled to the ground, a blue shirt, jeans and briefs in slow discard between soft kisses, teasing nips and ardent, hungry looks.

He lay beneath me, quiet and intense, as I took his long cock in my hand, wound my fingers at its base, and pressed it to my wet center. Armand's hands spanned my waist, grasped my hips, and as he helped me lean forward above him, captured my nipple between gentle teeth.

I quivered.

The bulbous head, the smooth velvet flare of his cock, parted my glossy lips, stealing my breath. I guided the head back and forth along my slippery opening, teasing us both. He felt hard, so very thick and warm, and swallowing each rigid inch I sank down, reveling in the slow pressure tightly stretching my inner walls. Heat, scalding pressure filled me.

My hands clung to his shoulders and his breath hitched, expelled in a slow sigh against my breast as the last inch of his cock slid inside.

I closed my eyes, breathing in short, lean sips.

Had he made love before out in the open beneath the stars? I wondered. I had never. Never before had there been a man who could make me lose all discretion. Dream or reality, sheltered or open site, it mattered not. I would have him. He was mine.

"All right?" he whispered, releasing my nipple.

I sat up and met his raw gaze, feeling his cock shift inside me with every movement of my hips. "Perfect."

"Yes, you are." He cupped my breasts.

A wanton rhythm began, slow gripping drags up, squeezing his cock from base to tip, and gradual downward glides, clenching around his every broad inch. Each slow plunge ended with a hip gyration, rubbing my bare wet flesh against his tuft of dark curls, eliciting dual groans.

I rode him slow, slower than ever before. Obscenely slow.

"You're killing me, *mon chou*," he grunted in a pained rasp.

"Do you happen to remember a few hours ago when you kept stopping and wouldn't let me come?" A mean smile twisted my lips, and I mimicked his accent. "*Mon chou*, thiz iz gewd for you, eet builds stam-ee-na."

He winced. "That's a horrible impression."

I wiggled on his cock and he groaned. "So sue me. Payback's a bitch, Buttercup."

It was as my gaze traveled his sensual features laden with lusty humor—the planes and angles of his face such stark masculine beauty—that something moved in my periphery. My hips stilled and I searched the thicket to the left, zeroed in on a dark silhouette.

The shadow, that dark foreign profile, stalked our dream. Again. It moved toward us slowly.

I breathed, "Shit," and went to free myself from Armand, but his hands gripped my waist.

"*Non*," he growled low, staring at the thing. My throat closed down as bitter words—obscure, hard, French—left his mouth in an angry stream.

The shadow stilled twenty feet away, standing tall and shrouded in darkness. It unnerved me but more, angered Armand.

"Let me go," I said, trying to tug his hands from me. If some weird mystical battle neared, if I had to fight that thing, I didn't want to do so with Armand's cock buried to the hilt and my knees clutching his waist. The more I struggled, the tighter his fingers bit into my skin.

"Listen to me, you're going to fuck me and ignore him."

"Wh...no to both, you jackass!" I grappled with his hold, then stilled. "Did you say him? Not an it, a him?"

"*Oui*." Armand's gaze and tone snapped.

"And you say it, he is somehow mine?" I stared at the shadow.

"He's here because of you," Armand said, then added quietly, "Desy, look at me." Anger, lust, determination stared back at me from his deep brown eyes. And love. Love gleamed there too, shining brightest of all. "Kiss me."

"You're absolutely mad."

"For you. Now kiss me." He released my waist, moved his hands to my upper arms and tugged gently.

An inch from his mouth I hissed, "What's going on? A setup? Will he attack? What—"

Armand's kiss cut off my ramble. *He poses no physical threat. Ignore him.*

His tongue pushed against mine in a wet nudge but I couldn't respond. Large shifting shadows tend to knock your libido down a few pegs.

Did that deter the Frenchman? Not hardly.

His hands closed over my breasts and he ground his hips up, shoving his rigid erection higher.

Oooh...God...this is nuts, I complained, sitting back up.

He tweaked my nipples and fire lanced a straight downward path, settling between my legs in a searing crackle. Breath wheezed from my lungs.

I looked down, entranced by the erotic picture of dark hair sprinkled on his forearms, the tight sinew that lay beneath, and his large hands molded around my breasts.

The night air swirled in a fragrant breeze, caressing my back, and the grass kissed my knees, my shins, in a cool tickle as his hips and hands circled over my flesh.

If not for the silent shadow, the dream would have achieved perfection.

Kiss me, he coaxed.

What is he? Who is he? I looked again at the dark form standing large and motionless. What? Why? Who? How? Armand knew of these things, but chose not to tell me.

Questions upon questions tumbled in my unquiet mind, thrusting me into confused stasis.

Kiss me, amoureux. Look at me…only me.

My head fizzed at his tone, drenched in sexual supplication and command, and I met his gaze. Had I ever before felt such radiating tension from him, or seen his eyes quite that fierce? Even in the low moonlight, they blistered with emotion.

Hell. I leaned down and nipped the thick vein that throbbed at the side of his throat. His pulse hammered and on his skin I tasted sharp need. Like a dry sponge, I absorbed it; his urgency became my own.

The tip of my tongue painted his full lower lip, and his deep moan flamed inside me, heating my desire to a rolling boil. My hips circled clockwise in counterpart to his pelvic grind and we began slow shallow thrusts, movements that teased and enticed. His cock slicked in and out.

He sucked my tongue deep within his warm mouth — heat sluiced through me at the first wet touch — and a tremor began at the base of my neck, traveling in a thrumming shake down my spine.

Tension lashed.

Armand, I whispered as he stroked me, immersing me within a world of our own making. He has a way of moving that is completely attuned to my every desire, using lips, tongue, teeth, and hands — those hips, that long thick cock. I quaked with a growing, stunning ache, knowing he would soon soothe me.

I swallowed his moan, he swallowed mine, as I began to lift and plunge in a wild whipping rhythm up and down his pulsing length, spilling hot juices onto his thatch, easing every fierce thrust, and he pinched my nipples, tugged, shoving high the pressure climbing inside me until it gathered in a tingling, molten knot.

Oui, he said, *Faster*, as my hips flew in churning digs—the squish of my plunges as loud as my moans—driving his cock high again and again. The steady friction of his strokes, his need, pushed my body into one erogenous mass.

Come, bebe, come for me. That unbelievable voice of his voice, laden with a sensual groan, seared the moment, curled and tightened within me.

The orgasm poured in hot, undulating waves, spreading, gripping his cock in a wet, scalding vise, dragging from me a sharp cry. Muscles tugged in violent spasms and his hands held my hips steady as he thrust with lunges both fierce and wild before pumping fast streams of semen.

His broken moan slid down my throat in one hot glide.

My hands clutched his shoulders, his hands—my ass, and as our spasms leveled, began to recede, our kiss deepened. Tongue licking tongue, he tasted so good, always so perfect—familiar, yet new...urgent, yet tender...demanding, yet giving.

I ate him up.

A sound, a footfall, reached me seconds after Armand's body had already stiffened. My head jerked up. The shadow had moved closer, standing not more than five feet away, and my entire body solidified with shock. I'd forgotten about it.

Another step moved it into a soft patch of moonlight. My heart stuttered, then pounded, and my voice emerged in a tight squeak.

"Nick?"

* * * * *

I lunged upright in Armand's bed.

He untangled his legs from mine and rose slowly, running a hand through his hair with a hard sigh.

I stared at him, wide-eyed, unblinking. "The shadow is *Nick*? In our dreams? Nick watched us screw? Twice?" The next question rushed from my mouth in a panicked squeal as if I'd sucked helium. "Nick saw me naked?"

"In his dreams," answered Armand. "Chances are he won't even remember."

"Chances are?" I vaulted from bed. "Chances are!" As I stormed from the room, I snagged his robe from a hook and threw it on. Nude, Armand followed silently as I thundered down the long winding stairs, calling over my shoulder, "Ignore him, you said! Look only at me, you said!" At the foot of the stairs I turned to him. "What in the hell were you thinking?"

"That perhaps I'm the aggrieved party here?" His lips wore a slight twist, as if he didn't know whether to smile or frown and fought both.

To the large foyer table I stalked, my feet slapping cold marble. The Jeep's keys bit into my palm. "You mishandled this badly, Creampuff. You should have told me it was Nick."

He leaned his bare hip against the table and crossed his arms. "He's been a clear presence since the hotel dream. You saw only a shadow. Obviously you weren't ready to see him." I huffed when he shrugged. "And I've not mishandled this." He raised my chin with a firm finger. "Your dreams play from your subconscious and until recently I've been the only man with you each night. But now you hold another in your mind. You've brought him into our dreams which means you're attracted to him sexually and —"

"That's not true," I said, searching his eyes. "Nick's always been my friend. I…I admit I'm more aware of him now as a man but I'm *not* sexually attracted to him. There's a big difference between admiring his looks and actually wanting him." My lips firmed and I poked Armand in the chest. Jab. "And I want only you." Jab. "You big French lug!" Jab.

He grabbed my finger, brought it to his mouth and sucked it whole. Immediately, my brain went soft. His teeth nibbled its tip on a slow release and he tugged me closer, pressing random kisses on my face. "I needed to hear those words, *mon chou*." A soft kiss to my forehead. "But because actions speak louder, I want proof." Lips pressed a feather-light buss to my cheek. "You'll speak to Nick about this," Armand whispered, kissing my nose. "Today." He kissed my lips. "Or I will." Another kiss. "And I promise you." A soft nip to my chin. "I won't be as diplomatic."

He swore lightly when I stomped on his foot.

"Oh gosh, I'm so sorry." I strutted to the front door. "You know how clumsy I can be sometimes."

"It's not even seven yet," he informed, limping toward me. "Where are you going?"

I flung open the door. "To clean toilets."

Wrens sang good morning as I marched to my Jeep. I had the door open when Armand called my name. "What?" I snapped, mad and aroused.

Nude, he leaned in the doorway with a smirk on his too-handsome face and an erection that cheerily waved good morning. "Come back inside."

I pushed wild curls from my face. "Why should I?"

"Because you're wearing a robe."

I glanced down. "Aw hell."

* * * * *

He almost made me late for work.

An uninvited guest, Armand joined me mid-shower that morning with a certain wicked gleam in his eyes and a hard-on enormous enough to whack through thick jungle weeds. I held up wet hands and told him his intent could be construed as an infringement of certain Witch Teamster bylaws. Right after pinning me against wet tile and plunging inside, he purred he would speak to my local union representative. I just held on and tried not to drown.

After a twenty-minute scuffle with him in the enormous room he calls a walk-in closet, where he caught me nude and unaware from behind, pounding away until our groans of release echoed through the house, I quickly dressed. "*Mon chou*," he said in a gloating voice, kissing me goodbye. "I accomplished my plan and you're still able to walk." To which I replied, "Yeah, but you're not," and I stomped on his foot again before sprinting to my Jeep.

I smiled all the way through horrendous rush hour traffic.

A casino sits in the shadow of the Billmark Hotel, and in early morning hours the moving catwalk connecting the two landmarks shuttles disillusioned gamblers reeking of alcohol and lost dreams. I'd seen my share of them the previous morning during a six a.m. stroll when I'd familiarized myself with the hotel's layout.

Thursday morning, though, I had just enough time to sling on my uniform before Mr. Adams called his nine a.m. staff meeting. A droning review of schedules followed and I sidled alongside Rebecca Carlton, who greeted me with a toothy grin, a whispered hello, and a cloud of hair product.

The housekeeping staff numbered just over thirty and ranged in age from high school dropout to retirement. Employees talked among themselves, successfully ignoring Mr. Adams.

"That wraps it up. Any questions?" he called out, tapping his clipboard. Our eyes met briefly before he wished everyone a productive day.

Rebecca spoke as we loaded the cleaning cart. "Thanks again for yesterday, Susan. Can I call you Sue?"

"Sure."

"Well, I got home just in time, if you catch my meaning." She snorted.

I gave her a smile as I grabbed some garbage bags. "No problem. Your mom okay?"

"As well as can be expected. She's on this new medicine—ends in an 'ix'. I can't even begin to pronounce it." Rebecca eyed the cart, added more rags. "Anyway, seems like it's helping a little better than the last stuff."

"That's good. I bet it's expensive."

We maneuvered the cart into the service elevator. I punched the tenth floor button.

"God, you wouldn't believe," she said, opening a new pack of gum. "Want some?"

"No thanks."

She poked a stick inside her mouth and promptly began snapping it. "And she's got shitty insurance too. Had to move in with me a couple months ago cuz she couldn't make rent."

I gave an empathetic hum. "That must be hard."

The elevator lurched to a stop and she shrugged. "Figure it's her turn to be taken care of. You know how moms are, they can drive you crazy but you'd do anything for 'em."

"Anything," I agreed. Perhaps even steal.

We resumed yesterday's routine, only this time I was a day older and wiser. After performing a magical whammy on each bathroom — one wave of my hand made porcelain and tile sparkle — I cracked open the door and watched Becca work.

She searched each room systematically — a glance at the nightstand's contents while she stripped sheets, a search of dresser drawers as she dusted, and a quick peek into any unpacked luggage, makeup bags and the like, before vacuuming.

The fifth room she hit pay dirt. Running water obscured the squeak of the bathroom door as I parted it open. Through the one-inch crack I watched her finish the bed, open the nightstand drawer, and withdraw a thin bracelet. She stuffed it in her bra.

It was an exact reenactment of the scrying bowl scene, complete with furtive look and practiced snatch. Magic is an eerie thing, I thought.

I flushed the toilet and over the gargling swish of water, made a phone call.

By the time we finished vacuuming, Mr. Adams and two security guards entered the room. He spoke quietly to her and stunned, dry-eyed, she turned around and fished out the bracelet. The closest guard returned it to the nightstand before he and his partner shepherded Rebecca from the room.

Mr. Adams stayed behind to talk to me. "She's been with us for over five years. Perfect record, too. Shame." His tone rang contemplative.

"Did you know her mother has cancer? She had to move in with Rebecca. They can barely make ends meet."

"That doesn't excuse her actions."

"I agree, but desperate people sometimes do desperate things, Mr. Adams." I held out my hand and he took it in a firm shake. "You'll have my report before the day's end."

Chapter Sixteen

"Is that a new belt?"

"Yeah," Nick said, fingering the black leather. "Like it?"

"It's beltacular."

He grinned. "Just give me a second. I have to powder my nose."

I waved him off and pecked away at my computer, ignoring the hardy rumble of my stomach. With just a few remaining keystrokes, I'd zap a copy of my final report on the Billmark Hotel case to Mr. Adams, with a second copy to Mr. Beckman of Townsend Investigative Services, who'd referred the case to us...if I could last that long without keeling over.

Sex all night, no breakfast, an argument, more sex, and my soon-to-be lunch partner continued to preen overlong in the office john. Ravenous, the stale mint that melted and stuck last Halloween to the bottom of my desk drawer began to look absolutely scrumptious. I embarked on a campaign to dislodge it with a letter opener and was chip-chip-chipping away when the front door swung open.

In strolled Nick's wife, the very last person I ever expected to see waltzing into the office (okay, maybe she wasn't the *very* last, that spot's reserved for any of Hollywood's A-list, but she definitely merited a top five rating).

I remained seated, still clutching the letter opener. "Anita...hi."

She looked uncomfortable and stunning, as if she just slipped away from her director during a hair commercial. "Hello." She motioned to the couches. "Mind if we sit? Do you have a minute?"

"Nick is—"

"I'm here to talk to you."

Could my day get any better? I mourned, completely unaware that yes, indeed it could. Two discoveries lay minutes away, one frightening, one shocking, and the real kicker—I wouldn't be eating lunch that day.

I looked longingly at the mint, veiled a sigh, and reluctantly set down the opener. Anita perched ramrod straight on the couch, her mile-long legs crossed and slanted to the left. I planted myself opposite her, my feet unable to touch the floor, on the lumpy couch that faces the office bathroom.

She gave me a disdainful look, as if I wore a fur and she was a PETA activist.

"I want to discuss your relationship with Nick," she said. Her tone cut stilted, frosty, and it said she perched high upon a snow-tipped mountain and deigned to notice little me, playing in the thick mud that lined the dirty valley below.

"Yes, let's do," I said with an easy smile. If pushed, I could be hoity and toity, too, although at that particular moment I'd rather have been trapped in an elevator with tambourine-playing Hare Krishnas who threaded wilted daisies in my hair.

"You love him." Nick chose that exact moment to reenter the main office area. He stopped short, silent, behind Anita as confusion knotted his brow. I didn't bat an eyelash.

"Do I love Nick? Absolutely."

"And he loves you." Both she and Nick stared at me; I acknowledged only her.

"Yes."

Her stiff shoulders loosened a fraction. On a less uptight person, I'd have said drooped. "Well," she murmured, cleared her throat. "Well, I wish you both happiness."

She uncrossed her legs, shifted on the sofa to get up, only to freeze when I said, "But we're not *in* love."

"What do you m—"

"May I be blunt?"

With the lithe crossing of her legs, her perfect brow raised. "You always are. Why stop now?"

I grinned. "You still wear your wedding ring. You drove here thinking Nick would be out of the office, to speak to the woman you not only believe stole him from you but who you'd rather spit on than talk to. Your eyes are a little puffy and you've actually chewed on your seventy-dollar manicure. You still care about your marriage, still hope to fix it, still are in love with him. Nick, on the other hand, tosses and turns each night on that couch—" I pointed to the one she perched on "— reading obituaries and—"

"Wait," she said. "Wait. He sleeps here? Not with—"

"Me? No—never has. Nick sleeps *alone* in this office and let's just say he's not been a happy camper. So frankly, if either of you sign divorce papers right now it would be utter lunacy. Have you seen a marriage counselor?"

Her stare continued, eyes of deep Smurf blue, and Nick's gaze shifted to her.

"He wanted to," she whispered. "I refused."

I blew a runaway curl from my face. "Because?"

Nick frowned when she gave a disparaging laugh. "Ego. I was an idiot."

"If he asked you to go right now, would you?"

"In a heartbeat."

I met Nick's intense gaze over her shoulder. "That's your cue, Cowboy. I'll take a rain check for that burrito."

He circled the couch, drew a stunned Anita to her feet, and I moseyed out the back door with a lightened heart into the harsh, gusting winds of a summer monsoon.

A sensible person would have brought an umbrella to work that day. After all, smiling weathermen on three competing television networks agreed that Thursday would see four or more inches of the wet stuff, and as a nifty preview of fall the temperature would plunge over fifteen degrees. A sensible person would have prepared. I guess I wouldn't know sensible even if it jutted out two fingers and poked me in the eyes.

Rain spit in a slanting sheet as I dashed to my Jeep. Four letter words poured from me to join fat raindrops as I fumbled with the wet door handle. I shook myself like a wet poodle in the Jeep's interior.

My nape prickled seconds before the sounds registered. A soft exhale. A slow slide of leg. A brush of fingers along my wet hair. My head jerked around. Warren.

"Good afternoon, Desy."

My heart soared to eagle altitude and a calm poker face slid into place, masking my fright. Warren Williams, reigning High Priest of my fair state, sanity-impaired thorn in my side, sat in my back seat. Smiling.

"Hello, Warren. Get lost on your way home?"

"I'm here to discuss important issues."

"Gosh, if I'd known I would have vacuumed back there." Through the rear window I saw a stretch limo pull in behind me, effectively blocking my Jeep. The words "royally screwed" surfaced on the empty stage of my mind and danced a jig.

"Firstly," he said, "I'm disappointed you lodged a complaint with the Council. They've scheduled a meeting for Tuesday to present me with formal charges. I must tell you it's quite an inconvenience. You'll rescind your complaint."

I made a vague sound in my tight throat, leaving him to his own interpretation while I concentrated on gnawing the inside of my mouth to a pulpy mess. Where were all the giant sinkholes when you really needed one?

"Secondly, Joseph has readied the suite that connects to mine. I think you'll find it most suitable. We chose blue."

"Okay, you lost me. And I'm getting a crick." I sat forward, met his eyes in the rearview mirror. "Joseph who? Suite where? Blue what?" My left hand edged along my waist, where my Taser sat clipped.

"Joseph, my interior designer. He's done wonders in so short a time. The perfect bedroom suite awaits you now in shades of blue." His wide hazel eyes sparkled.

"Oooh, did you use any toile?" I bubbled, unclipping the Taser, slowly sliding it from its holster. "I just love blue and white toile."

His voice climbed. "We've used it in the draperies."

"Wow, toile draperies. Anything else?"

"And on some pillows."

"I meant any other important issues?"

"Oh yes, where was I?"

"On thirdly." I clutched my Taser. There'd be no fourthly or fifthly.

"Thirdly, I've called together my coven leaders in this county for tomorrow evening. Midnight. I'll send a car for you. Any questions?"

"Questions? Oh, my yes. Lots. Like why do they put Braille dots on the keypad of the drive-up ATM? Why do we drive on parkways and park on driveways? Why don't you ever hear about *gruntled* employees? If one synchronized swimmer drowns, do the rest have to drown too? And oh yeah—what in the world makes you think I give a rat's ass about your blue bedroom suites, your Council inconveniences, or your midnight coven meetings?"

"Because I've made sure you will." He held out a slim rectangular package wrapped in red paper and tied with a neat white bow.

"No thanks. I was taught never to accept gifts from strange men."

"Oh, you'll want to see this. I'll just leave it here." Warren set it on the back seat. "Tomorrow at midnight, Desy. You'll come alone. Together we'll release fellow witches from centuries of hiding and persecution." He opened both the door and his umbrella (even a psychopath was more sensible than I), and wished me a pleasant day. The waiting limousine whisked him away.

Warren left behind a foreboding stink no spray could eliminate.

I wrinkled my nose, hit the all-lock button for my Jeep and melted into the seat with a hard sigh. My head fell back against the headrest, my eyes closed, and my mind slipped into the outstretched, welcoming arms of deep denial.

I could already taste the creaminess. In the worst way I craved a McFlurry, and not just the child size I allowed myself on occasion. Nothing would do but supersized — so big it can't fit in your cup holder. Little chunks of broken cookies swim in thick ice cream to treat your swooning taste buds to an incomparable contrast of smooth and crunchy. Each bite is better than the last until you can no longer feel your tongue or gums, and you scrape your spoon along the bottom of the cup to scoop the very last bite and sigh contentedly as it slides down your numb throat. Total bliss.

I was going to have to kill the bastard.

A cookie! That's what I really needed. Not the stale generic type you find wrapped in plastic trays on your grocer's shelves, no, it would have to be homemade, hot from the oven — so big you need two hands to hold it. And it would have chocolate in it, lots and lots of chocolate chunks that would melt in your mouth and on your fingers. You'd lick each hot buttery splotch, every crumb, and sigh contentedly. Life would be swell.

I'd have to kill him because it was obvious he just *wasn't* going to go away. And the Council with all their appointments and formal complaints and red tape couldn't be counted on, in my opinion, because look how long they'd allowed him to rule in the first place. No, there seemed no way around it. I'd have to open an entire can of whup ass on Warren. Probably on his posse, too. Hell.

Sticky buns. Humongous sticky buns, fresh from the oven, the kind my aunt makes on Christmas mornings. Whole pecans and cinnamon and yeasty dough rolled together and slathered with white icing that dribbles down the sides. You unwind the layers, break off long pieces, and coil them on your tongue where they melt in a sweet explosion. No napkin required. You'd lick each finger clean, every hot, sticky inch of skin, and never feel happier.

And after I killed him, witches statewide would be left with no ruler. Anarchy would ensue. Council eyes would turn to Armand and me with expectations that would slowly wind around my neck in a suffocating squeeze, like a hungry jungle python. Soon my free time would be spent settling petty disputes. Coven A would petition to purchase charms wholesale while coven B would dispute their suit, citing it would bring undue attention from non-Wiccans. To end their bickering I'd have to step in and propose a rousing game of rock-paper-scissors.

I would kill Warren just for placing me in that hellish position.

Maybe I really needed salt. Chips or nachos or pretzels. Aunt P always stashes something from the greasy salt family in the pantry. She often—

Aunt P…Aunt P–Aunt P–Aunt P! I dug out my cell and jabbed her number. No answer. She always answers! Well, nine out of every ten calls. Maybe that particular try she was out gardening…in the rain. Maybe she ignored the phone because a climatic scene was unfolding on her soap operas. Perhaps Marco just discovered Shane was the true father of his illegitimate son with his thrice-removed cousin, Tiffany, who'd given the baby away to her estranged long lost twin, Trinity, currently suffering from amnesia and a rare eye disease.

Or maybe Warren the weasely witch had paid my aunt a visit.

I raced home beneath a dark ominous sky with the windshield wipers dancing on high, a sick feeling churning deep in my gut, and no notion whatsoever of the shocking sight that would soon nearly turn me blind.

The first piece of clothing I encountered, a demure leopard print dress with a wide purple belt, lay in a sorry mound on the living room floor. The knot in my stomach tightened, my brow furrowed, and I pushed forward on shaky legs. Soon I found pink panties on a lampshade, a matching bra hanging from a chair, a man's plaid pants, the loops still threaded with a worn brown belt.

Sick with worry, my brain skipped past the logical, the obvious, and focused only on Warren. What had he done? I couldn't call out my aunt's name, couldn't even swallow.

I skirted around a stripped cotton shirt on the floor, a pair of white boxers dotted with yellow smiley faces, and entered the sunroom.

Aunt P lay on the couch...nude...moaning. Franklin Crenshaw also lay on the couch...also nude...also moaning. They were. He was. She. They.

My eyes bulged, my hand covered my mouth in a hard slap, and I began to back out of the room. I turned around and smacked face first into a wall. "Shit! Hell!"

"Desy?" Aunt P called. Frantic, nude senior citizen whispers followed.

"Um...uh, don't mind me," I chirped. "I'm just leaving." I rubbed my nose. "I didn't see a thing. Honest. Go back to...just keep..." Aw hell. "Bye."

I dashed back out into the rain, again sans a sensible umbrella, and found myself ten minutes later parked in front of Armand's house. I don't remember driving there. My Jeep sat beside an unfamiliar car, newer model, black and sleek.

Catalina let me in, jabbering away about taking better care of myself, and left me standing in my own widening puddle to get a towel.

Armand entered the foyer and just as a smile began to crook my wet lips, I saw at his side a stunning blonde dressed in a clinging apricot pantsuit. Beautifully styled, her hair lay in obvious obedience (unlike mine). When she shopped for pants, she never had to look for the words short or petite on the tag (unlike me). And her skin shone a milky white, possessing not one freckle (unlike mine). I hated her on sight.

She gave a husky laugh as they talked and touched his arm.

I stood there and dripped.

"And you have my number," she said in a silky voice, which I hated.

"*Oui.* I'll call you next week." A wide smile broke across his face when he noticed me. "Desy." He turned to the mystery woman, whom I hated. "Amanda Preston, I'd like you to meet Desdemona Phatt."

I had to hand it to her; she didn't bat an eyelash over my last name or at having to shake a cold, wet hand. She seemed cheerful, polite. I hated that.

"It's a pleasure," she said, pulling a collapsible umbrella from her purse (how very sensible) before strolling to her sleek car that I hated.

"*Mon chou*," Armand said with that soft, low, seductive purr. "You're very...wet."

"Wet's the word." I felt something dribble down my cheek, probably my waterproof mascara.

Catalina bustled back, still prattling about my health, and handed me a thick white towel. She strode off to make me tea. I hate tea.

He took the towel from my numb hand and began to gently dry my face. "You're a little pale, *amoureux*."

I blurted, "She's beautiful."

The towel softly stroked my nose. "She is."

"And she touched your arm."

He grinned. "Jealous?"

A puff of disparaging air, heavy with disdain, left my mouth. "Pfft. Of a tall, curvy blonde with long sultry hair and no freckles? Are you insane? What could possibly give you that idea?"

"Perhaps because your hands are clenched into two tiny fists?" He patted my hair with the towel.

"That's just rigor mortis. I've had one too many shocks today. I'm actually dead. You're patting my remains."

"And what lovely remains they are. Even dead, no other woman can match you. Not even tall, curvy blondes who are happily married with three children and facilitating my donation to the children's wing at Clemont Hospital."

My numb lips managed to curve in a small, rueful smile.

"Let's get you into some dry clothes and then you can tell me about today's shocks."

I sighed, thinking he shouldn't be subjected to my pisser of a mood. "No, I've got to go. I promised Nick I'd babysit the real estate agent this afternoon."

"You spoke to Nick? Everything's straightened out?"

"Well, not exactly." Armand's lips tightened and I hastened, "Now don't go getting your designer shorts in a knot. There hasn't been time yet."

He cupped my face, searched my eyes. "Desy, why are you here?"

"For some tea?"

"You hate tea." He kissed me softly on the lips, making me ache for more. "You came here needing to talk, so treat me to a few minutes of your time and tell me about your morning." He led me toward the stairs. "We'll get you into dry clothes, you'll drink some tea to spare Catalina's feelings, and if you're really good I'll loan you my umbrella before you return to work." Warm lips pressed against my cold knuckles. "*Oui?*"

"*Oui,*" I said. "But prepare yourself. One shock involves Warren and the other, the real doozie, entails senior citizen couch nookie. *Naked nookie*, Armand."

"That is how one generally has nookie."

Chapter Seventeen

Despite the blonde wig, despite the schoolgirl outfit complete with white knee-highs, it was definitely Denise Campbell, real estate professional, loving wife of our client Todd Campbell, mother to Brittany, Lauren, and toddler Christopher.

And our hidden cameras captured her every naughty deed in living techno color.

The man she "entertained" in the home's concealed basement room stood of average height and build. A unibrow the thickness of a raccoon's tail stretched above his eyes but the rest of his body hair was sparse—a thin sprinkle on his chest, a short ring around his balding head, and way down below, near his plumbing (which, too, was quite average by the way) sprang a meager patch of light brown.

The two had been going at it for hours.

Not in the traditional sense, more in the role-playing-tie-me-up-leather-whip-spanking kind of sense (which made no sense, if you asked me). BDSM does absolutely *nothing* for me. Parked down the street, I watched them on our remote monitor for three hours that evening before I had to rush inside (I'll get to that part soon) and it was less titillating than Gilligan's Island reruns. Yawn.

They enjoyed plentiful use of wrist and ankle cuffs and blindfolds and leather belts and fantasy outfits and some kind of upright restraint frame thingy. To each his own, right?

As the man bent Denise over his lap (for the umpteenth time), pulled down her schoolgirl white cotton panties and slapped her reddened ass, my mind wandered (also for the umpteenth time) to Armand.

During my short afternoon visit he used his considerable charm and calmed me, made me laugh, forced tea on me, and listened as I spilled my guts, starting with Nick and his possible reconciliation with Anita. His eyes hardened then to a flinty brown when I described Warren's visit, making me feel almost sorry for the unbalanced High Priest. Retribution shone clearly in Armand's hard gaze. I suspected his vengeance might involve one or more bodies composting in a distant landfill.

But as I described Aunt P and Franklin, pink panties on lampshades and walking into walls, his eyes softened, lit with humor, and I laughed so hard with him tears ran down my face. Seeing it through his eyes helped me focus on the comical absurdity of the scene rather than my horrified chagrin.

Most likely she would be wearing clothes when I returned home, but even so I felt unready to see my aunt. I asked Armand if I could spend the night. He pulled me close and said, "Never ask, love, my home is yours. And why you insist on knocking at the front door instead of just coming inside is beyond stubborn."

I hugged him and thought I could forever listen to the dip and sway of his accent, the sexy drag of vowels, the way every "s" slid into a "z" and the unbelievable timbre of his voice and how he tilts his head just so and the way he touches me and his scent and the…(insert soft, long sigh here).

I know. I've got it bad.

Back to the basement couple. Up the street from me Average Joe's Saab sat parked at the curb with a vanity license that said "Tiger". Kid you not. I added it to our long list of plate numbers Nick slogged through daily, compiling quite an impressive background on each male customer.

Most of the men were married. I was shocked. Not.

Tomorrow, nine a.m. sharp, we'd present Todd Campbell with evidence to pursue a divorce. The case file listed a precise chronology of his wife's covert pastime, clear stills and video of Denise's face and form in compromising positions, and for his promised five thousand dollar bonus, detailed backgrounds on a week's worth of Johns.

On the monitor I watched as Denise allowed herself to be strapped to the upright frame again. Flexible cuffs encircled her widely spread wrists and ankles. Erotic? No. Uncomfortable? You betcha. I began a slow slide into a semi-brain-dead state (the kind you fall into whenever acquaintances insist on showing you their vacation pictures) when Average Joe stuffed Denise's mouth with what looked like wadded red silk. He hadn't done that the last time, and she didn't look happy about it.

I sat up, leaned closer to the monitor.

He began to rip her clothes, handle her roughly. Was this role-playing? I wondered, if-you-take-a-little-pain-and-fight-me-there'll-be-an-extra-Ben-Franklin-for-you role-playing?

Denise pulled at the restraints in frantic tugs, shook her head wildly, and suddenly I felt convinced the terror on her face was not acting.

"Shit!" I sprinted through torrential rain (my third time that day) to the house.

The women thought they played it smart. Two or three of them always manned the house to prevent just this type of thing from occurring and to monitor the front door for actual prospective homebuyers. That night Denise's coworker, Heidi, thumbed through a thick magazine at a small desk, the only piece of furniture on the main floor. Her head jerked up when I burst inside.

"Where's the door to the basement?!" I bellowed, striding toward her.

She shot up. "Hey, you can't come in here."

"Denise is in trouble," I said, pushing past her. I tried the door on the left, a green-tiled bathroom. I spun and Heidi rushed in front of a second door.

"You can't go down there. Who are you? How do you know Denise?" Fright clouded her green eyes.

"Listen, the man down there is hurting her. Move aside."

She shook her head. "I'm not supposed to let anyone in. How—"

"Tough titties!" I got in her face. "Move aside *now*."

"I'm...I'm going to call the police."

"That would be dandy." I pushed her out of the way. The door opened with ease, banged against the wall, and I rushed below. The only closed door in the basement was locked; the handle jiggled uselessly in my hand. Muffled sounds emerged from within. An angry masculine voice. A garbled cry.

I took a deep breath and called my magic. It wakened in an ebullient pulse, flushing me with power. The knob turned.

The scene that greeted me was unpleasant to say the least. I rushed into full-blown, royally-pissed-off mode.

Average Joe turned to me as I strode toward him. "Who the hell are you?"

"I'm the woman who's going to rip off your stripes, Tiger."

He snorted, then smiled—two things he really ought not have done. If I had been less angry, I could have used magic, frozen everyone, and trussed him up like a pork loin. Problem solved. But I felt so furious, so blistering enraged nothing would satisfy me but the feel of his bruised skin beneath my fists.

I went at him and he swung the long leather belt as a whip. The tail lashed around my wrist and forearm in a hard sting—I wouldn't feel the burn until much later—but I caught a piece of it and his smile slipped when I yanked, rushed forward at the same instant, and plowed my fist into his face. His head snapped back with an audible crack. It was a nice sound.

I jabbed my thumb in the spot where his collarbone met his shoulder, a really nifty pressure point that sends a brilliant sting down the arm, and the belt dropped from his numb hand.

Behind me, through the silk that filled her mouth, Denise mewled, "Hit him hard," or perhaps, "I can't breathe." It was hard to tell.

Tiger's left fist swung. I ducked and swung my own fist right into his balls.

He made a girly sound and promptly dropped to his knees, a perfect height to grab his Dumbo ears and smash my raised knee into his unibrow. I sidestepped as he fell forward. The hollow sound his head made as it hit the floor was not unlike that of a pumpkin being thrown against leaf-strewn cement.

I checked his pulse and felt a strong beat. How unfortunate.

It was hard to resist kicking him; the urge raged so strong, but that would have been ill done of me. Childish even. Instead, with my body blocking Denise's view, I waved a hand over his flaccid penis and thought one word—"*minuscule*". You can imagine the results.

Denise coughed after I tugged the wet silk from her mouth.

"Are you okay?" I asked. She hacked some more. "Of course you're not, that was a stupid question. Here." I began to work on the restraints.

"Denise hon? I'm so sorry. I didn't know." Heidi came up beside me with her hand splayed over her heart and worry pulling her round face into a tight pinch.

We helped a wobbly Denise to a chair. Heidi pulled a blanket from a closet behind the upright frame and draped it over Denise, whose body had begun to shake with delayed shock.

"Who?" she breathed in a scratchy voice, as if she'd swallowed 350 grit sandpaper. Denise swallowed, stared at me, and tried again. "Who are you?"

"My name's Desy." I chose not to elaborate. She didn't need bad news at that precise moment. I asked of Heidi, "Did you call 911?"

A blush stole over her white skin. "No, I was too scared."

"That's when you're supposed to call."

"I know. I was too scared."

She stood beside me weaving like a bobblehead. "Here," I said, directing her to a bench. Three sets of hooks attached to its sides (I didn't want to know why). "Sit. Everything's okay now." I eyed the nude, unconscious, diminutively endowed man, and smiled, feeling warm fuzzies for a job well done—a true Kodak moment. "Got any rope?"

* * * * *

I made four calls, the first to Armand to tell him I'd probably be very late and not to wait up; then one to Nick to get his butt over to Hazel Park and help; next Aunt P, who I told not to expect me that night; and my last to 911, requesting EMS and police.

It was a long night.

"Well, Des," Nick said as he walked me to my Jeep. "You did a number on that guy."

"Not really. He's still able to walk."

Paramedics treated Denise at the house. Heidi drove her home. But EMS took Tiger, a.k.a. Mr. Jason Parks, to the hospital for observation. Blurred vision made them suspect a closed head injury.

By two a.m. the police were satisfied with our various statements, the rain had stopped, and as Nick and I cut across a lawn the grass protested with loud squishes. I still felt wired and turned to Nick at my Jeep. "Want to get a piece of apple pie at the diner?" Apple pie's his favorite. Besides, it would give me a chance to discuss (and hopefully put to rest) his proclaimed mushy feelings. It would make me feel better, not to mention a certain Frenchman.

He looked sheepish. "Anita's waiting up for me."

"That's nice, Nick, no problem. Nine sharp, Todd Campbell. See you around say eight-ish?"

"Eight-ish it is." He tugged lightly on my hair and we said our goodnights.

I drove to Armand's mulling about the crazy moments that composed my day, all the while completely forgetting about the small package on my backseat. I'd even forgotten to mention it to Armand. Dumb. But then again I suppose I should be forgiven. It's not every day one is an unwilling eyewitness to senior sex.

I wouldn't remember the gift until the following evening, prompting me to always look back and wonder if recalling it earlier would have helped. All I can say is I really don't know. And sometimes, that's just not good enough.

By the time Armand's front gates swung open, my adrenaline high had waned. His bed came to mind, the absolute decadence of it. Sheets from Egypt, an acre of hand-tufted mattress, a down pad custom-made by nine Tibetan monks (okay, I might be exaggerating a smidgen, it was probably only six monks), but the point is his bed's an unparalleled out-of-body experience.

I pictured myself on it, melting into its softness, as I quietly let myself into his home. Low lighting illuminated the foyer, gleamed off marble, winding staircases, rich woods and Armand's face.

"Oh! You scared me."

"I've been right here." He cupped my cheeks. "You're dead on your feet. How did it go?"

I gave him the highlights and he stroked my hair as I talked. With all the drenchings my curls underwent that day I'm sure they were a frightening sight, as if I'd French kissed an electrical socket.

"Hungry?" he asked when I'd finished.

"Yeah, but I'm too tired to chew."

"Bed then, *mon chou*." He kissed my forehead and as his hand slid down my arm in a warm caress to clasp my hand, a slight gasp escaped me. "What is it?" He lifted my hand and turned it over. His face tightened and when he looked up, his eyes met mine with an exacting stare. "He did this to you?"

"It looks worse than it really is." If I told him the truth, that my wrist and forearm stung worse than a third degree sunburn, he'd probably call Sam and then the highly anticipated pairing of my tired body and his bed would be delayed that much longer.

"How?" he asked.

"How can it look worse than—"

"How did he do this? It looks like a welt. A burn."

"Leather belt thingy. He used it like a whip."

"And somehow you neglected to mention this when you called." His lips firmed when I shrugged. "I'll call Sam," he said. (See?)

I began to tug him upstairs. "It's almost three in the morning. You're not calling Sam. Bed," I sighed. "A naked Frenchman. Those are the only two things I need."

Had there always been this many stairs to his bedroom? I wondered. It seemed to take forever to get there. I felt as if I plodded through dense mud, the heavy muck of it weighting my every step.

"Here." He carried me the remaining way. Setting me on the bed as if he handled something priceless and fragile, Armand began to gently undress me, shooing away my hands each time I tried to help.

Too tired to object, I let myself enjoy it and just purred when he tucked me in. Seconds later, with only a slash of moonlight illuminating the room, Armand joined me in bed. I rolled to him, draped half my body over his, resting my head on his firm chest, and his arms curled around me.

I sighed. "God, you feel good." My speech dragged slow, drowsy. "You should charge for this."

"Come closer, *mon chou.*" He shifted me until I sprawled on him like a lumpy blanket.

I sighed again, wallowing in complete bliss. "What does that mean, anyway? *Mon chou.* I've never known."

His palm slid down my back and fondled one cheek of my butt. "It means *my little cabbage,*" he murmured, squeezing the plump mound.

It took several seconds for my brain to grapple with what he said, but when it finished my brow furrowed and I pushed from his chest. "What!" I stared down into the shadow of his face. "All this time you've been calling me a damn *cabbage*?!"

He gave a soft chuckle. "It's a common term of endearment in—"

Armand grunted when I pinched his nipple. "You Chowder Head! I can't believe this! What's next? Come here, *my tiny green onion*? Take off your panties, *my sweet rutabaga*? Pass the salt, *my divine potato peel*?"

He chuckled again, caught my hand before I pinched a second time. "Desy, I adore you. Go to sleep, *amoureux*."

I settled back, burrowed my face into his chest. A few moments of silence passed, then I grumbled, "I suppose *amoureux* doesn't really mean sweetheart, does it?"

"No. It means turnip."

"Tell me you're kidding."

He kissed my head. "I'm kidding."

Chapter Eighteen

A kiss from Armand never fails to give me elevator stomach.

With a coiled stride and blistering stare so intense it held me immobile, he crossed the large room and I knew the very second he reached me, we'd kiss and it would be magnificent, marvelous, memorable, and a bunch of other M adjectives.

That look was on his face, fierce hunger, unwavering need; it was in the way he walked and moved with leashed heat struggling for release, and in those eyes of his, those stunning eyes, where it glittered and burned, darkening them a deep black.

I quivered as he neared, feeding off his beauty and passion, his urgency.

His large hands framed my face, slid in my curls as he leaned down and took my lips in a stunning kiss. His mouth wasn't tentative; it plundered. His tongue didn't flirt; it conquered. His movements weren't soft or coaxing or sweet; they raged raw.

I felt that familiar, thrilling oomph in my gut and moaned.

His rich voice, usually so suave, so smooth, rasped in my mind with a grating bite. *I have to have you – this very instant.*

God, yes, I answered.

In a rough motion he turned me, bent me face-down over one of the long tables, and flipped up my skirt. I smiled against fake wood grain, hearing his harsh inhale pierce the silence.

Jesus Christ, he groaned.

Thigh-high stockings hugged my legs in jet black, topped with spandex lace and matching garter belt. I wore three-inch heels…and no panties.

Oh Christ, he breathed, running his hands over the white, rounded globes of my ass. His breathing quickened, turned thick and hoarse, as he slid his hand between my spread thighs, pressing his fingers, palm, then the wide heel of his hand against drenched skin.

Flushed, my cheek lay against the table and my eyes fluttered closed as he rubbed. A heavy, sweet ache throbbed.

I heard rustling after his hand left me. My excitement climbed higher, awaiting his next touch. Would he use his hands? His mouth? His cock?

In a circling squeeze he kneaded my ass, pulling my cheeks up and apart before spearing his tongue inside my creamy center. I jerked. *Oh god.* He shoved higher, wiggling his tongue madly, giving me what I needed, but more, exactly what I wanted.

There was a sensation of floating, of time holding still—just for a moment—before I fell back into my body and came.

Armand began to eat me as though taking savory bites from a juicy summer peach. He grunted between my thighs as his lips opened and closed over my spasming center.

With his hands plumping my ass cheeks round and round, his thrusting tongue, scraping teeth and hot mouth plundering my drenched core, the orgasm splintering through me spiraled higher, somehow dug deeper, forcing a spate of low guttural moans from my throat.

His tongue began to lave in scalding swaths from my drenched lips to my anus, up and down and back again. My stomach seemed to jump with every caress.

Again, he ordered. *Come for me again.*

I could only pant and clench in tight fists the far edge of the table. My fingers bit into wood.

A drop of juice rolled down my inner thigh. I felt its hot trickle seconds before Armand lapped it up. Air shuddered from my lungs as my ass was slowly filled with the tapered width of one long finger.

He timed his thrusts carefully so the slow plunge of his finger coincided with the flick of his tongue's withdrawal and then the reverse, his finger's hooking retreat happened in concert with the wet thrust of his tongue. Slurping noises and wet suctioning, a double rhythm, and masculine hums of pleasure consumed me.

Now, he grated, pressing a finger on my clit, rubbing its slippery hood with fast, hard strokes.

I bucked, stiffened, then soared.

Amid a hot flush searing my skin, a stark cry that broke from my lips, he breathed a hoarse *Yes bebe*, as I once again climaxed.

His teeth scraped along my ass, bearing down for a hard nip, not enough to break skin but with enough pressure to thrust me toward a pleasurable pain. I shook, sucked in greedy gulps of air, and grasped the table harder when first his teeth left me, then his finger slid from my ass.

I heard him shift, felt the heat of his hands as they ran over my back, skimmed along the dip of my waist and the curve of my hips. One hand left me and I felt a stiff nudge against my entrance, the smooth head of his cock prodding there.

Even with my eyes closed I knew what Armand looked like behind me, the fascinating picture he made. His sensual features would pull tight in concentration as he fought to temper his rocketing need and his dark eyes would blaze with heat, shadowed beneath lashes laying at half-mast.

His hand would wrap around the thick column of his cock that stood tall and rigid, heavy, as he guided the long length inside me.

And because he likes the sight so much his gaze would be fixed below, watching as he took me, made me his, joining our flesh as one.

My need for him held a desperate edge. I vibrated with straining desire as Armand began to enter an empty ache we both wanted filled. *Tight*, he hissed, and the muscles in my belly drew up. His voice sounded so dark.

Sawing back and forth in ever-lengthening thrusts, his cock drove home. We shared a moan, then two when he ground his erection deeper. His hands held my hips in a firm clasp and Armand began to rock back and forth behind me, slipping in, pulling out until my lower lips clung to just his wet tip, then sliding back in again.

Careful thrusts soon turned fierce, possessive, and his pelvis rapped against my ass with each pass. Bruising urgency spurred every thrust, his powerful rhythm—

torrid and swift—hammered into me from behind, and then he groaned with his release, pumping me full of bucking cock and thick, spurting cream.

His pelvis slowed from hard slaps against my ass to mild taps that soon yielded to lazy, gentle grinds.

You are amazing, was his soft whisper and I tried to say "Ditto" but my larynx wouldn't cooperate, so I gave a shaky little hum instead. I knew he understood. He'd heard it many times before.

His large hands palmed my tush and there was a squishy sound as he pulled his cock from me.

"Getting up, *mon chou*?" he asked, giving a squeeze to my buttock and lowering my skirt.

I heard the rasp of his zipper and cleared my throat. "When the blood rushes back into my brain."

"Let me help you."

His hands eased under me and lifted my upper body, boneless dead weight, and he pressed my back against his chest, swooped down to nuzzle my throat from behind.

In a soft purr against my flesh he whispered, "A library?"

"Yeah." I leaned into his talented mouth. "A library."

I dreamed of the large library I visited as a child. The central room holds rows of long wooden tables and colorful plastic chairs. Multi-paned windows reach toward the arched ceiling and case after case of books hug the walls.

Aunt P used to take me every Sunday afternoon and when I grew older, middle school age, girlfriends and I would peek at anatomy books in the back row and giggle ourselves silly.

Of a simpler time, my memories sparkled like sun on snow.

"Promise you won't laugh?" I asked and he said, "Promise." I felt his lips curve against my throat. "When things get too crazy in my life," I confessed, "I have this weird fantasy of becoming a librarian."

Armand muffled a snort.

"You promised," I admonished, reaching behind and attempting to pinch his rock-hard butt. My thumb and index finger just slid off his pants and I huffed.

"Sorry," he said. "Continue."

"Well, just think about it. It's quiet here, peaceful, and the only stress you'd experience is finding a John Steinbeck novel mistakenly shelved in the romance section."

He turned me around, met my gaze. "You'd be bored to death after one day."

"Not if my coffee breaks were spent bent over a table."

Armand stiffened and shot his gaze over my shoulder, to the left. I whipped around. The shadow—Nick—stood several feet away and although still a blurred form, I could see him clearer in that dream. He seemed to gain substance with each subsequent appearance.

I breathed, "Oh hell." Armand's hand tightened painfully where it rested on my waist. I winced and looked back over my shoulder at his furious face. "You're hurting me," I said, and looking down at me—fire raging with naked pain in his eyes—he said, "And you're killing me."

Poof. He disappeared. Gone.

With his name on my lips I woke in his bed. Early morning sun smiled into the room, uncaring of the current turmoil within. Armand sat on his side of the bed, his back to me, and I crawled over the mattress (my injured wrist gave just the barest twinge), slid my arms around his waist and pressed my breasts to his wide back.

Resting my head near his left shoulder, I chose my words with care. "It's amazing to me what I feel for you, scary — it's, it's so big, and feeling the way I do I don't understand why Nick is in our dreams. I really don't. But I tried to talk to him yesterday, more than once, and — " I sighed. "This morning, at eight, I'll talk to him."

"And this morning," Armand said, "at eight, what will you say?"

"I'll tell him there's a certain Frenchman in my life I'm absolutely nuts about and of all the men in the world who are wildly attracted to me — let's face it, we could be talking in the thousands here — he's the only one I want."

I breathed a sigh of relief when his hands moved over mine in a soft caress.

* * * * *

Nick sat on the office couch — no drool-dotted pillow evident — with the contents of the Campbell case file spread out on the coffee table. He'd rolled out our small television from the closet to review the latest discs of Mrs. Anita Campbell in full color tie-me-up-tiger action.

"Morning, handsome," I said, plopping on the couch opposite him. "We've got to talk."

"Morning and yes, we certainly do."

My eyebrow arched over his tone and the quizzical look settling on his face. "Ladies first."

He leaned back. "Fine, shoot."

"You're a wonderful, gorgeous man and I love you." He smiled. "But it's a good-pal-known-you-forever-sister type of love, Nick, and it can't evolve into something more." There, I said it. Finally. His smile fled.

"Des," he objected, obviously upset. "You can't know that for sure. You haven't given us a true chance."

"There were true chances, lots of opportunities in our past," I countered, searching for the right words, "when we were neck-deep in the dating scene. We could have pursued a different kind of relationship with each other then. And we didn't. I think you knew then what you've lost sight of now, our friendship is too special to mess with."

"It's Armand, isn't it?"

I blinked. "Do you have waxy buildup? This isn't about Armand, although yes, I'm very serious about him. But I could be dating Jack the Ripper, my feelings for you would be the same." I sucked in some air and continued with the patient kindness of a nun, which was trying for me because I'm not Catholic. "You're confused right now and I want to help in any way you'll let me, but what happened yesterday should have shed some light."

He rubbed the back of his neck. "Yesterday. Light." He looked bewildered.

"Yesterday in this very office you had a wife and you had a lunch date with a friend and a big beef burrito. Whom did you leave with?"

"But—"

"And last night, you had a wife waiting for you and a friend who desperately needed a piece of pie. And you chose?"

"My wife."

"There's something there, Nick, something between you and Anita that's obviously worth fighting for." I leaned toward him. "I want you to be happy. I've always wanted that. Concentrate on your marriage because I have nothing more than friendship to offer."

He said nothing and it grew awkward. I shifted on the couch, cleared my throat, picked at imaginary lint, and thought of Buff the cabana boy. But this time Armand sat beside me on the beach, and he was naked.

"You're sure Des?" he said, and my head whipped up. Hurt hid behind amiability on his handsome face but not well enough. I saw its raw edge and within me a kindred pain stabbed. I hated to hurt him. I nodded yes. "If that's the way you want it, if that's the way it has to be," he said, "I'll concentrate on what's left of my marriage."

We shared a look and I cleared my tight throat. "What do you need to discuss with me? Something about the case?"

Nick spoke after a long moment. "Yeah." He picked up the television remote and turned on Thursday night's disc of Anita. "Mind explaining this?"

The film showed me whupping Mr. Jason Parks' (a.k.a. Tiger's) ass. I grinned. Unfortunately, it also showed in glowing pixels my hand waving over his nude privates and his then rapidly diminishing penis. My grin rapidly diminished as well.

"What exactly am I seeing?" Nick paused the tape.

"Obviously a faulty tape. We need to splice that part."

"I thought so too, at first, but I've examined the tape thoroughly. It's accurate." He studied me with the kind of fascinated curiosity one might grant a rare exotic slug. He looked again to the tape. "Explain to me what you're doing."

"Let's discuss something more interesting," I suggested gamely, "like head lice."

"The tape, Des."

I've always known someday I would tell Nick about witchcraft, but on that Friday morning it felt too soon. I still wallowed in comfy denial, where I never fail to find warmth and safety in the complete illusion everything's perfect. I didn't want to leave its embrace, certainly not after just stomping on Nick's heart. Now I would smash his conceptions of reality to smithereens. Two scoops of fun.

I filled my lungs with a fortifying breath and let it out slowly. "Okay, there are a few things you don't know about my life. I'm a witch. Armand's one, too. But here's something much more shocking." I leaned toward him. "Aunt P…has…sex."

If I'd flashed him, he couldn't have looked more shocked.

"It's true. She's doing the dirty with a widower. He lives right d—"

Nick held up his hand. "Go back to what you said just before that. You, uh, you think you're a witch?"

"I know I'm one." I pointed to the television. "And Tiger there really pissed me off. I shrunk his, his thingymajobber."

"Shrunk…his…thingymajobber," he repeated slowly, testing the words, and I sighed.

"You think I'm a nutcase, don't you? A freak. A loon. A—"

"You're not any of those," he assured, "and with a little medication, perhaps some therapy, soon you'll be—"

"Nick, I don't know about vampires or werewolves or abominable snowmen, so I still have my doubts. But as for witchcraft? Magic? They're real. They exist. And you've got me on tape as proof."

Perplexed, I'd say, cautious, with climbing frustration swirling with healthy dollops of incredulity and skepticism. I felt a little sorry for Nick; his eyes shone with such varied emotions. In my opinion no one should have to discover magic is real while completely sober. I tried not to smile, it wouldn't be nice, but my facial muscles proved stronger than my conviction. My mouth curved high.

"C'mon, Des," he scoffed.

"Want a demonstration?"

A puff of cynical disbelief left his mouth. "What the hell—yeah."

Chapter Nineteen

I called my mojo and its reply was one of surging, eager energy.

Months ago I felt as if magic was an entirely separate entity trapped within me, always straining for release. I battled for control, supremacy, each time I allowed it free rein, but over time I've come to realize it's just another part of me, like a heart or lung, and the more I exercise it, accept it, the better it thrives.

Armand once counseled, "Don't fight it, be as one." At the time it seemed a ludicrous proposition. The power within me rages bold and aggressive, dominant, just downright pushy. Who wants to be one with that?

Those traits have always been a part of me, though; they've just been tamed by civilized manners (and the threat of Aunt P's boot in my backside). Magic is simply stripped-down force, unencumbered by societal rules. It's raw and powerful. With each use I continue to grow into a heady, reluctant acceptance, one that isn't quite so scary anymore, and it is simply this — I am a witch.

Nick stared at me, the skin around his eyes pulled tight as if he'd just received an injection of botox, and a tic began to jump in his clenched jaw. I knew the picture I made and what a virgin viewer found most frightening with a high witch in full power. The eyes. The whites give way to pitch black like two dull lumps of coal, and the sight is frightening, inhuman.

Would Nick find *me* frightening and inhuman now too? I knew him well enough, hoped I did, that after spending a short interval holding the cold hand of shock he'd accept the "new me", although my stomach held a flutter of unconvinced nerves.

With my power comes a warm breeze that lifts my hair in long, wild ropes of curls. I control the air better now (my first few attempts were like battling gale forces), but to give Nick the full effect that morning I allowed the current its will. The small leaves of our corner ficus began to rustle.

As his hands curled into fists I used one thought to close the window blinds. They snapped shut.

"Desy. What the hell's going on?"

"Magic, Nick."

"It's not real."

I gave him a sad smile because let's face it, a reality pill is sometimes hard to swallow. "It's real," I said, waving a hand over the case file strewn about the tabletop. Papers and 8 x 10 glossies soared in the air, shuffled into order, and slipped neatly into the waiting manila folder.

The paused film began to play, minus the proof of my magic, the cut seamless, and it flew from the disc player to settle gently in my palm.

Shock washed all color from Nick's face, turning his skin Casper white, while dazed astonishment twisted his handsome features.

Divergent emotions fought within me, remorse for burdening him with magic and relief he finally knew the truth. The latter displayed clear victory by curving my mouth in another small smile.

I closed my power, tamped it down, and with uncanny timing our nine o'clock appointment—arriving fifteen minutes early—pushed through the front door.

Nick's head turned with a slow mechanical swivel toward our guest.

I set down the disc and crossed to greet him. "Mr. Campbell, hi, I'm Desdemona Phatt. It's a pleasure to meet you." We shook hands. "Care for some coffee before we begin?"

* * * * *

The coming evening would prove to be quite a humdinger.

I remained unaware, of course. In hindsight, being completely oblivious probably worked in my favor; otherwise I'd have teetered through my day not unlike Chicken Little ranting about the falling sky, accomplishing nowhere near what I actually managed to that Friday.

At work, I happily toiled through two background checks, one for a couple from Birmingham on a prospective nanny, who checked out fine and dandy, and one for a securities firm, corner of Eight Mile and Woodward for a prospective employee, who checked out neither fine nor dandy. His application held more falsehoods than a presidential campaign.

Following our meeting with Todd Campbell, Nick skedaddled, citing pressing business elsewhere. Far, far elsewhere. I pretended to believe him, poor guy. He needed nothing more than time away from me to gather his scattered wits, and mull. Nick's a muller, and I had no doubt he would present me with numerous concise questions, all tidy from careful mulling, the following

Monday. (Unbeknownst to me, it would actually be that very evening, before spaghetti and meatballs.)

Afternoon paced along in a mundane manner and on my way home from work I picked up the collective dry cleaning for Aunt P and myself. I mention this little tidbit only because later that day it would play a large part in sucking every bit of calm from my evening.

An earlier phone call from my aunt resulted in a dinner invitation for Armand and me with of course, the ubiquitous Franklin. We four assembled in the living room prior to the meal for some drinks and conversation (stilted on my part). I pretended I didn't know a tiny brown mole sprouted square in the middle of Frank's left buttock, but to be honest it was a challenge. Even after three glasses of wine, every time I looked at him the sex scene from the couch flashed brightly in my mind.

It proved highly distracting.

Before midnight I expected one or more of Warren's minions to arrive in a limo to whisk me away for that night's mandatory coven meeting. I also expected to impart some hard truths to said minions before I sent them home alone.

Was I a tad nervous about their arrival? Yep. Truthfully, though, I anticipated nothing more than a small verbal skirmish and if perchance it evolved into more, on my side I had guns, witchcraft, and Armand.

My Frenchman sat close beside me on the loveseat, resting his hand on my thigh, sometimes stroking his fingers along the thin cotton of my pants, and I found myself looking at the strength of his large hand, the veins just beneath the skin, the dark hair sprinkling his forearm.

"Don't you agree, sweetie pie?"

My head jerked up. "I'm sorry, what?"

"I said, don't you agree a barbeque at Frankie's next Saturday sounds delightful?"

Armand pinched my thigh. "Delightful! Absolutely."

A knock sounded at the door and Aunt P beamed. "Oh, there he is!"

As she stood I asked, "Who? Who's here?"

"Why, Nicky. I invited him to join us. Anita sent her regrets." Aunt P always graciously invites Nick's wife and Nick's wife always graciously declines with an equally gracious excuse. It seemed an all-around gracious arrangement.

My heart dropped somewhere in the vicinity of middle earth. "Nick's here?"

Armand stiffened beside me.

"Yes," she said, already moving to get the door. "I'm so glad he could make it."

Seconds later Aunt P ushered him in. Armand stood. Franklin and I followed suit. Introductions were boisterous between Nick and Aunt P's beau, lots of hearty, "Heard a lot about you's," and backslapping.

Nick turned to Armand and the levity fell as flat as my chest in fourth grade. The two men spoke each other's name in a brisk manner. They'd crossed cautious paths only twice in the three months I'd known Armand. Nick turned to me and tweaked my nose by way of greeting.

Aunt P began to shoo us into the kitchen, gaily reciting the menu.

Nick said, "If you don't mind, Aunt P, I'd like to borrow Des before we eat. Something important just cropped up at work. I need to discuss it with her. Only take a minute." He flashed his charming smile, the one that melts anyone with breasts in a ten-mile radius.

She tittered, "Of course, dear," and looped her arm with a smiling Franklin. The happy couple left the room.

Armand stood beside me as unobtrusive as a lion amidst gazelles and silently crossed his arms against his chest. The two men's stares clashed. Visually they were nearly polar opposites. Nick towered with his cropped blond hair, jock's build, and his features screaming good looks. Armand's hair fell dark and long, his build was strong but natural, and his handsomeness whispered with deep sensuality.

The room filled with silent tension, thick enough to cut with a spork.

I blurted, "Okay—everyone—group hug!" The men didn't appreciate my jocularity.

Nick told Armand, "Excuse us, please," to which Armand replied one simple word, "*Non.*"

By that point excessive amounts of testosterone wafted through the air and I'd inhaled enough to grow chest hair. Enough was enough. I asked of Nick, "Is this really about work?" and when he paused overlong I said, "I thought not. Anything you have to say can be said in front of Armand."

Nick raked a hand through his hair and gusted a sigh. "Fine." He stared into my eyes. "You haven't been a witch all your life or I would have known. Did *he* turn you into one?"

Armand stiffened further. "*Non,*" he answered before I could. His voice was cold steel, the kind that's thin and pointy and shoved into enemies. "One is born a witch, we are not turned or made."

Nick continued to stare at me. "But you weren't like this all your life."

"Armand revealed my powers to me," I said. "But they've always been there. They're part of who I am, Nick."

Armand's stance loosened with that declaration and he pressed his lips to my temple. I grabbed his hand not only because I love the feel of it against my palm but also to hold him back should he decide to lunge for Nick's jugular.

A line of concentration creased Nick's brow. "What can you do, what powers do you have?"

"Oh, well," I said, "I have a nifty cosmic freeze ability and a blue gamma ray thingy for fighting and —"

"Desy's power is limitless," Armand said. "The more she practices her craft, the stronger she'll grow. She will know no boundaries."

Although not the first time I'd heard those words from Armand, they sank home in that moment with equal parts excitement and trepidation. Boundless power. Yikes. Sort of like Superman without the troubling kryptonite.

Nick continued, "But how c —"

"Dinner!" Aunt P called.

"We're being rude," Armand said. "We'll continue this discussion another time." And with that proclamation he led me from the room. A silent Nick followed.

From the many gushing compliments, I gathered my aunt's spaghetti and meatballs tasted scrumptious. Being the sole recipient of frequent manly stares from Nick and Armand, feeling their underlying tension, the rumbling of it so palpable it felt as if the house sat on train tracks, I tasted only sawdust.

After dinner our party of five moseyed back to the living room where the discussion meandered from the latest hit movie (great special effects) to the fast-approaching fall season (the first leaf raking is pleasurable; each subsequent one is a chore), and somehow touched on least-favorite errands (like dealing with dry cleaning).

"You did pick it up, didn't you, dear?" my aunt asked.

My mind sprinted around helplessly, then landed on the answer. "I left it out in the Jeep." I popped up. "I'll just run out and get it."

"Honey Bunny, tomorrow's soon enough."

"No. I insist." I dashed outside for some much-needed air.

Dusk greeted me, already a moon glowed overhead, and from somewhere down the street I heard the distant revelry of a late summer party. With the assistance of a long protracted sigh, tension eased and I opened my passenger door. The interior light blinked on with a soft yellowish glow. I leaned in to grab the mass of hangers, the plastic-covered clothes, and when my eyes caught on a splash of red in the backseat, they widened.

Warren's gift. Red paper. White bow. Forgotten.

"Need some help?"

I jumped, banged my head on the doorframe. "Shit! Ow! Damn!"

I stood and rubbed my head.

"Here," Armand said, removing my hand. "Let me see." He probed lightly. "Should I kiss it and make it better, *mon chou*?"

"Sure, but I see three of you," I grumbled. "You'll have to form a line." He smiled, leaned in and I felt his gentle lips. "Why didn't I hear you coming?"

"You were mumbling to yourself."

"Was I saying anything like 'Please God, take me now so I won't have to go back inside'?"

"That bad?" He brushed his knuckles over my cheek.

"Uh, *yeah*. I have no doubt somewhere over the rainbow you and Nick will be grand friends, but right now? It sucks lemons to have you both in the same room. I need an antacid."

He gathered me close, rested his chin on my head, and into the warm haven of his chest I mumbled, "About Warren? I forgot to tell you he gave me a present yesterday. It's on my backseat."

"What is it?"

"Don't know; it's wrapped."

"Well, let's find out."

Armand retrieved it and I ripped off the paper, speculating on the contents. A bracelet, I thought, because of the box's size, or perhaps a folded invitation to his grand Wiccan gathering.

I whipped off the box's top. Gasped. Recognition dawned swift and ugly, sinking my heart into my summer sandals. Armand swore. Atop a pristine bed of white tissue lay Sam Bearns' glasses, broken, splattered with blood.

The box's top fell from my hand unnoticed and in a sickened tone I breathed, "What have I done? My god. These have sat on my seat since…since…"

"Desy." Armand slapped the box onto my hood, drawing me into his embrace. "This is Warren's doing." He squeezed me tight, swept up his hand to cup the back of my head. "You've done nothing."

I'd done nothing, all right. What had that maniac done to poor Sam? Sam, who wouldn't hurt a tick sucking his last drop of blood. God. I pushed from Armand's chest, met his concerned, angered stare. "Let's go kick some serious High Priest butt."

Chapter Twenty

The Hulk drove me to the meeting.

He seemed grumpy and disinclined toward conversation. En route I attempted all the tried and true icebreakers—a banal discourse on the weather, a hearty show of hometown spirit for the winless Detroit Tigers, a thorough rundown of my favorite restaurants in order of cuisine and geography, and still not one grunt from him.

I chewed on the soft tissue of my mouth.

If I wasn't a witch, a High Priestess, the harshest thing I'd ever have to battle would be water retention, but battle that night I would, and there wasn't time beforehand for hand wringing or slinking into warm denial. I couldn't pretend I was really skipping through a patch of summer daises while singing Carpenters songs. Sam needed my help, Armand's help, because he wasn't strong enough to protect himself. That's what high witches are for, to lead and protect the Wiccan community below them.

Understanding that tenet had been a long time coming for me, but as I holstered my guns that night, felt cold hard anger knot in my stomach (and all right, a healthy dose of fear, too), it crystallized in that moment. I finally understood.

Earlier Armand used some fictional song and dance about my sudden, debilitating migraine to rid the house of guests. When Aunt P learned the truth from him that night, she clucked around the house like a nervous hen running from a hungry farmer, and turned her worry toward baking snickerdoodles.

Because we didn't know the meeting's location, Armand tailed the limo. I found it hard not to peak out the rear window and look for him so I chatted, shifted, scratched, coughed, and squirmed away the half-hour drive, all the while praying Sam was all right.

The Hulk pulled into Warren's drive and followed a gravel path, just wide enough for one car, beyond the side garage to the far recess of the property. An outbuilding dawned large against midnight stars. Dozens of cars sat parked in neat rows.

I'm sure Warren violated several city codes not only with the monstrosity of an outbuilding he built but also by holding such a huge public meeting. If I were still alive in the morning, I vowed, I'd make some phone calls and rat his ass out good.

The Hulk spoke his first words of that evening. "Stay here." He lumbered around the limo, opened my door, and when I slid out, blocked my path with his impressive girth. "Your guns," he said, reaching to pat me down.

I wondered if he realized he often spoke in two-word sentences and stiffened as his hands neared. I peered up into his shaded face. "Touch me and I'll chew you up and spit you out."

"One phone call and your friend will hurt some more."

Hurt *some more*. Oh Sam. I spread wide my arms and spouted the Nike mantra. "Just do it."

His hands searched everywhere, and unfortunately, found everything. He pocketed my guns. Royally ticked, following in his huge shadow, I cast furtive looks for

Armand. Nothing. The big guy and I went to the building's rear entrance. It was a long walk.

He ducked inside, turned left down a dim, narrow back hall. I followed, girding myself for battle, eating the carpet with my bold commanding stride. I was confidence personified, capable and fierce. I was a lioness in the jungle, a top CEO of a Fortune 500 company, a monster truck with a Hemi, a telemarketer at dinnertime. *I was unstoppable.*

He opened a door, motioned me in. "Wait here."

"But—"

The door closed.

I huffed and my shoulders sagged. I wasn't a lioness, a CEO, a truck or anything else. Unstoppable? Ha! I was unarmed, alone, and—I tried the doorknob—obviously locked in. The room held neither window nor furniture.

I could pull a MacGyver, attempt to use my belt buckle and some underwear elastic to jimmy the door lock. Nah. Magic immediately answered my call and bubbling with renewed confidence, I tried the locked door again. The knob wouldn't turn. I kicked the door, succeeded only in stubbing my big right toe, and as I hopped around swearing, Armand's smooth voice flowed into my mind.

Desy, tell me you're okay.

I'm fine, I huffed, rubbing my toe. *They've locked me in a room and for some damn reason my magic can't open the door.*

Must be ensorcelled, he said. *I'm at the building. Where are you?*

Forget about me, find Sam.

Desy. Frustration and worry tainted his voice.

I'm safe, Sam's not. Please, Armand.

I heard his uneven sigh. *First Sam. Stay safe.*

You too. I yanked on the doorknob.

This was *sooo* not what I had expected. Where was Warren? Where was the pre-battle, pithy exchange of words? The skirmish between good and evil? The ultimate victory, where my side wins and his loses in humiliating defeat?

My mind morphed into a Nascar track—my thoughts, speedy theories that raced vroom vroom vroom in endless circles. Warren had obviously expected Armand and planned to keep us apart. He'd be better able to deal with us separately. I never said he was stupid, just insane.

He was also dead meat because when I finally got my hands around his scrawny neck I'd squeeze until his skin turned a nice purple hue, reminiscent of eggplant.

You might think me bloodthirsty, and all right I admit sometimes I can be, but I'm also of the mindset violence should be used only as a last resort. The only problem that night? It *was* my last resort.

With Warren I'd tried reasoning, which proved as effective as worn tires on snow. I'd used the law—Wiccan law—and lodged a formal complaint with the Council, who wouldn't make time to see me until it was just too goddamn late. There are no spells (except for binding one's mind) that can be used against High Priests or Priestesses—we're just too strong for them. My freeze power? It works only against lesser witches and non-Wiccans.

Death seemed the only thing that would stop Warren.

I tried the door again, pounded on it. Like that would help.

Desy. Armand's voice sounded odd, sluggish.

My heart sprinted. *What's wrong?*

I found…Sam. He'sss under a binding ssspell.

What's wrong with you!? I croaked.

No response.

Armand! Something was wrong, terribly wrong, and just the thought of Armand hurt sent my body into a sick shudder.

His voice a bare whisper, it slurred through three distorted words. *Drugged. Neeeedle. Don't —*

I heard only his quiet sigh.

Oh god. Oh-god-oh-god-oh-god! Fright and desperation lurched within me, merged with my roiling power and on unsteady legs I stepped back from the door. Hot energy hurtled down my arms and flew from my fingertips in bright streams of blue. The door stood unaffected, mocking me in an untarnished walnut grain.

My chest rose and fell in fast spurts and I aimed my next attack at the wall alongside the door. It exploded on impact, sending chunks of drywall flying into the hall. I passed through chalky dust, wispy smoke, and out the large hole I'd made.

A sprint took me down the hallway. Heading right would take me back outside so I kept to the left, pounding through the winding maze before dashing up a short flight of stairs. Through low lighting I ran over carpet, then tile, down a twisting corridor edged with painted cinderblocks, praying I chose the right way. It had to be the right way.

A low murmur of voices snaked through the air with the smoky scent of burning incense and my lungs burned as I sprinted all the faster, rounding a corner to the left. My heart and legs skidded to an abrupt stop in a long narrow passageway.

The dance of candlelight swayed along a huge back wall, pitch black, and opposite it in front, drawn curtains in long bolts of soft black velvet. The opposing ends of the room gaped open. A stage, I thought—somehow fitting for the scene the High Priest set before me.

Warren held reign in an ornate throne that would do a gothic castle proud, backed by the Hulk, Ugly, and two other monstrous goons whose sheer size made nightclub bouncers look like underfed kindergartners. Beside an empty chair to Warren's left stood Sam. A binding spell hazed his eyes—bruises, small cuts, marred his face. Near Warren's shiny black shoes lay an unconscious Armand. In the shifting candlelight his skin gleamed pale, his chest rose and fell with a shallow rhythm.

A queasy sob broke from my mouth.

"Desy, welcome," Warren said, gesturing to the chair on his left. "Please, have a seat."

He expected me to walk, when my legs were thin jelly. He expected me to actually step over Armand, when all my strength expended just to stand upright. He expected me to sit beside him, when all I wanted was to see him good and dead.

Cold sweat erupted on my skin, seemed to seep into my bones, and as I grew lightheaded fine tremors began to rack my body. I bit down on the side of my mouth hard, tasted blood, and the familiar pain helped me focus. "Let Armand go free, and Sam. Then I'll sit next to you."

Warren laughed, looked over his shoulder. "Do you see why she's perfect? Even now, she tries to negotiate." His paid apes stood unsmiling. "Desy," Warren said, shaking his head, patting the chair. "Sit." His expression said "you poor delusional child—you've lost".

My eyes fell to him. Armand. Still, so still. Like a loose mooring, within me something large shifted, a rending from my tenuous hold on sane logic and the one small part of my brain still functioning whispered of Warren—he wanted only one thing—me. If I sat beside him in this macabre calculated scene, how would that help Armand or Sam?

"No," I whispered in a small girl's voice. Magic slithered inside me, restless.

"Then perhaps you need one more persuasion." At the quick snap of Warren's fingers, the two unknown goons behind him exited the stage.

Delight swirled in Warren's hazel eyes. Victory. It boiled my milk. Anger slowly filled some of the emptiness inside me and when he smiled I cocked my head, pointed at his teeth. "Porcelain veneers?" His smile slipped. "And the paisley tie, Circus Boy?" I crinkled my nose. "It turns your skin sallow."

No longer smiling, he looked down and fingered his tie. When he frowned, I felt only trivial pleasure. It seemed doubtful I could insult him to death.

The goons returned dragging a large man, and although trussed like a Thanksgiving Butterball, he still struggled against their hold. They drew near, through flickering light and shadow, and confirmed what I somehow already knew. Cold and hot tingles pricked my skin; the precursor to a dead faint, and my heart pounded a strange rhythm, bellowing an erratic roar in my ears.

Each heartbeat said No...no...no.

I managed his name. "Nick." Did that thin, hollow voice belong to me? It couldn't have.

His head whipped forward. "Des—god, you're all right." His eyes closed briefly in relief and he jerked against the goons' hold. "Sorry," he told me. "I followed you."

"Wh…why?"

"You were upset at the house—I saw your face—and you don't have migraines. I thought you might need my help." He spoke from only one side of his mouth. The other side swelled thick, trickling with blood.

"Oh, Nick."

A high giggle burst from Warren. "Your face is priceless, Desdemona. Come, sit." He patted the empty chair again. "Before you fall."

Nick watched me, how I began to weave slowly on trembling legs. I felt buoyant, as if I could fly, and he struggled harder with Warren's henchman. The bigger of the two men, the one who resembled a huge G.I. Joe doll with lifelike hair, frowned and punched Nick in the kidneys. I screamed as Nick dropped to his knees.

Pain lanced his face. Warren stared at Nick with hard concentration and the realization the High Priest was casting a binding spell stole my last drop of sanity.

Later I would deal with cause and effect, how I reacted that night and if I could have done anything differently. Time would help with future guilt, because no matter what I am—witch or P.I.—taking a life is an act that shifts forever restless on your soul.

Later too, Sam would describe how the solid black of my eyes gave way to an incandescent red. He would tell of how my feet left the ground and I levitated in midair. My hair, he would say—"Honest, Desy, you should have seen it!"—seemed to electrify and stand on end in wild, glowing curls.

In that quiet moment I knew only sick anger filled me and when it grew larger than my body could contain, my magic accommodated it, transformed it, so the quivering woman standing there just one blink ago was no more.

I burst with power and the wind answered with a gusting wail, ripping the velvet curtains from their rod behind me, extinguishing the candles. With one jerk of my hand the two henchmen holding Nick flew backward, striking high on the far wall. They slid down its dark surface to land on the stage floor.

Gasps sounded behind me but were as important as the buzz of a fly.

I saw everything with crisp clarity and with each breath my power grew, began to mix with an answering masculine energy. Armand. His magic—aggressive, powerful, commanding—flushed through me with bold force from our merging spell months ago.

Ugly tried to tug a resisting Warren from his chair to safety while the Hulk pulled my Springfield .45 from his pocket. He widened his stance, aimed up at me.

Energy shot from my fingers not in familiar blue but in blazing scarlet and with the precision of a laser it sliced the Hulk's chest open. His body pitched forward, smacked the floor, and the gun skittered several feet away.

More gasps of alarm buzzed behind me, chair legs squeaked against wood.

From his pocket Ugly drew a knife and with a flick of his fat wrist the wicked blade spun toward me. End after end it sliced through the air—the tip, the black handle, the tip again—glinting silver and sharp.

I spoke one word through unmoving lips. *Feather*. The air shimmered, seemed to flare with warmth, and the knife was no more. A tiny feather, downy and gray, floated to the stage floor.

As I lifted Ugly straight up in the air with just the barest motion of my hand, I felt Warren attempt to bind my mind. The first time we met, his spell had lashed powerful, full of agonizing pain, and if not for Armand he would have succeeded. Warren's magic burned so very strong. But on stage that Friday night his attempt felt no more than a child's effort, inept and awkward, coloring outside the lines.

I was not a lioness in the jungle, a top CEO, a monster truck. I was simply me—a High Priestess, a Wiccan Queen.

Ugly dropped from a height of thirty feet with a hearty thump to the floor. He didn't get up.

Frustration shone on Warren's face, slow realization his binding spell failed. He raised both hands and shot fierce blue streams of power. They arced toward me, rushing true, and bounced off my body in a wilted sputter of pale indigo, like defective Fourth of July sparklers.

I felt a warm tickle, nothing more.

The wind began to shriek as I stared down at Warren and the three men he'd hurt.

A bruised Sam stood impassive, barely blinking, aware of his surroundings but unable to move without Warren's guidance. Nick lay on the ground, trussed and perhaps unconscious, his eyes closed. And Armand. My Armand. He lay on the ground so still, so wan, with something foreign winding through his veins. The wind had blown his hair onto his face and I wanted to smooth it back, stroke his pale cheek.

I trembled with hurt, with anger, with rising boundless power.

As he watched, resignation crawled over Warren's face. He didn't run. I raised one hand and he soared in the air to float level with me.

The frantic talking behind me stilled.

I cupped Warren's face, met his wide frightened eyes, and felt searing heat travel beneath my skin, rolling waves of boiling energy that began to seep from me…to him.

Shudders racked his body. He began to shriek and buck, tug at my arms. Beneath my palms his skin heated and the air thickened with the stench of burning flesh. His screams hurt my ears, echoed there, and abruptly stopped.

His eyes bulged.

His body quaked.

And he burst.

Not with splattered gore and blood—but with magic.

Warren simply disappeared.

Chapter Twenty-One

Behind me a chorus of gasps sliced the air, soon followed by a swell of frantic whispering. I focused solely on the men below me as I glided to the stage's floor.

Warren's binding spell disappeared with him and Sam immediately darted toward Armand to kneel at his side. As I crossed to them he began to heal Armand and I waved a hand in Nick's direction. The ropes binding him disappeared. His eyes slowly opened.

I kneeled beside Sam. "Will Armand be all right?"

Concentration knotted Sam's brow. "Calm the wind please?"

I looked up with the slow realization the wind still gusted and moaned, beating against us with forceful slaps. One command stilled the air.

Sam mumbled a distracted, "Thanks." His eyes closed, his hands trembled.

"Well?"

"Wait," he whispered, engrossed.

Every second his answer delayed felt like drops from Chinese water torture and within me panic began to climb inch by inch, churning sour all the hope I held. It didn't help that Sam's upper lip beaded with sweat, that he swayed and shook.

When I first met Armand I couldn't wait for him to return to Paris. The grit of his arrogance rubbed me like a cheap emery board, his knowing smile flashed too cocky, his every mannerism set me on edge and now, now I couldn't imagine one day without him. Couldn't even begin to imagine the possibility.

How had this happened in so short a time? I wondered. This connection, this all-consuming emotion, palpable and immense, that bound me to this man so tightly, our lives forever altered and entwined. I'd lost part of myself to him, and he to me, and somehow in the giving we gained something larger than the two of us, something priceless and immeasurable.

I stroked his cheek, willed him to wake. He would wake dammit, *he would,* and he would fix those bewitching dark eyes on me, curve those beautiful lips, the same ones I've sipped from countless times but never enough, no never, and he would call me that ridiculous vegetable endearment and then and only then would I be able to breathe again.

I smoothed Armand's hair, held his limp hand, and with Sam's whispered, "He's okay," a small sound eased from my throat—relief soared with a hard shudder to a fathomless height, calming within me the two roiling forces.

Sam leaned back, breathing hard, while magic swirled in his black eyes. "He'll wake in a minute."

"Can you see to Nick?"

He nodded.

Color seeped slowly back into Armand's skin. Soon Nick and Sam joined my vigil while behind us the buzzing volume of voices grew. I had eyes only for Armand and softly I spoke his name. No response.

"Des," Nick said, stroking my arm, "he'll be okay, hon."

Quivering, I whispered, "He has to be," and leaned down to press my lips to Armand's. "He's my world." Dark with magic, Armand's eyes slowly fanned open, swept the faces hovering around him, paused in confusion on Nick, then fixed on me. A slow smile began to curve his lips. "*Mon chou*," he rasped, "you're all right? You did it? Where—"

I lunged and squeezed him until he wheezed, laughing, and I pressed sloppy kisses all over his face like a lovesick puppy. With his power still humming inside me I said, "We did it."

Armand rose to his elbow, cupped the back of my head for a thorough kiss, this one soft and lingering, and as he made to get up Nick's palm shot out offering assistance. The two men shared a look; Armand grasped Nick's hand.

The next few seconds are a cloudy memory as if my mind wrapped the scene in gauze and tucked it away in a dark corner of my subconscious. Armand and I stood, embraced, and just as my eyes closed in relief—he was safe and well and perfect—Armand slammed me against the hardwood floor. My elbows hit first, zinging pain up my arms seconds before the rest of my body thumped horizontal beneath Armand. A gunshot rang out. Shouts. Before I even understood what was happening Armand flung out his arm, hurtling blue death across the stage.

One of Warren's underlings, G.I. Joe, survived his earlier toss against the backstage wall and crawled unnoticed to my gun, firing straight at me. The man jerked, gasped at the violent impact of Armand's magic, and lay motionless twenty feet away.

Nick felt for a pulse. "He's dead."

Armand, sprawled on top of me, met my gaze and we said in unison, "Are you all right?"

I grinned, then gasped as he jerked me to him in an embrace so constricting I felt as though I'd attempted to squeeze into an old training bra. He must have heard the last micron of air release from my lungs because his hold loosened. "Sorry," he whispered with a small laugh, assisting me up. A spattering of applause erupted as Armand and I stood. I whirled around.

Not a pond, nor small lake, but a vast sea of men and women stared back. All witches. They were the leaders of covens in only one county, I thought, amazed. Exactly how many witches practiced in Michigan?

Over the din Sam's voice rang out. "Blessed be, sisters and brothers," he called, motioning toward Armand and me. "Your new Priest and Priestess."

As the entire auditorium bowed, a frown began to work at my mouth. If I closed my eyes, maybe they wouldn't see me, and just as my eyelids began to clench tight, Armand spoke.

"Desy." He held out his hand, fixed me with clear midnight eyes, eyes that sat in his stunning face and promised wanton things, eyes that challenged me to be all I can be.

I knew what he wanted, what it would mean if I took his hand. The moment ripened with choice. Like a sudden fork in the road, one path led toward Armand and magic while the other path curved toward a destiny unknown. My gaze swept the sea of expectant witches, slid to Sam and Nick standing off to the side, then locked with Armand's intense stare.

Did I say I had a choice? Who was I kidding? Everything I could possibly want waited for me in his warm eyes. I placed my hand in his—saw those eyes flare with happiness—and we turned to the assembly.

"Okay people," I called in a loud echo. "New rule. No more bowing!"

* * * * *

Carefully I inched the sheet down his back, over his taut butt, down his long legs where dark hair swirled, while early morning sun played on his skin, coloring it light gold. On his stomach, his arms and head buried in the pillow, I filled my gaze with Armand. I usually got a good eyeful of that particular stunning view only as he walked away.

A rich slide of hair obscured his profile in a wicked tease, only hinting at features so beautiful, so masculine, I still find myself trying not to stare. The rounded muscle of shoulder, long sinew of back, the tight globe of buttock— this intoxicating anatomy I explored first by eye and when I could no longer resist, with hands and tongue and teeth.

He spoke softly in a sleepy tone. "No Nick."

My lips smiled against the small of his back. "No Nick," I agreed, thinking of the dream that had just ended.

We walked, the previous night, the streets of Paris.

My mid-Western eyes mooned over each new sight as Armand held my hand through a strolling tour of his favorite haunts. I saw the Eiffel Tower, the Seine, countless cafés, restaurants and boutiques. He led me to his favorite open markets along the busy stretch of Rue Cler market street where he told of spending many an early Sunday morning.

Within our dream, as summer sun gave way to summer moon, as his hands began to linger, speaking silently of his need along the curve of my waist, the flare of my hip, the curl of my hair, we made our way to his Paris home.

There my feelings grew bigger than me, bigger than the moment, bigger than the dream trying to hold them, and Armand, always somehow sensing my needs, silently led me to his bedroom. We spent the remainder of the dream talking and making love. Nothing marred our hours together...no shifting silhouette...no shadow...no Nick.

I woke with a lightened heart.

The pad of my forefinger stilled over a thin raised band of skin hidden in the crease behind his left knee. A tiny scar. I'd never noticed it before and I fingered it, wondering how it happened. Had he injured himself once during battle? Had he—

"*Amoureux*," he murmured, the sexy timbre of his voice somehow both smooth and raspy. "What are you doing?"

"Subatomic particle research."

When he turned toward me on his side, I lost my breath.

My heart chugged a thick beat and I held his stare as I lay beside him. His eyes probed mine as his mouth curved in that trademark slow, sexy smile, the one that never fails to ignite my panties.

My gaze swept over his southern hemisphere, took a slow sightseeing trip back up north. Legs long and muscular, sprinkled with soft hair of dusky brown led to a bulging sac, the balls within swollen with seed and shadowed beneath a long thrust of cock.

From base to tip his erection strained, pulling away from his stomach to lean toward me in rigid enticement. Veins coursed the thin skin, skin I've licked and sucked and pumped within my hands, skin that has pushed inside me time and time again, but somehow never enough. And at its tip flared a wide crown of deepening red topped with a luminescent pool shimmering just for me.

I licked my lips, unaware of how long I lay staring.

"*Mon chou*," he whispered and my head lifted. In his eyes a tempest swirled.

"Sorry," I said with a growing grin. "Got distracted." I reached for his hair, smoothed some wayward strands. Why is it bedhead looks sexy on him but on me it would frighten small children? "I've come to the conclusion I'm an Armand-oholic."

He rose to his elbow, curious, trying to gauge my mood, and spoke as he took my hand to his mouth for a soft kiss. "I don't believe I've ever heard the term."

"Well, the cravings are relentless," I informed, sitting up and gently pushing him to lie flat. He wore a slight smile and my gaze swept his face, my hands—his wide chest. "Close proximity is the only way to manage it. Four out of five doctors agree."

"Des."

"My condition is acute because you are simply the most beautiful man I've ever known." My hands swept over soft fur, the rounded strength beneath, to relish the sensation of his smooth nipples beading beneath my touch. "And the most arrogant."

His eyebrow arched.

"In fact," I said, shifting up to nibble his chin. "Don't even get me started on that particular personality trait. I could rant for hours." My teeth nipped his chin. "Perhaps days and months and years." I kissed my way along the strength of his jaw to his ear and softly blew in it. "Another thing? You never put down the damn toilet seat. I fell in again last night."

"Desy."

"Shhh." I scraped my teeth on his lobe. "Your French nose stabs the air each time I dare to mention fast food. I've had to pass up a lot of Whoppertunities because of you. And sports? *Please*. What self-respecting man can only discuss the Tour de France and soccer?" My lips brushed his nose. "It's sadly pathetic."

I shifted closer, caught his face, and whatever he read in my eyes completely froze him. A slight furrow of expectation lined his brow. "Your patience always surprises me, how very kind you are. You're just…good. A good man. You want to lead covens here not for power but because you care about people." My voice strengthened with each new word. "Funny and smart, generous and strong, and so much more. I know you, Armand, see all of you, and I want every part."

He recognized those words, knew what followed, and as my name left his lips in a soft, soft whisper, I watched his eyes flare and darken with loving expectation.

My fingers curled in his shiny mane. "You're mine," I vowed, searching his eyes, and then I spoke words that had long awaited release. "I love you."

With my name carried on a masculine groan, "My Desy," Armand cupped the back of my head and drew me down where he plundered my mouth in a kiss both sweet and carnal, quickening an already unsteady pulse. Armand's low hum reached inside my tummy and flipped everything upside down. He rolled toward me, slid his heavy leg between mine, and nudged his cock where a fierce Congo beat throbbed.

His hand—so large, so gentle on my skin—danced along my hip, and my heart sped as he grasped himself. His thigh lifted mine slightly and Armand pressed against me.

'Round and 'round swirled our tongues, and I felt his fingers slide in my wetness, open me, then the bold push of his cockhead. The very center of me stretched, filling inch by inch with the solid heat of him, and my hands cupped the back of his head as he pushed in, and in, and in, all the way home.

Against my lips he said, "Tell me again." His usual smooth-as-velvet voice held coarse gravel and the friction slid deep inside me to rub all the right spots.

"I love you."

"You can't know how much I've wanted to hear those words. I love you, *mon chou*." He shifted. "You feel like heaven."

With tangled limbs, bodies crushed together, warmed by the summer sun, our gazes latched tight, and he began to thrust in a dreamy rhythm, flexing his strong abdomen against mine, his furred chest against my nipples, his cock in and out and in again. A sizzling tingle buzzed beneath my skin, like every cell was on fire as we rubbed together on the sheets, and my leg tightened around his hip, pulling him closer.

Armand pushed me back, rolled on top, and as my inner thighs clutched his moving waist, his cock plunged in a new angle, rubbing slowly against my rigid clitoris. I rocked beneath his large body, my breasts swayed, and he dipped his head to bathe my nipple with a hot swirl of tongue.

"Armand." I breathed his name, arched into his mouth, and his teeth raked over the sensitive tip in a stinging caress, causing me to wonder what exactly was a fit of vapors and if somehow I was at that precise moment experiencing one.

A shudder rolled through me and didn't stop until my toes went numb.

He laved the valley between my breasts, trailing his tongue up the other rounded swell to suckle at its crest, and I thrust back my head, feeling that those three little words—I love you—made everything we did in the bed that morning—every touch, every look—more special. A low noise rumbled at the back of his throat a second before his cock withdrew in a noisy slurp, and Armand began to nip my tummy on his way to lower things.

Impatient, needy, I sat up and pushed on his shoulders, watching his eyes flash as he allowed me to press him back flat. In a shiny mass, his hair trailed over the bed's edge. Stomach to stomach I straddled him, facing toward the thick pillar of his erection, and captured his sticky length in two fists. My tongue swept his spongy cap.

The taut muscles beneath my stomach jerked and I felt the warm pressure of his hands glide up the backs of my spread thighs. "You're beautiful, Des," he purred, playing his fingers along my cleft. "Pink and wet." My vision blurred with the first long swipe of his tongue.

I filled my mouth with Armand's glistening cock, one hand gripping his wet base, the other stroking his tight sac, and his hips rocked a slow rhythm, swaying my body back and forth, stroking his cock in and out of my mouth, while his tongue slid along damp, tender folds weeping for his touch.

Each slow thrust slid his cock deeper into my relaxed mouth until my every swallow constricted around his broad length in tight suction, eliciting muffled grunts from him, exaggerated hip thrusts, and dragged him to an orgasm he could no longer delay.

Long inches of Armand bucked inside my mouth and he shuddered, groaned as hot spurts of come streamed down my throat. The rise and fall of his hips jerked in wild thrusts the longer his contractions squeezed and within my palm his large sac drew tighter still.

I rode his storm, luxuriated in his body's thundering release, and as his come slowed to a bubbling trickle, as I swallowed the last salty drop, felt his long sigh of completion feather against my sex, he unexpectedly slid his finger into my ass.

I tensed slightly, eased his cock from my mouth as he rubbed along the tight tunnel of nerves, and I felt my breath drag from my lungs when he buried his finger inside. I shuddered, closed my eyes, and nuzzled into fragrant pubic curls.

As if relishing the last ice cream cone of summer, he lapped my center, and I could no more hold still my hips than prevent the rippling approach of my orgasm. I followed his lips with the part of me that throbbed and tingled and pulsed.

"You're so close," he crooned, slowly pushing his tongue past tender folds, fluttering it in a hot pool of arousal, swallowing and coming back for more, all the while sliding his finger in and out of my anus where dark pleasure tightened with every thrust.

Our stomachs rubbed together in sweaty friction, and the scent of ripe sex permeated the air as he slurped and licked, nipped and kissed me toward a high crest. Tingles skittered, soon rolling into delectable waves, and my clit sang beneath his stroking tongue, drawing from me a gush of juice.

A hoarse cry sprang from my lips as my center contracted and all the nerves that banded together earlier suddenly dispersed with a tight jump of muscle.

Armand pushed a second finger into my ass as I came, forcing my hips to buck, a scream from my throat, and my hands to anchor at his hips so I wouldn't fly away as the orgasm soared.

With a slow flex, Armand withdrew his pumping fingers and had me on my back before I could utter more than a startled gasp.

He mounted me and plunged.

His body pressed down heavily but I had the buoyant sensation of floating weightless on a cloud. I searched his eyes and found magic swirling in their depths. The air thickened, the room shifted, and I looked toward the bed. It sat several feet beneath our joined bodies.

We were floating.

A joyous sound, his laughter. I felt the startled surprise on my face bloom into a rosy smile. "This is incredible," I breathed, and he began to move his hips. "Being inside you is more so."

Pleasure came off Armand in waves. I could feel every happy ripple. We rolled, placing me on top, then rolled again with my handsome witch plunging down to meet my rising hips, using nothing but air and magic for leverage.

There was a sense of falling and my stomach jumped with a surprised lurch. I clutched at Armand and landed somewhere not wholly unexpected, somewhere hot and exciting in a tangle of sheets with a French voice crooning how beautiful I was, how perfect, and a large amorous man thrusting between my legs.

His hair flowed around my face as he took my mouth in a lush kiss. I dug my hands in the dark mane, pressed my heels to the twin globes of his gorgeous behind, and lost myself in steady friction.

Far too soon my hands fisted in his hair, he swallowed my soft cry, and I came with a hard shudder just before filling with long streams of pumping cream.

He grunted, slowed his rhythm, and I felt his cock squish back and forth within its large pool of seed until Armand stilled.

Damp with sweat and happiness, I loosened around him—my hands from his hair, my legs from his waist—and enjoyed long minutes of a languorous kiss, one in which his tongue slid with mine, licking with obvious enjoyment.

"I have something for you," he murmured, nibbling my lips.

Several inches of cock, spent but still rigid, bucked inside me. My eyes flew open. "Holy mother of god, Armand, I need a multivitamin to keep up with you." I gave him a quick peck. "Give me a minute?"

A half-snort, half-chuckle wafted against my face. "That wasn't what I had in mind but hold the thought." He leaned, squishing me slightly, and dug around in his nightstand drawer, withdrawing a small black velvet case. A case that looked just the right size to hold a ring. A case that trapped my next breath inside my lungs, spun my head with dizzy heat. A case the fiendish Frenchman chose to show me only after he'd purposely turned my legs to rubber so I couldn't run away.

He watched my face. "Don't panic."

My answer emerged in an embarrassing wheeze. "I'm not panicking." I pushed at his shoulders. "Off—off! I can't breathe!"

Armand levered himself up and his cock slid from me in noisy disagreement. Beside him I lunged upright, gulped air, and he opened the box, withdrew a ring that twinkled so brightly, my eyes squinted. I gulped more air and began to choke on the excess. While I coughed up my spleen the diamond sparkled in the morning sun and he clasped my limp hand.

I swallowed, lifted my gaze. "Is…is this a proposal?" My voice hovered between a mouse's high squeak and the low bawl of a rutting moose.

"*Non*," he said with a secret smile, sliding the ring onto my third finger, left hand. It fit perfectly.

"No?"

"*Non*, because you'll just run scared. So I have a plan."

"A plan?"

He nodded. "I'll first ask you to move in with me. It will feel less threatening to you." His hand played in my bedhead. I didn't have the sense of mind to warn him it might become permanently stuck.

"Less threatening?" I glanced down at the ring. It felt odd, heavy.

"Then I'll gently ease you into the idea of marriage. Move you in that direction so slowly you'll be unaware of your growing acceptance."

"I'll be unaware?"

"And before you realize it—" he flashed his pearly whites, snapped his French fingers "—you'll be mine always, Mrs. Desdemona Bellamy." He palmed my belly. "And someday, *mon chou*, you'll have my child."

I slid my hand over his. "Our child."

His gaze burned brighter. "Our child. And she will be as beautiful as her mother."

"He," I countered. "*He* will be as handsome, as wonderful as you."

Armand began to swim before my eyes, and softly, so very softly, he kissed my lips, whispering words of France, something wanton I'm sure. "*Amoureux*, don't cry."

"I'm not crying, it's—"

"Just allergies." With a growing smile and love shining brightly in his eyes, Armand said, "I know, love."

Epilogue

The first meeting with the High Council went smoothly, even though I found the thirteen witches to display more liver spots than true initiative. In a formal ceremony next week they plan to acknowledge Armand and me as the state's new High Priest and Priestess. Sam hasn't stopped grinning for days.

Nick's left hand once again sports his wedding band. He and Anita see a marriage counselor once a week. The sessions must be working because my lifelong friend and cohort has a new spring in his step, and it isn't due to a Dr. Scholl's insert.

Franklin's barbecue fete, the one Aunt P thought sounded delightful, turned out to be just that, made all the more so when Frank surprised my aunt with two tickets for a cruise to Alaska, a place she's always yearned to travel. Her cheeks bloomed a pretty pink and in that luminous moment, when I saw how happy she was, how happy that made him in return, the retired accountant completely won me over. Even though they're not leaving until late next week, an ecstatic Aunt P is already packed. She's taking more luggage than could fit in a midsized U-Haul.

Aunt P knows she'll return to an empty house; I'll have moved in with Armand by then. I don't know who's happier at the news, the Frenchman or her. Armand is trying hard not to gloat over my easy acquiescence, actually believing everything is following in accordance to his plan. (I did make mention of his arrogance, did I not?) But I believe it's my mission to always keep him slightly off-balance, so I've devised a plan of my own, one that involves a simple gold band—masculine but elegant—some heartfelt words, and just in case, red lacey lingerie.

Because with Armand I can be all I'm meant to be, a better me. He sees my foibles, my triumphs, the light and shadow of my soul, my very essence…and loves me. So wish me luck with my fine Frenchman.

Tonight, I'm proposing.

Enjoy this excerpt from

Empath Wanted

© Copyright Jacqueline Meadows 2003

Planet Earth

The Year 2037

Isabelle Pentriss, 26-year-old self-proclaimed failure, sat in her small Kansas apartment fretting. She'd just lost another job, this time through no fault of her own, and her spirits were now as flat as her wallet.

She was on a one-way road to loserville and desperate to find a detour. A job, she thought, a good job. That wasn't too much to ask. And it wasn't as if she lacked skills—why, she could...a fatalistic sigh escaped her mouth; she couldn't do much of anything, really.

The only talent she had was her life-long ability to "read" people. She'd always been able to judge basic character by viewing a person's aura, to feel their emotions through touch—even picking up an actual stray thought or memory on occasion. But rather than revel in her empathic abilities, Isabelle found them to be isolating and often a burden. And they certainly couldn't pay her rent.

Snapping out of her pity party for one, she focused on the central tele-communicator before her, its screen displaying today's galaxy--wide job opportunities. Eyes scanning the ads, she paused on one for a minimum wage bagging position at the corner Piggly Wiggly grocery store. Yeah—right! She was desperate but not yet suicidal. Snorting, she read the next ad and her breath caught in her lungs.

Was this a joke? Shaking her head, her eyes scanned the telecom screen once more as her hand absentmindedly moved to her hair and wound a cropped brown curl around her finger. Unbelievably, the advertisement still read the same the second time around:

WANTED

Female Empath

No Formal Experience Necessary

Planet Fortuna, House of Borgio

Start Immediately

Call for Personal Interview

Starcon 955

Fascinated, Isabelle stopped toying with her hair and slowly reached for her communicator pad, entering the ad's number before second thoughts, saner thoughts, changed her mind. After all, she really had nothing to lose.

* * * * *

Planet Fortuna

House of Borgio

The Following Day

She was here! His long wait was over. Body tensed, he watched her through the monitor and thought her to be the most gorgeous creature he had ever beheld. Zeff softly traced her body's image on the monitor's screen with his thumb. Isabelle Pentriss. Finally here, and mine, all mine.

Taking a deep calming breath, he dragged a hand ruthlessly through his thick ebony hair and stalked towards the formal waiting room to meet her.

Down the hall, Isabelle fretted. Fretting was something she practiced routinely. She had fret down pat.

"I must be nuts," she muttered to herself. Agitated, Isabelle shoved herself up from the waiting room's couch and started pacing. "It's not like I have a chance in hell of getting this job. I'm just wasting everyone's time. And on top of that, I'll probably somehow manage to make an ass of myself." Placing a hand on her stomach to calm the butterflies raging inside, she settled back down on the couch. Her nerves were already shot and she hadn't even had the interview yet. Ruefully, she rolled her eyes.

The waiting room's door clicked and began to open. Isabelle jerked back upright to stand on leaden limbs. Nervously she smoothed her sweaty palms down her apricot silk pantsuit and turned toward the opening door.

Her eyes widened and the butterflies in her stomach started dancing around to the rumba instead of a waltz. The man standing in the doorway was unbelievable. Tall and solidly built with sleek muscles and classic features, he just oozed testosterone. His hair was longer than hers, jet-black and brushing along his broad shoulders. His soft smile was at odds with the burning intensity she saw in his light blue eyes. And oh shit, he had dimples! She was such a sucker for dimples.

The man's aura, though, just might be the most incredible thing about him, mused Isabelle. Blinding white for integrity, some violet for humor and enough red to signify quite a libido.

Reaching out to shake her hand, he introduced himself. "Welcome Isabelle, my greetings to you. I am Prince Zeff Durel Santoa Borgio. I hope your transport here went smoothly."

Flustered, Isabelle cleared her dry throat and tentatively extended her hand. "Prince Borgio, I'm honored."

She always steered clear of touching others unless her protective mental shields were firmly in place, but her thoughts and nerves were too jumbled to think clearly. The second her hand touched his, though, reality crashed down on her. "Uh oh," she whispered as her eyes rolled back in her head, legs buckled, and all went black.

* * * * *

Isabelle roused to warm hands on her naked skin. Still in a dreamy state, she felt firm lips nuzzle her ear, nipping lightly on the lobe. Breathing a moan, she tilted her head to the side to allow better access to her ear and neck. The large hand on her waist moved slowly to cup her round, pert breast, palming it and gently squeezing. Her nipple tightened and beaded. As the lips left her ear to trail over her cheeks and eyelids, the hand at her hip slid under her, grasping her rounded buttock rhythmically. Moaning louder, Isabelle restlessly shifted and opened her legs.

"Yes, Belle," a masculine voice crooned. "Open for me."

At the sound of the voice, Isabelle's eyes snapped opened. Slamming her legs closed and whipping her mental shields up, she croaked, "What's going on?" Her amazed stare collided with his. Stunned, she questioned, "Prince Borgio? What are you doing? Where am I?"

His hands stilled but held her firmly in place. "Easy, Belle. You are in my chambers, in my bed, and I am helping to wake you." A small, fleeting smile curved the prince's mouth before his warm tongue traced her lips. He added, "You fainted."

"I did?"

"Yes, my sweet. Are you feeling better now?"

"Uh, Prince Borgio? I'm naked. You're naked. Maybe on your planet this is how you wake up job applicants, but where I come from this is considered quite, well, forward. Maybe even illegal."

About the author:

Jacqueline Meadows, wife and mother, lives in Michigan's thumb area where she feeds her addiction to steamy romance—the hotter the better—with large daily doses of reading and writing.

Jacqueline welcomes mail from readers. You can write to her c/o Ellora's Cave Publishing at 1337 Commerce Drive, Suite 13, Stow OH 44224.

Why an electronic book?

We live in the Information Age—an exciting time in the history of human civilization in which technology rules supreme and continues to progress in leaps and bounds every minute of every hour of every day. For a multitude of reasons, more and more avid literary fans are opting to purchase e-books instead of paperbacks. The question to those not yet initiated to the world of electronic reading is simply: *why?*

1. *Price.* An electronic title at Ellora's Cave Publishing runs anywhere from 40-75% less than the cover price of the <u>exact same title</u> in paperback format. Why? Cold mathematics. It is less expensive to publish an e-book than it is to publish a paperback, so the savings are passed along to the consumer.

2. *Space.* Running out of room to house your paperback books? That is one worry you will never have with electronic novels. For a low one-time cost, you can purchase a handheld computer designed specifically for e-reading purposes. Many e-readers are larger than the average handheld, giving you plenty of screen room. Better yet, hundreds of titles can be stored within your new library—a single microchip. (Please note that Ellora's Cave does not endorse any specific brands. You can check our website at www.ellorascave.com for customer recommendations we make available to new consumers.)

3. *Mobility.* Because your new library now consists of only a microchip, your entire cache of books can be taken with you wherever you go.

4. *Personal preferences are accounted for.* Are the words you are currently reading too small? Too large? Too...**ANNOYING**? Paperback books cannot be modified according to personal preferences, but e-books can.

5. *Innovation.* The way you read a book is not the only advancement the Information Age has gifted the literary community with. There is also the factor of what you can read. Ellora's Cave Publishing will be introducing a new line of interactive titles that are available in e-book format only.

6. *Instant gratification.* Is it the middle of the night and all the bookstores are closed? Are you tired of waiting days—sometimes weeks—for online and offline bookstores to ship the novels you bought? Ellora's Cave Publishing sells instantaneous downloads 24 hours a day, 7 days a week, 365 days a year. Our e-book delivery system is 100% automated, meaning your order is filled as soon as you pay for it.

Those are a few of the top reasons why electronic novels are displacing paperbacks for many an avid reader. As always, Ellora's Cave Publishing welcomes your questions and comments. We invite you to email us at service@ellorascave.com or write to us directly at: 1337 Commerce Drive, Suite 13, Stow OH 44224.

Discover for yourself why readers can't get enough of the multiple award-winning publisher Ellora's Cave. Whether you prefer e-books or paperbacks, be sure to visit EC on the web at www.ellorascave.com for an erotic reading experience that will leave you breathless.

WWW.ELLORASCAVE.COM